Some readers' comments

'The Lily stories exhibit a fine and yet creative attention to detail. The type of attention that is introspective of ideas, but observant of the surrounds. For example, in one story we have: "...her ability to see the magic. Within a year almost every tree of interest in the woods had names——and the children down the hill, who had joined her in discovering the wonders of cow paddocks, knew all the names, and had added a few of their own." These stories are uniquely beautiful and indicative of deep insights and thoughtful observations of human internal and external levels.'

Geoffrey Campbell

'Finely familiar, and idiosyncratic, these are intriguing characters and relationships and with sharp attention to matters of time and place. Jennifer Code's prose is beautifully measured, her glimpses of life indeed moving.

Brian Edwards

'These stories keep you interested from the beginning to the end. They are told with utmost attention to the details of surroundings and characteristics of people portrayed. As the reader you are there and live the story with them.'

Barbara Westwood

'That clear young voice, painting such clear pictures, of the people, the land, the library, the ice, skates; I hope my memory never loses those images. I think the first story I heard started with a child walking down a steep hill in the dark, immediately you are drawn into the tension of the narrative.'

Heather Tobias

'I loved the Lily stories, especially the tales of her as a child -- her innocence was captured so beautifully.'

Stephanie Mariani

'Jennifer Code's Lily stories make addictive reading. They conjure up a world we experience through the eyes of a child, where terror rubs shoulders with wonder in the day-to-day encounters that echo through adult life...This detail builds a strong sense of place that locates us firmly in each setting. As Code guides us into the makeup of each character and how it formed, we find some degree of empathy with even the most awful-seeming.'

Jackey Coyle

'The stories carry a personal theme and a relationship with the reader that one could relate to one's own personal experience. Jennifer Code's craft shows in her ability -- allowing them to unfold on their own. Somehow the stories take off in a direction of their own. The Lily stories remind us of family lives in the content and context style of the writing. As the reader we could relate and identify to characters -- be they mother, daughter and siblings -- and observe how they carry a feminine narrative without labelling them feminist and pretentious; they are devoid of sensationalism and sentimentality but rather often self-reflexive in a language which is measured and structured in such a way that when read aloud is easy on the ear. A fine testament in storytelling from one of our beloved literary writers working in good prose.'

Phil Constan

The Mad Angel

THE MAD ANGEL

An original episodic novel

Jennifer Code, PhD.

Ódrerir Books

2021

Published by Ódrerir Books
Dromana, VIC 3936

ISBN: 978-1-922270-62-7 (pbk) eISBN: 978-1-922270-63-4 (ebook)

A catalogue record for this
book is available from the
National Library of Australia

For my husband Trevor Code and our two daughters,
Genevieve Twomey and Ingrid Code

FOREWORD

This novel, *The Mad Angel*, is set mainly in Worcester County, Massachusetts, USA, as the protagonists move in an unsettled search for stability, economy and identity, in two village towns of Worcester city in mid-twentieth century America -- Oxford to the near south and Hubbardston to the near northwest. Lily is the child of a dysfunctional family of partly alien Australian Betsy and afflicted ex-marine Charlie. In that sense, both Lily and her mother are outsiders looking for association and acceptance in their society. Sometimes it becomes a study in child development: how can the sensibility cope with recurrent alienation? It is Lily's mind, consciousness, memory and reflections which create this novel, through dreams, nightmares, vagaries of family, violence, alcoholism, language, calamities, the discovery of libraries and reading, snow storms, reunions, friendships, village traditions, skating, and one long excursion into the southern states. These lead eventually to adult survival, some humour, and resilience. Many scenes proceed through realistic dialogues between characters in revealing confrontations. And that old biblical question, "What is true?" As Lily's narrative creates them, the mind and memories continually open up to further incidents, depictions and reflections. While not tragedy as such, there is a sense of dislocation for some characters -- a downhill inevitability.

This book includes important appendices by the author in which she discusses her writing processes for the reader.

CHAPTER 1

1982–1947

Lily Pays a Visit or Two

Betsy and Lily were sitting on the deck at the back of the house. It was a beautiful midsummer day in Massachusetts and a rare thing for them to be sitting together like this, with nothing to do but enjoy each other's company. Lily, her husband William, and their two little girls, Josie and Anna, had arrived from Australia just a few days before and rented a house about fifteen miles away. They were to stay for a whole year.

Betsy had invited Mrs. Foster from up the hill as well, for it was a special occasion, as everyone knew, and besides, Betsy never did feel comfortable to be entertaining with just family around her.

Mrs Foster had known Lily since she was a child and was very glad to join the family in welcoming her home. There would be so much to talk about, she thought, and she was looking forward to it. Even so, she looked sober as she walked down the road to Betsy and Charley's house. She had long ago learned not to look too pleased about anything. She knew that things have a way of biting you—if you let them. Nevertheless, she couldn't help thinking in a level-headed, straight-

1

faced and without exclamation marks sort of way, 'My goodness. Lily was only eight years old when she first came here to live, and now I am a childless widow and Lily is a mother. It has been such a long time and so much has happened since then. Yes, I think it will be nice to see her again.'

She had always liked Lily. She especially remembered the days of one summer in particular, when she had seen her playing by herself at the edge of the big field between their houses. It was the one memory that had stuck in her mind—that and the day when Matty and Alan had locked Mr. Foster in the barn for the whole afternoon. Well, of course you would remember a thing like that, she thought. It was such a piece of mischief! But she was quite certain that she was the only one who had ever really noticed Lily when she was playing alone and attempting the impossible. How many times had she looked out that window and seen her standing just a few feet away, at the exact spot where the Foster's lawn ended and their field began? From the corner of her dining room window, just out of sight, she could see how Lily would look down the field as if plotting a course, and how she would look up at the sky and put out her hand as if to catch the wind at the exact right moment, and how she would lean forward then and race off down the hill with her arms spread out wide—like wings. She had asked her about it once and Lily had told her that she was trying to fly. She had seen herself flying over the field in a dream, she had said. She even knew how it felt and she had told Mrs. Foster, with an earnest little frown, that she was quite sure she could do it, but it all depended on the wind—on whether the wind would catch her as she ran and lift her into the air. She admitted that it had never worked, but she would keep on trying, she said.

Now Mrs. Foster was walking past that same field, wondering just how many years it had been and thinking to herself as she walked, 'There she is, down at the house again, a fully grown woman with children already half grown up, and hasn't she just flown all those miles across the Pacific Ocean? Yes, she was bound to fly, one way or another.'

For a moment or two she cast her mind back into her own childhood and wondered whether she had ever thought of flying when she was a child. The answer which came to her rather too abruptly was no, of course not. Little girls didn't do such things in those days. She sighed and looked even sterner. She had never had a daughter and now her only son was gone—killed in an appalling accident. She could never think of it without wondering if he had done it on purpose. They had told her afterwards that there were drugs in his system, but they never thought of the whole picture—of Vietnam and the haunting that ravaged his mind so relentlessly that they sent him home—so damaged that even his childhood home seemed dangerous to him, especially at night.

Perhaps he killed himself. It was her first thought on that awful night and from then on she too was haunted—as if it was an inheritance of sorts—a haunting transferred. She could never understand why he drove at such a speed through road works clearly marked with signs and barriers and lights, unless he meant to kill himself. But now, on her way down the hill, she wondered why she would be thinking of this again for the hundredth or thousandth time, when it was all such a long time ago and there was no point in being wistful about it. Certainly not! Surely she had learned her lesson well enough by now. It was as plain as could be. Whenever she thought of how her life had been, she was quite sure there was no point at all in wanting to live it over again. Good heavens, no! Didn't all the people she knew just keep on doing the same things over and over again, no matter how silly or stupid they were? No matter how painful. Why couldn't they see that?

Why was she thinking of Alan again now? Because Lily and Matty and Alan were children together—three years between each of them— in that order. Lily, who was six years older than Alan had minded him when he was just a boy—the closest he ever came to having a sister.

She remembered the first time Charley took him skiing with Lily and Matty. Alan had never been skiing before and was afraid—especially afraid of the rope tow he told her when he came home that evening. He had fallen over when he tried to grab it and had got into such a tangle. It was scary, he said, and he wanted to go home again, but then Lily came along behind him and swooped him up. With her skis outside his and her arm around him, she grabbed the rope and up they went. By the time they got nearly to the top she had taught him how to do it himself, and then she had let him go to finish the climb on his own. Ah well, Mrs. Foster thought as she walked down the hill, there is more than one kind of memory. It was the look of sheer happiness on his face when he came home that day.

Betsy had arranged some food for afternoon tea—enough to occupy them all for at least a couple of hours and, it being a very sunny afternoon, she had ordered Charley to fix the sun umbrella in just the right spot, so that she would be protected from the glare without it casting a shadow on the others. She wanted to be able to see the faces of her guests. It was important, she thought, to be able to see them clearly. "I need to be out of the sun, you know," she announced when they arrived. "I am allergic to it."

As they gathered around the table, Charley brought in the afternoon tea. "Afternoon tea" is what Betsy called it, according to her own rules of amusement—although she knew better. There was food—a good-sized bowl of peanuts and another bowl filled with small nibbles in the shape of fish which she was sure the children would like. There was plenty to drink, both soft and hard.

"There's tonic for the girls," she said, and smirked at them. "Ask your grandfather to show you where. There's a fridge full of them in the cellar. Go on now! Go get yourselves a drink."

As Charley went off to show the children where to find the soft drinks, Betsy shouted after him, "Charley! I'll have a gin and tonic—and one for Lily too!"

He turned back towards the table where William had just sat down, sighed patiently and said to all except Betsy, "There's beer and soft drinks—several kinds of each—and gin. What would you like?"

William chose beer and got up to help Charley. Lily, who knew her mother well, agreed to the gin and tonic, although she couldn't remember ever having one. Mrs. Foster asked for lemonade.

"William! Sit down!" Betsy ordered. "There's no need for you to be helpful. Charley knows what he has to do." And with a frown, she said to Charley, "Don't you make Lily's drink as strong as mine! Do you hear me? She's not used to it."

There followed some moments of uncertainty as those who remained at the table settled into their chairs, unsure of what would happen next. Betsy, however, was never one to waste time on the comfort of niceties and pleasing manners. She was miles ahead of them already. "William," she said, "you can help Charley with the barbecue in a while. We're having hot dogs and hamburgers. And I made potato salad and coleslaw myself. How's that?"

Before he could open his mouth to reply, she focused briefly on Lily, then turned to Mrs. Foster and said, "What do you think, Grace? Doesn't she look good?"

Mrs. Foster looked at Lily and shook her head. "I don't think so," she replied, looking at Lily. "You're too thin. Much too thin. You look gaunt."

Lily laughed, then immediately apologized. "I'm sorry," she said, "I don't mean to be rude. It's just that the thought of me ever being too thin is so funny. You have no idea how hard it has been to keep my weight down to even a reasonable level."

"You're too thin," Mrs. Foster insisted. "You used to be so lovely. Such soft, smooth skin you had."

"Well, I'm not fifteen any more, and I've just flown across half the world, which is the most exhausting thing. It plays havoc with your skin, you know. Dries you out…"

"That's not true!" Betsy said, glowering at Mrs. Foster. "Gaunt, you say. She's not gaunt!"

She rose from her chair and leaned across the table, knocking the bowl of fish snacks as she did, and, unaware that her own face was now in the sun, she stretched out to within four or five inches of Lily and peered at her face. She squinted, inspected, scrutinized and said, "Gaunt! Where did you get that idea, Grace? Come and see for yourself!" she demanded, waving her hand at Mrs. Foster. "There isn't a single wrinkle in that skin. Look! You would think she was only twenty-five years old."

Peering into another person's face wasn't something Mrs. Foster could do, and she wasn't too happy to see Betsy doing it either. Her mother would have said that it was just plain bad-mannered. She sat back with a firm look on her face and said to Lily, "Perhaps it is the flying, but you don't look really well. You should take better care of yourself."

Lily smiled at Mrs. Foster and thanked her. "I'm sure you are right," she agreed. "I am always so busy with other things that I scarcely ever pay attention to myself, unless I'm dressing up to go somewhere. And I stay up too late."

Mrs. Foster seemed pleased with that and Betsy, who had sat down again and possibly felt that she had missed something in the moment of her sitting, pointed her finger at Lily and said, "Just because you don't have any wrinkles, don't let it go to your head. You might not remember it but I do—you were an awful child! A perfectly awful child!"

Lily was accustomed to the twists and turns of her mother's mind and usually managed to keep up to some degree at least, but this time she was quite taken aback. She had assumed that the novelty of her arrival after so long away would have brought her ... well ... a warm welcome perhaps, or at least a bit of leeway. She looked at Mrs. Foster, hoping for a clue, wondering if she really had been such an awful child. She was glad that it wasn't some stranger sitting there.

And seeing how Lily looked at Mrs. Foster, Betsy snapped, "Oh, you think you were an angel, do you? Ha! Let me tell you, you were the most impossible child. You were always running away from home. No one could ever keep track of you. And you never told us. You just went. First thing we knew about it was that you weren't there and nobody ever knew where you'd gone! Explain that!"

Lily was thoroughly confused by then and her mother's face had become unreadable. The only thing she could think of to say was, "I don't remember ever running away from home."

"Oh, no, of course you wouldn't remember," Betsy replied. "You were only five months old the first time you ran away."

Charley had brought the drinks by this time and Betsy was holding her gin and tonic close.

Lily held her own drink close—to cool herself down, or steady herself perhaps, as she asked, "Five months... How?"

"Oh," Betsy replied, "you just crawled down the front path to the gate and then got your head stuck in it."

"How? I-I mean, was there no one to stop me? Was I out in the yard by myself?"

"Of course you were. We were all busy doing things. You just sneaked away."

"Sneaked!" Lily exclaimed. "I don't remember sneaking away."

"I suppose you think you're being funny," Betsy replied, "but it's true. You were everywhere. Once you began to move about of your own accord, there was no stopping you—and no knowing where you might be."

Lily, thinking of what her own children were like as babies, asked, "How exactly did I get there? I mean, was the front door open? Surely

7

I couldn't have reached high enough to open the door. And you told me once that there were steps—that the path was at least five or six feet below the front door."

"Oh, you didn't have any trouble with that. You went down backwards. It was just that gate. Once you got your head stuck in it, you weren't going anywhere."

Backwards, Lily thought. Of course! But how could... It was an unfinished thought, drowned in a wave of exhaustion. It was all that travelling, or was it that she had just remembered what her mother was like when she entertained guests. Old friends or new acquaintances, it was all the same to her—an opportunity to perform. This wasn't just the twists and turns of her mind, it was a blatant performance. She was sure of it! No doubt her mother would have been great in vaudeville, but only if she was the centre of attention.

The trouble was that Lily could never be sure whether anything her mother said on such occasions was truth or fiction—or a concoction of both, but if there was ever any doubt, Charley would quash it with his wide-eyed look and his best advice in a deep voice, "You better believe it." It had made an impact. Even after all those years away, she knew better than to doubt. Instead she stifled a sigh and asked, "How did you know I was stuck? Was I yelling?"

"It was Mrs. Peach who was yelling," Betsy said with a hint of triumph—the look of a person who had won the point. "She was on her way home from the shops and found you there. You were a bit frustrated, she said, but you weren't yelling. Poor old Mrs. Peach tried to set you free, but couldn't, and as long you had your head stuck in the gate, she couldn't open it either. So it seems that you were both stuck. It was very funny, I must say."

She smirked—pleased with herself.

Good Lord, thought Lily. What could a five-month-old possibly have been frustrated about? Surely if she had managed to open the front door, get down the steps and make her way to the gate, she was well on her way, although perhaps she was just *a bit frustrated* because she forgot to pack her suitcase, or call for a taxi, but she had better stop thinking like this or her mother would soon be reading her mind. The real question was how to distinguish—in any of her mother's stories—the difference between fact and fiction. Is this the invention of the moment, she wondered, or the gin?

"I know what you're thinking," Betsy said with a frown. "I can read your mind. You think I'm making it up, but I was there and you weren't. I know what you did."

Lily chose not to argue the point, because of course there was a difference between the baby who was there and the adult who wasn't and there was no possibility of her remembering what happened when she was only a few months old. In fact, she was having trouble remembering what it had been like when she was nineteen—before she left home—or right now, for that matter. She wondered whether her mother had always been like this. Dramas and story-telling were her *forté*, yes, but—like this? Had she really forgotten? She didn't dare to look at Mrs. Foster for fear of being accused of conspiracy.

"Well," she said, "someone must have got my head out of the gate."

"Oh yes! It was your Uncle Max. He was a most resourceful man. He came along on his bicycle at just the right time. Poor Mrs. Peach was at the end of her tether by then. It all depended on the angle, he said. Once he turned your head in the right direction, you were free. As simple as that! Can't imagine why you didn't think of it yourself. He told me you laughed at him. Cunning little thing you were. But you were crazy about your uncle Max. He used to take you for rides on his bicycle—in a basket attached to the handlebars. He said you loved it. Of course, the front gate episode was just the beginning. By the time you were nine months old we had learned to pin your sheet to the mattress with great safety pins when we put you down for your nap. We had to, because the moment we put you down you were up again and there was no controlling you. Your cot was right next to the window and we didn't want you jumping out of it."

Lily frowned—remembering her own children. The thought of pinning a sheet to a mattress had never occurred to her, although she recalled that about the same age, Josie had once climbed over the side of her cot and landed with a crash. But then her cot was next to a wall and after that first noisy landing—miraculously without injury—Lily decided to leave the side down and give Josie the option to come and go, which was surely better than having a catastrophe.

"Of course, that was just the beginning," Betsy went on, duplicating Lily's frown this time. "You were such an *impossible* child, and it was a *hot* summer day. We had the window next to your cot open so you could get a breeze to cool you down a bit. We were all outside drinking tea. Next thing we knew there you were standing on the window ledge, looking down at us. It gave us all quite a shock! The window must have been at least seven or eight feet above the ground. It was high drama for a minute or so. Your grandmother rushed into the house and your aunt stood under the window in case you jumped. 'Imagine that!' your grandmother said, when she'd got hold of you. 'She undid the safety pins herself.'"

Lily sighed—just a little sigh—and turned to Mrs. Foster, for she was sure that she would want to talk about something else after all those years. Mrs. Foster smiled a small proper sort of smile and Betsy pounced once again. After all, the party belonged to her and she wasn't likely to let anyone forget it.

"So you don't like having your past history aired in public! Well I can assure you there's plenty more. You got much worse after we came to America. We were living with your grandparents then and you were always running down the drive to the highway. You weren't much more than thirteen months old. I can't think how many times your father's dog saved your life. Barney was his name. A big German Shepherd. He would grab you by the seat of your pants and pull you back again. In the end he was hit by a car and killed. You'd think you would have learned to be sensible after that, but no! And I have never forgotten the time when you ran away from home on your tricycle. Went to your grandmother's house, of all things! Really! We lived in Park Street then. It was miles! You were just three years old. Of course, you won't remember a bit of it. Children of that age have a very a short-term memory."

"Oh but I do remember it," Lily said. "I can even remember it in colour—the trees, the houses, the sidewalks... I have always thought—after I grew up, I mean—that it was quite astonishing that I carried it out right to the end. I was so small."

"That's not true," Betsy replied. "You are just pretending. You couldn't possibly remember all that!"

"Oh yes, she could," said William. "I can assure you that Lily has a prodigious memory, and I know the story so well I could tell it to you myself."

Underneath the umbrella, a cloud came over Betsy's face—a clear and visible shadow in the midst of an otherwise beautiful warm day. Suddenly, it seemed, a storm was looming—or was it a fog? Betsy, who had apparently just lost purchase on her own party, took a good long sip of her gin and tonic. And Lily frowned at William, hoping that it was the end of it—that her frown would be taken as a signal to change the subject, because in answer to the question of Lily's memory, there was a good deal to say and there was no doubt that if it were said, it would wind her mother up into a hysterical fit.

Later on—that evening perhaps—she wondered if it really was all about memory, but whose? For her it was just a matter of how the mind works—in this case how a child's mind might work. Lily as an adult could remember that day very clearly, but her mother couldn't, or wouldn't, believe it possible. Why? She wondered whether her mother had ever understood what it was about that day that made her decide to go to her grandmother's house.

And that thought made her wonder where her mother had got her ideas about bringing up children, because she was sure they didn't come from her grandmother Tilly. She had never forgotten how kind her grandmother had been when she came to visit—all the way from Australia—and how she had kept an eye on her 'so that she would be safe.' That's what Lily had heard her grandmother say to her mother. She thought about it for a minute and realized that her tricycle visit to her Grandma Linnea came first. Tilly came later. How much later? Days? Weeks? She couldn't remember. She came because there was a new baby.

Lily had no idea how the brain stores memories. She just remembered. She knew that memories can be strange and unreliable, but this particular childhood memory, she was certain, was so intrinsic to her own being that it remained constant—not always there, but when called upon, always the same. She knew exactly what happened that day, and how, and when. It was the 'why' which took time to understand. That came later. At the time, she thought, it was just a feeling and a need, but of course that thought was coming from the mind of an adult—and from that point of view all the rest made sense. She remembered because in all that she did that day she was entirely alone and her mind had been fixed on reaching her destination safely. No one spoke to her. No one even seemed to notice her. There were no distractions except the worries that travelled with her.

So here it was again, that particular memory, brought to mind this time by her mother, on a day on which there were surely more important things to think about. It began with a new baby in the house. In all of Lily's life prior to that time, there had never been a baby in the house, unless it was a visitor's baby. But this baby was there to stay. He was called Matty and he was her little brother. He was very small and he yelled a lot, and her mother was always fussing over him, and patting and cooing and changing his nappy and feeding him and smiling at him and sighing... And all during the day, every day, Lily was told to stay outside. Betsy didn't want her around being a nuisance. "Go out and ride your tricycle," she told her.

On any ordinary day, there would have been kids all over the neighbourhood riding tricycles or bicycles, playing games, running about... But on this day there was no one. Lily had no idea where they had gone. She rode her tricycle from one end to the other of that part of the street where she always played, and no one came outside or answered her calls. It was a hot day in July. She thought that perhaps they had all gone to the beach.

She had become quite accustomed to riding her new tricycle. Her parents had given it to her on her third birthday in May and she loved it. But what was the good of riding up and down all day when there was no one to play with? As she sat on her tricycle that day wondering, a forlorn feeling had come over her and it made her thirsty. She went into the house to get a drink and once again her mother sent her outside. And again her mother said she was a nuisance. How many times had she said it? A nuisance, Lily knew—because her mother had told her—was a person who was 'bothersome'. So she went out again without a drink. And what was a child who was unwelcome in her own home supposed to do?

Lily, who could see Mrs. Foster on the other side of the table looking at her thoughtfully, remembered that by the third or fourth or fifth time she had been sent outside on that day, she was feeling extremely lonely—miserable, in fact. Even now, she remembered that she had ridden up and down the street again, not knowing what else to do. And not knowing whether her mother would ever let her in the house, she wondered one more time why there was no one to play with. That was when she thought of her grandmother Linnea. It was a thought that seemed to come of its own accord, quite out of the blue, and it brought with it a lovely warm feeling. Not hot like a July day, just warm, because whenever she went to visit her grandmother she was always gathered up in smiles as if she was a treasure.

If the adult Lily had to question her memory of that day, now would be the time to do it—in the midst of her mother's performance. Was that the right word for it—this travesty of a reunion after so many years away? Who knows? She wondered whether she—the child Lily— had hesitated on that day. Perhaps. Did she think of asking her mother for permission to ride such a long way from home? She couldn't remember, but little Lily must have known that if she had asked the answer would have been no. Her mother didn't like her grandmother. She knew that. Did she run away from home? No. She went to visit.

It was a mile or so from where Lily lived to where her grandparents lived, and to get there, she would have to cross two roads and one set of railroad tracks on which trains came by on regular schedules. The trains that went through were mainly carrying things like coal, and they were often very long. But Lily had been back and forth to her grandparents in her father's car so often that she knew exactly where to go. And she had crossed both the rails and the streets many times when she walked up to the shops with her mother. And every time, she knew that her mother would say, 'Be careful. Stop here. Look both ways twice before you go. Never cross the street if the light isn't green.' Lily knew all this and thought it would be easy.

And it was easy up to a point. She rode her little tricycle to the end of her street, turned left and continued on until she reached the train tracks, where she stopped, looked and listened, and it was the same for the traffic lights in the centre of town, where she had to cross twice to make a right-hand turn. She was beginning to feel a bit confident as she rode past the hardware store and the town hall. But then there was Front Street to cross and it didn't have traffic lights, so she had to be really careful. She remembered how pleased she was that she did it all by herself and there weren't any cars to run over her that day. And then there was the library. And next was the big house where Sarah and Betsy and Ruth lived. And then there was a school, and then more streets and the doctor's house, where there were great maple trees with reddish-green leaves, and a sign to tell people that a doctor lived there. His name was Dr. Hale and he was a very nice man. Lily liked him a lot. A bit further on she came to no-man's land, where both the yards and houses suddenly became smaller and more crowded, and some of the houses were almost touching the road. Although she had seen it all many times from her father's car, it seemed very different when she rode past on her tricycle. She became quite nervous in that strange part of town where she didn't know anyone. She was not at all sure of herself and she was beginning to feel tired. It was much further than she had remembered. For a moment or so, she thought she might be going to cry, but then the road curved a bit and at the end of the curve she could see the big gas station and she knew exactly where she was. There was just one more quite big house with a quite big yard to get past, and immediately beyond it was her grandparents' house with the long curved driveway.

She rode her tricycle faster then. She was pleased that she was able to ride up the little slope without sliding backwards, and as she came around the curve, feeling so happy to be there, her grandmother came out of the house smiling at her and calling out, "Why Lily! What a lovely surprise it is to see you!" But even as she was looking at Lily, she seemed to be looking beyond her as well. Looking for something else and puzzled at not seeing it, she asked, "Where is your mother, Lily? Have you been riding so fast that you left her behind? Maybe she's tired. It's quite a long way to be walking with a baby in a carriage—and so soon too!"

"I came to see you by myself," Lily said.

As the older Lily remembered it, her grandmother had exclaimed, "Oh my goodness!"

As memories go, it was at that point—and only at that point—that

15

Lily began to realize that she had done a wrong thing, but it wasn't until years later that the thought occurred to her that her grandparents might not have been home that day—and what would she have done then?

What followed was a glass of milk and a cookie for her at the kitchen table, and a phone call to her mother, who apparently had no idea that Lily wasn't still riding her tricycle up and down the street outside her house. Her grandmother—the only woman in the family at that time who could drive a car—took her home 'in a little while.' Lily had no recollection of being punished. Quite the contrary, it was more like a thing put in the closet. Were there words like, "Don't ever do this again!"? She couldn't remember.

How long does it take to think a memory through? Scarcely seconds it seemed, because in the time it took for it to go racing through her head, in technicolour, William had managed by some magic of speech, to bring her mother down to earth again and engage her and Mrs. Foster in a much more sensible conversation. She could hear Charley and the children in the kitchen laughing. She sat back happily and had another sip of her gin and tonic. It was quite nice, she thought, but on the whole she preferred tea, or a nice glass of wine. It is a very strong drink, she thought as she had another sip.

She wondered how a person as small as her mother could possibly drink as much as one, let alone two or more. She saw that her mother was concentrating on her drink at that moment and wondered why, after all this time, she still found her intimidating. It must be habit, she thought, or the grief that followed if... If what? It had never really made sense. She cast a glance in the direction of Mrs. Foster and was rewarded with a warm and supportive smile. She knows, Lily thought. She always did. How easy it is to know a thing when nothing changes! While her mind was muddled by a jumbled confusion of past and present, caused by her mother who couldn't seem to see anything on a straight angle, there was Mrs. Foster, perfectly relaxed, as if accustomed, in the same

way that she was accustomed to tying her shoelaces. Watching them—
William and Mrs. Foster—chatting comfortably was a lovely thing to
see. She took a deep breath and relaxed for the first time that day.

Was that really how it was? she wondered. She could never be sure
of it, not even in retrospect, because the rest of that day had disappeared
from her mind altogether, possibly overshadowed by her mother's
antics. But she was willing to bet that some time in the afternoon, or
early evening, there was a barbecue with hot dogs and hamburgers and
potato salad and coleslaw. And perhaps her mother had hugged her
good-bye at the end of the day—if she was up to it.

CHAPTER 2

1948

The Lie

Lily stood very still, looking into her mother's eyes and concentrating with all her might. She was searching inside herself for "the truth"—the thing that her mother wanted to know. Her mother held her firmly by the shoulders and stared into her face, as if she could see right into her, in underneath her skin and bones. As if she could see what Lily was really thinking—if only she looked hard enough... She was being serious in a way that Lily had never encountered before. And there was something else too—in the way that she was sounding so confident in Lily—something artful. This was not the way her mother usually spoke. So it seemed to her that her mother was trying to find a way to make her say what she wanted to hear. This was why she was concentrating so hard—trying to think what it was she should say. But she could not understand why her mother would not accept what she had already told her.

"I know that you are a good girl," Betsy said. "I know that I can rely on you.

She waited a few moments for this to sink in, watching Lily's face.

"Do you understand," she went on, "what is the difference between the truth and a lie? Do you?"

"A lie," Lily answered, "is not true."

"But what is true?"

"What really happened."

"What really happened then?"

"I told you already," Lily said, beginning to feel confused. "If I tell the truth, it is true. I can't say different. I don't know."

She hung her head.

Betsy was getting impatient. "I want you to understand this," she insisted. "It's very important. You have to tell me the truth."

"But I already told you."

Her lip was beginning to quiver. She didn't know what more to say if her mother wouldn't believe her.

"Mrs. Beauregard told me you lied," Betsy said, watching Lily's face intently. "That you lied against Ellie on purpose. You tried to get Ellie in trouble because you were really the naughty one."

She paused, waited, and then went on, "You should not be afraid to tell the truth—even when you are bad. It is always the right thing to tell the truth."

She waited again. Then she asked, "Why won't you answer me? Do you want me to think that Mrs. Beauregard is a liar? She asked Ellie what happened. Ellie said you lied."

Lily remained silent. She was thinking—trying to sort out her confusion. Mrs. Beauregard was a grown-up. Grown-up people told children the right way to be. Behave yourself, they said. Mind your manners. Be a good girl. Don't pick your nose. Hold your fork the right way. Don't hunch your shoulders. Go to bed. Did they tell lies too? But then, she thought, it was Ellie who lied. Mrs. Beauregard was just saying what Ellie said. Mrs. Beauregard believed Ellie. Ellie was bigger than she was—much bigger—almost a grown-up herself. She was eleven. Lily was only four.

She tried not to cry. She did not really understand this, but she knew, even though she was only four, that the Beauregards were nasty people. Perhaps because sometime she had heard someone talking or because the other kids in the neighbourhood didn't always want to play with them, or because they always looked so dirty, even when they had only just come out to play.

Ellie was the oldest of nine ragged, snotty-nosed kids. And all of them—even their mother—looked the same. Like a whole family of paper dolls that had been left to fade in the sun and rain, they had dry, straw-coloured hair and pale blue, washed-out eyes, and stubborn faces and worn clothes. They lived, not on the wrong side of the tracks, but almost exactly on the tracks, in a shabby, patchwork house which appeared to lean precariously on the edge of the railway embankment.

It made sense to live there; Ellie's father worked at the train station in Oxford. There were a lot of trains that went through in those days. Some of them stopped in the town to pick up passengers, but mostly, there were great, long freight trains that rumbled on through, while lines of motor cars waited at the flashing red lights, and the people in them counted the freight cars, every time. There were so many and they had such interesting names painted on their sides that, for children, it was a reading lesson and a counting lesson all in one. Sometimes at night, when they came back from somewhere, Lily would hear her father say, as they drove over the tracks, "Must be a train coming through soon. Bo Beauregard's out with his lantern again." And sure enough, she would see a light bobbing around in the dark down near the tracks.

In the daytime, Lily could never cross over the tracks without looking back to see if the Beauregard's house was still there. One day, she thought, it might just lean over too far and slide on down the embankment to meet the next train. And the train might come along and take the whole thing away to another town. The thought pleased her. The house had always made her nervous. The people in the house had always made her nervous. She never went too close to it, or them, if she could avoid it. In fact, she never once went inside it. A train might come and take her away. Besides, the only time she had ever been bitten by a dog, it was the Beauregard's dog. So she stayed close to her own house, which was straight and snug. It was painted red and had a big garden with tomatoes in it.

"Perhaps," Betsy said, "you have forgotten what really happened."

Another pause.

"Are you paying attention to me, Lily?"

Lily looked at Betsy again—meaning to pay careful attention.

Betsy sighed, a little exasperated.

"Maybe you need to think about this some more," she said.

Lily tried again to remember what had happened. No. She already knew what had happened. So now she tried to remember if some other thing might have happened instead. Was it possible, she wondered, that the thing she knew was not true? Was it possible that she only remembered it as she did because she didn't want to think she was really a very bad girl? She began to feel awfully tired.

Betsy sat for a while longer saying nothing. Waiting. This must be very important, Lily thought, because her mother hadn't spent so much time with her all at once for as long as she could remember. Her mother was always too busy. They had a baby that yelled a lot. The baby was yelling right now, upstairs in its crib. But what else could she say? She couldn't think of anything else.

Betsy was tired too. She had begun to regret that she had been so hasty in ringing that sharp-tongued Beauregard woman. And Matty was crying again! She sighed. It was either messy pants or an insatiable appetite. One way or the other, it added up to one very demanding baby and no peace for her.

She took Lily by the shoulders and looked into her face once more, impatient to get this over with. "I want you to know," she said, "that

I will have to tell your father when he comes home. I want you to understand. It is very important for you to learn to tell the truth—more important than anything. Only bad people lie. If you don't want to grow up to be bad, you must start now. Tell me the truth."

Lily was silent. The baby was still crying. Betsy sighed again. She was tired of the baby. Tired of Lily.

"All right then," she said. "I tell you what. I will make you a promise. I promise you that if you tell me the truth, no matter what it is, you won't get a spanking. Now, you will go to your room and think about this. You will stay there until you remember what the truth is. And when you remember it, you can come and tell me."

"But I already told you. I don't know."

She meant to say, 'I don't know what you want,' but it didn't come out that way when she spoke. She was getting mixed up.

"I said go to your room until you remember. Go!"

Betsy pointed to the stairs and gave Lily a push. Such an aggravating child, she thought. It was enough to drive a person crazy. All that bother! It had been going on for hours. She would need to make herself a cup of coffee—and see about that baby.

Lily went up the stairs slowly, hanging her head. She was tired and hungry. She knew that her mother believed Ellie and she wondered again if it was true—that she could have forgotten what really happened—or, perhaps she had lied by accident. She thought, as she walked up the stairs, that she should try her very best to remember, for if she could remember, then surely her mother would see that Ellie had lied. And then, maybe, her mother would give her a hug and pat her on the back and say, "There, there..." She would really try. It was very important. Her mother had said so.

When she got to her bedroom, she sat on her bed and looked down at her dress and tried her utmost to remember 'the truth'—the one really true truth that her mother wanted.

❧

Her mother had made her a new dress. She certainly did remember that. It was blue with little pink flowers on it, and it had a white collar. When she tried it on, it had felt good. The new material was crisp, and the skirt stuck out a little and swayed when she moved. It was tied at the back with a big bow and it had pretty pink buttons. It had made her feel like a princess in a fairy tale—so pretty that she wanted to show off. She wanted to wear it outside. Her mother had said no.

It had been raining. But now the sun was shining and it was warm. "Please," she had begged—her face earnest and shining, "Please Mom, can I just go over and show Carol? I'll be good."

Of course she would be good. Without being able to express it, she knew that. Didn't her mother know? Didn't she know that when you feel like a princess in a pretty new dress you can walk around for hours and not a speck of dust will touch you? Didn't her mother know that in a new dress, you have a special magic?

Perhaps Betsy did know it, because the next moment, she changed her mind. "Okay," she said, "but only to show Carol."

She could agree to that, she thought. After all, it was only a few yards. Carol lived just across the street. Besides, she didn't mind doing a little showing off herself. She was very proud of her skill with a needle. No one else in the street could sew like she could.

"But first, you have to look neat all over," she had told Lily. "I can't have you going out looking like some beggar child and shaming us."

She had got busy rearranging Lily so that by the time she set out to cross the street, Lily was wearing not only her new dress but also clean white socks and summer-white sneakers and a big white ribbon in her hair.

Carol was Lily's friend. She was bigger than Ellie—nearly fourteen. Betsy always said she didn't want Lily hanging around being a nuisance to Carol all the time, but Carol would just laugh and say she liked having Lily come to visit. It was true. Carol made Lily welcome— fussed over her, read her stories, played jacks with her, cut out paper dolls for her. She almost always had time for Lily, if she was home.

When you went to Carol's house, Lily knew you never knocked. One day, when she was smaller, she had stood outside banging and banging on the door until Carol's mother had finally come out. "Carol's not home," she had said, "but the next time you come, don't knock. Just stand outside and yell, 'Carol!' If she comes, then you can be sure she is home!" She had laughed and sent Lily away with a cookie. Carol's mother laughed a lot. Lily liked her too.

Today, Lily didn't get to yell Carol. Carol was already coming out the door as Lily reached the steps.

"My goodness, how nice you look!" Carol had exclaimed when she saw Lily. "Is that a new dress? I'll bet your mom made it! It sure is pretty."

Carol kept on walking as she talked. She was on her way out and in a hurry. When they got to the street, Lily stopped. She wasn't sure what was happening.

"Come on!" Carol said. "I'm just going over to see Lorraine. You can come with me. Lorraine won't mind."

Lily shook her head. "My mother said not to go anywhere else."

"But it's just across the street," Carol told her. "It's okay. I'll be with you. Your mother won't mind. Really she won't. Don't you want Lorraine to see how pretty you look?"

Lily hung back, not knowing what to do.

"Come on!" Carol said. "I'll take you home afterwards myself. Come!"

She took Lily by the hand and they began to cross the street. Lorraine's house was just a little further down on the same side as Lily's. If she was with Carol, she thought, it would be all right to go to Lorraine's, for just a minute. But still she hesitated, pulled against

Carol, tried to release her hand. Carol seemed not to notice and Lily began to think, as Carol hurried her up the street, that her mother really wouldn't mind. Not if she was with Carol.

But then, halfway to Lorraine's house, events took a different and unexpected course. Lorraine—instead of sitting sedately inside her house waiting for someone to knock on her front door, as Lily had expected—came running out with a bunch of the neighbourhood kids around her, all jostling and jumping and shouting with excitement. Lorraine herself was waving urgently for Carol to join them. "Come," she cried. "Quick!" And before Lily could discover what it was about, the whole crowd was heading in a great hurry towards the end of the street down by the turkey farm—and Carol was with them. She had simply abandoned Lily, or failed to remember that she had promised to see her safely home.

Without Carol's hand to hold, Lily didn't know what to do. She thought she should go home, but she also felt that she belonged to Carol—that she was in a sense still visiting her. So—like a cork caught up in a heavy sea—uncertain and erratic—she followed the crowd as it hurried up the street. She wasn't at all sure of herself. She wanted to be with Carol, but she also knew that her mother would be angry if she went somewhere else. She was still thinking about this when she saw that Carol was out in front—laughing and chattering, leading the others on and getting further and further away without ever once looking back.

She stopped, unable to understand how Carol could so easily have forgotten her. But then it occurred to her that Carol might think she was still there, running along with all the others. So she ran to catch up, but she didn't think to call out and, although she was running with all her might, she couldn't narrow the gap between herself and the others. They were so much bigger and faster. She began to feel miserable and wondered again why Carol had left her behind. Hadn't she promised?

She stopped again. This time, she looked down at her shoes and hung her head so that her hair fell across her face. Looking down in this way was a thing she had done for a long time whenever things went wrong. It was a way to hide her thoughts, or feelings, because she knew that you had to hide your face sometimes. Faces could be read. Her mother had told her so—many times. "Don't think you can hide anything from me! I know what you're thinking!" is what she always said.

When Lily looked down, she saw her new dress. In all the fuss and hurry, she had quite forgotten why she had come out in the first place, but when she saw her dress, she knew immediately that she should go home. She also knew that she needed to hurry to get there before her mother got mad. But as she turned towards home, she saw that she was much further down the street than she had ever been. Further than her mother had gone, she was sure. Her mother never walked beyond Lorraine's house. For Lily, this part of the street was a foreign place. It made her nervous. If her mother wasn't there, there might be dogs— big dogs that barked and scared her. So she stood in the middle of the street and turned her head back and forth—looking one way to see if she could catch up with Carol and the other way to see if her mother might come out and see her standing there. If her mother came out, she thought, she would be able to run back home. But finally, with neither a crowd nor a mother to attach herself to, and feeling utterly alone, she turned and ran as fast as she could to catch up with Carol— who was not really so very far away.

As they reached the house opposite the turkey farm, all the boys went racing ahead up the steps. Tim Nelson lived in this house. Lily had never met Tim, nor seen him at her end of the street, but all the kids who went to school seemed to know him. His house was small and green and perched so close to the corner that between the front door and the street there was scarcely room for more than a set of wooden steps. On each side of the steps, a tiny patch of lawn formed a border between the house and the street, which curved around past it and continued on over a railroad bridge so narrow that only one car could cross over it at a time. Even from a child's point of view, it seemed such a small house and such a small yard—squashed between the street and the tracks—that it was like a toy from an electric train set on a table too small to contain all the pieces.

The thing that was happening at this end of the street was Tim Nelson's birthday. His mother had sent out the message that all the kids in the neighbourhood could have some cake if they came. She might not have known when she said it that there were so many children in the neighbourhood. Even Ellie Beauregard was there, looking grubby as usual, standing at the bottom of the steps, making up her mind whether to go in or not.

When she saw Lily coming up the street looking so clean and new her eyes narrowed and her mouth hardened and she moved away from the steps—back into the street—and she bent down, as though she might be going to pick up a stone or something. Lily saw this and sped up so that she could get closer to Carol who, by this time, was standing amongst the small crowd of girls who had been pushed aside by the boys in their rush to be the first through the door. As she reached the steps she squeezed her way through the girls, slipped her hand into Carol's, and breathed a sigh of relief. She looked back for a moment at Ellie with the hard face and pushed to hurry Carol into the house.

In the hallway a plump lady with dark hair and black-framed glasses came up to her and exclaimed, "My oh my! Is it your birthday too, my dear? My! My! Such a pretty dress! You do look so pretty! Whose little girl are you? You must have some cake. Come in and meet my Tim."

"No ma'am," Lily whispered. "It's my summer dress. My Mummy made."

She meant to say she had to go, but Mrs. Nelson had already bustled on to organize another batch of children. It was probably the only time in Tim's life that he would have so many at his house all at once and it was such a muddle and noise. Lily was anxious. Kids all over the place were bumping into her and she was afraid that her dress would be spoiled. Her mother might be looking for her by now. She'd been gone too long and too far. She turned to tell Carol that it was time—but she couldn't see her anywhere.

Oh no! Lily thought. She went without me.

She started down the steps in a hurry, looking to see where Carol had gone. Carol was nowhere to be seen outside or in. Only Ellie was there, standing in the street next to a big puddle, a foot or two from the steps. She glared at Lily and hissed. She laughed at Lily and made it sound menacing.

Everyone else knew that Ellie was tough—that she liked scaring people. The other children would always laugh and hiss back at her but Lily was small and didn't know. She hesitated, not knowing what to do. She began to think that Carol must have got mixed up with another part of the crowd and was still in the house. She would go back in, she thought. But before she could move—in the blink of an eye—Ellie jumped smack into the puddle in front of her and splashed mud all over Lily's new dress.

"Smarty pants!" Ellie yelled, jumping up and down in a fury. "Smarty pants! Pee in yer pants! Ants in yer pants! Ha! Think yer so smart! Think ya! Ha! Ha ha ha ha ha!"

She kept on jumping and splashing mud in all directions.

Lily stood fixed to the spot—horrified—looking at her new dress all limp and stained with mud.

Mrs. Nelson must have heard the noise outside—the angry noise that threatened to spoil all her happy birthday noises—because she came out of the house to see what was happening.

Lily was still looking down at her dress.

Ellie, the moment the door opened, jumped back from the puddle and burst into howls of outrage.

"Look!" she yelled. "Look! Lily made me all dirty! She thinks she's so good! Look! She got all dirty too! When she splashed me! Look! Oh look!"

And she cried. Furiously. Convincingly.

Lily gasped when she heard this—a deep, sobbing gasp. And without waiting for Carol or anyone else, she ran, shrieking the whole way home, entirely forgetting that she was alone.

That was all she could remember, no matter how much she thought about it. And no one had seen it except herself and Ellie.

She sat on her bed and thought some more. She knew what her mother wanted her to say. But she couldn't understand why she wanted it. Why was she supposed to say the same thing Ellie said? Ellie's mother was nasty. Lily knew she had demanded an apology from her mother. She had said how dare Betsy complain about *her* Ellie? But why didn't her mother say that Ellie should be punished? Why didn't her mother tell Mrs. Beauregard that Ellie had lied? Why wouldn't her mother believe her? Was she just too small to believe?

She thought for a long time. It seemed an awfully long time until, finally, it occurred to her that she might never leave her room again, not if her mother wouldn't believe her when she told the truth. She could sit there forever. She might never get to eat again. And she was hungry. Her mother had forgotten all about lunch when she had come home all ruined and shrieking.

Lily could hear Matty banging a spoon on his high chair downstairs. She heard her mother moving around in the kitchen, banging pots. She heard her talking to him. Cooing at him. She could hear him blurting his food. Making buzzing noises. Chuckling. He was having fun with his food.

All at once she knew what she had to do. It would be okay, she thought. She would be allowed out again. Her mother had promised that she wouldn't be spanked, no matter what. It would be okay.

When she went downstairs to Betsy, Lily was smiling happily. Betsy was still feeding Matty, not really thinking of Lily at all by this time. Such a bothersome day it had been. She was not aware of the child standing next to her. She started when Lily spoke.

"I have thought," Lily told her, "and I remember what happened. I did it myself. I jumped in the puddle because I got mad at Ellie."

Betsy stopped feeding Matty. She stared at Lily for a few moments, saying nothing. Then her face went a deep, furious red. She smacked the spoon down onto the tray and jumped to her feet in a rage. "What are you saying?" she shouted.

She grabbed Lily and shook her till she began to get dizzy. "Why? Why? Why did you lie?" she yelled. "You disgraceful child! You bad, bad, bad girl!"

She began smacking Lily all over. Hitting and batting and shaking and shouting. She was beside herself. "You wait till your father hears about this," she shouted.

Betsy's words were clipped off short with a snap. She smacked and hit—grabbed Lily by the chin—shook her head back and forth—yelled. Then, gasping for breath, she stopped. She had worn herself out. She seemed smaller then, and very tired. Why bother, she asked herself. She should leave it for him. Yes! She would!

"You are going to get such a spanking when your father gets home!" she said. "Go to your room! Now! Go! Stay there until your father comes. He will deal with you! And you will have plenty of time to think about this while you wait!"

She began to push Lily towards the stairs. Then she stopped again, struck by another thought.

"No! Wait!" she said, narrowing her eyes as she looked at Lily. "First, you have to apologize to Mrs. Beauregard!"

Betsy grabbed the top of Lily's arm very tight and pulled her over to the phone, held her as she dialed the number. Her hand was shaking. Tears were pouring down Lily's cheeks. The once cheerful ribbon hung down over one of her eyes making her look lopsided and crumpled. Someone answered. Betsy pulled herself up straight and spoke into the phone, all haughty and abrupt.

"Mrs. Beauregard!" she said. "My daughter has decided that she has something to say to you."

Betsy handed the phone to Lily, scowling.

Lily wasn't very good at telephones—wasn't good at this kind of thing at all. It was one thing to say what she thought her mother wanted to hear and another thing to talk to Mrs. Beauregard. She stood with the phone in her hand, saying nothing for a moment.

"Speak!" her mother snapped. "Say it!"

"I'm sorry," Lily whispered.

Although her mouth was touching the phone, she was barely audible.

"Tell her," Betsy hissed, "Tell her you lied. Tell her!"

Lily looked confused. She could hear Mrs. Beauregard on the other end, her voice high-pitched and cutting, like a hacksaw. "Foreigners! Dirty foreigners!" she was saying.

The phone went dead and Lily held it away from herself, as though there was something wrong with it. Betsy frowned and grabbed it, opened her mouth to speak, then stopped—caught, as in a photograph—puzzled to find a dial tone where a voice should have been. She was taken aback for a moment. Then she looked at Lily again, Lily so wrecked and forlorn, and she went into a rage all over again at the sight of her. She shoved her towards the stairs, pulled at her hair, hit her on the legs and shouted at her as she tripped on the steps.

"You promised me!" Lily cried as she stumbled. "You said if I told the truth!"

For a long time, Lily lay sobbing on her bed, streaked with dirt still, and damp and sad. The magic was gone from her dress.

She could hear her mother moaning downstairs, "A new dress! Brand new! My own beautiful work! She promised me! She promised to keep clean. She is such an irresponsible child! Such a stupid, stupid child!"

Upstairs, as she sat sobbing, Lily was still trying to figure out why she hadn't been able to get it right. She had told a lie trying to get it right. She sat up suddenly, shocked at the thought that had just come to her. She had told a lie. She really had told a lie. Her father would never believe her now.

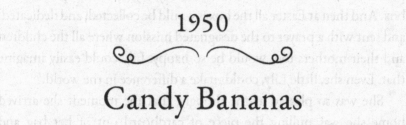

CHAPTER 3

1950

Candy Bananas

When she was about six years old, Lily began to have problems with language. She found it confusing that very simple words suddenly seemed to have quite different meanings—social and political meanings far beyond her understanding. Furthermore, she discovered that some words meant quite different things to different people. How was she to know who was right when that happened? How was she supposed to get it right if the grown-ups didn't agree?

Well before Lily added the word "impaled" to her vocabulary, but sometime after she had discovered the meaning of "obstreperous," she came home from Sunday school one day with her cup overflowing with goodness and mercy. In those days, she often went to Sunday school alone. Betsy and Charley weren't in the habit of attending church regularly, but Sunday school was a regular business for Lily who certainly needed such a good example, in their opinion.

It was the beginning of Lent and Lily's church always gave "mite boxes" to the children then. Every year at this time, when they got the boxes the children would be given a little sermon about the missions and the poor hungry children of the world who went around dressed in rags—or nothing at all. Lily had seen pictures of them. Sometimes not even their mothers had shirts. She had seen it in the pictures.

Pennies were all that was required for the mite boxes. All the spare pennies a child could find for the next forty days should be put into the box. And then at Easter all the boxes would be collected, and dedicated, and sent with a prayer to the designated mission where all the children and their mothers too, would be so happy. Lily could easily imagine that. Even she, little Lily, could make a difference in the world.

She was so pleased at the thought that the moment she arrived home she was pulling the piece of cardboard out of her bag and showing it to her mother. She needed some help to punch it out and make it into a box. "Fold on the line," it said—here, and here, and here.

Her mother was in the kitchen hanging up her dish towel. She was smiling. What a glorious day! It was early spring. The snow was melting and on the radio they were playing Lily's favourite song—tra la la, tra la dee dee, it gives me a thrill"—and Lily was humming along as she handed the piece of cardboard to her mother.

"So, where are they sending the mite boxes this year?" Betsy asked.

"Japan," Lily answered.

"Where," Charley asked, looking up at her over his Sunday newspaper. His face was stiff and there was an ominous chill in his voice.

A frown skipped across Betsy's face. She looked at Charley anxiously and put the piece of cardboard down on the table.

Oh no! Lily thought. Something is the matter!

The sun was streaming through the window, yet it seemed cold all of a sudden—and so still—and Lily knew that she was going to give the wrong answer.

"Japan—they said."

She spoke in a voice so soft and hesitant that if there had been any other sound, Charley wouldn't have heard her. But he could hear a pin drop. It was the wrong answer.

The whole house seemed to explode then. The glass that Charley had been holding in his hand shattered against the kitchen wall with a noise that far outweighed the size of it. Pieces of glass sprayed around the room, echoing as they landed. Some pieces hit Lily with a sting. She might be bleeding, she thought, maybe, but Charley was coming at her with such a wild look in his eyes that she imagined she would be the next thing to shatter against a wall. Pieces of Lily would be everywhere, she was certain.

"Charley!" Betsy shouted. "Charley! You stop it now! Charley! Stop it, I say."

Betsy pulled at Charley's arm. She yelled at Charley to make him pay attention. "It's not Lily's fault," she yelled. "She couldn't possibly know. Stop it, Charley!"

Charley stopped. Or, as it seemed, all his energy took a sudden detour. It fixed him to the spot and came shooting out of his head instead. As if he could actually feel it happening, he put his hands on top of his head and it looked like he was holding it on. And he began shouting. "Hell! Goddam it! It's incredible!—People died!— Hundreds! Thousands! My friends! In jungles ... spiders ... gigantic ... dead ... my friends. Dirty Japs! Slit-eyed little yellow bastards! They want me to give them money? I'll kill them! I'll kill the bastards!"

"Charley! Calm down!" Betsy insisted. "I'm sure they were only thinking of the children. The children haven't done anything wrong, you know."

"Yeah? Sure! Goddam it! Let's feed the damn children. So in ten or fifteen years they can send them out too and do the whole goddam thing all over again. Bloody Japs! I'll kill the bastards! Right now! Goddam it!"

Charley's energy took off in another direction then and he headed out the door in a fury.

"Charley!" Betsy yelled after him. "Stop! What do you think you're doing? You come back here! It's lunchtime! Come on now. Let's have some lunch."

Charley kept on going down the path to the car. He was wild.

"Charley! Stop! Charley, where are you going?" Betsy yelled after him.

"To Grace church," he shouted over his shoulder. "To the goddam vicar! That idiot! Mr. Paine! I'm going to kill him."

While he was gone, Betsy and Lily cleaned up the mess, got the lunch ready and waited. They were nervous the whole time Charley was away. Another of Lily's favourite songs came on the radio, the one that Betsy always turned into a game, the "Anything-you-can-do-I-can-do-better" song. They had a competition over it, just like in the song. "No you can't. Yes I can." They played the game every time the song came on whatever they were doing. Betsy could dry dishes better than Lily. "No you can't." Betsy could sweep the floor, "yes I can," tie her shoelaces, "no you can't," make a cake, "yes I can." But right now wasn't a good time for games. Neither of them was really listening.

Lily was thinking. If Mr. Paine had told them what a good thing it was to send mite boxes to Japan, how could her father get so mad? Didn't her mother and father always tell her that she had to go to Sunday school, even if it was a nice day, because she had to learn to be good? And her parents were good too; they were parents. But if one good person said mite boxes for hungry children and the other good person said "kill the bastards," somebody had to be wrong. They couldn't both be right.

Lily knew of course that there had been a war. Her father had married her mother in that war. Ozzie was the best man. They had pictures of it, the men in uniforms. Ozzie and Charley always laughed at themselves when they saw those pictures. "Big Swedes down-under!"

they would roar and, "Remember Heather!" They laughed wildly at that, whooping and slapping their sides at the memory. Heather, Lily thought, must have been a very funny woman "down-under".

"Stupid Swedes!" Betsy called them. Or "stubborn Swedes". Either way—and here she almost invariably and quite unconsciously reduced the whole to the specific, to an image, not of Swedes in general, nor of Charley and Ozzie, but of Charley and his mother—they were in her opinion interchangeably "stubborn" or "stupid". She had in fact on a number of occasions pronounced with a singular dryness that you could apply a whole lot of words to Swedes—a good many of them not suitable for the ears of children.

In truth, Charley and Ozzie were Americans with at most a dozen Swedish phrases between them. As boys they would follow the men who worked on the farm. *"Riktiga grisarna,"* Charley heard them say. "Dirty pigs!" is what he always said it meant. As a child, he had repeated it in delight, "Rikti greesolar!" "Rikti greesolar!" Again and again he repeated it, spreading his mouth wide each time in a silly grimace on the last syllable. Years later, the adult Charley was still repeating it, in precisely the same way and enormously loud at family gatherings. "RIKTI GREESOLAR!" he would roar. And he'd laugh his great squealing laugh. But Charley was thoroughly American—cut off from his forebears by this third-generation language gap—and the grafting of a Yankee strain.

Notwithstanding the compelling reality of those photographs of a wartime wedding, which loomed over all other evidence in Lily's mind, there were other reminders of the war around still. They had air raid drills at school. The local Civil Defense Corps trained every week. And she had seen her mother and grandmother mixing the "oleo." She loved to see the colors gradually blending together until the darker yellow had completely disappeared and it was all one smooth color. Her grandmother told her they had to do this because of the war—

because of rations, or shortages. Not because it was fun to watch the colors getting all mixed together.

Lily also knew that her father hated all things Japanese. He would never let them have anything that had "Made in Japan" written on it. Not even if it had been a gift. Junk, he said, it was all junk. Everything Japanese was junk. You had to learn to read the labels to make sure you wouldn't get fooled. It was worth it, he always said, to pay a whole lot more just to make sure you weren't getting cheap Japanese junk. He was fanatical about it.

Now Lily was having to think some more. Wasn't it logical to see that the children of a country that could only produce junk might be hungry—Especially if no one ever bought anything from their parents? Even Lily could see that. Her mother had told her that if everyone kept on going to the supermarket for their meat, Mr. Moshinsky, the local butcher, would soon be hungry. Mr. Moshinsky was a nice man, Lily thought, so the Japanese children must be really hungry by now. Something wasn't right, she knew. It was very confusing.

Charley returned looking pleased with himself. Sat down to lunch without a word. Betsy watched him shove a great chunk of bread into his mouth. She waited and, finally, she asked if he'd managed to see Mr. Paine.

"Oh sure," Charley answered through his mouthful.

"Well? What did he say?"

Charley went on munching as though he meant to keep her in suspense, but it was an awfully big chunk of bread he had stuffed into his mouth—a clear miscalculation if a dramatic effect was what he had intended. It took him a long time to chew it. A long time before he could look at Betsy with a perfectly composed face and ask, "What are you fussing about? I've fixed it all up."

And then he had to swallow a couple more chunks of bread before he got around to telling her that Mr. Paine had agreed to send Lily's mite box to an Indian mission out west instead. Betsy looked relieved. Charley concentrated on his food till his plate was empty. Then he sat back, stretched, and ended his meal with an enormous belch.

He did this every time. It was an art, he said. He had perfected it in the Marine Corps. He was the best belcher in his company. It was a mark of honor he told them, and true appreciation, if you could belch a perfect belch at the end of every meal. It was even, he argued in a contradictory way, an ancient oriental custom. Betsy loathed it. It was a primary bone of contention between them for years. She endured it if they were alone, warned him seriously every time they had company coming, and nearly died of mortification if he did it in a restaurant. Privately, she thought she had been deceived by a military uniform. The civilizing of Charley was proving to be a much greater task than she had originally anticipated.

With Charley's belch, the mite box crisis came to an end. Peace returned to the household. But the day didn't seem quite as glorious to Lily as it had been. In fact, she lost interest in the mite box almost entirely. Betsy assured her that the American Indians were no less worthy a cause, but Lily did not yet have the personal confidence to swim against the stream. It simply didn't feel the same to be the one person in the whole Sunday school who was doing something different.

Her mite box sat mostly neglected in a corner of her room throughout the remainder of Lent, with the result that when Easter Sunday finally arrived, she was astonished to find how heavy it had become. She had no recollection of having put all those pennies into it. It was even more amazing than her Easter basket full of candy sitting high on the shelf where Betsy had put it "till later." Lily stood quietly, weighing the mite box in her hand with a puzzled look on her face until downstairs her mother yelled hurry. It must have been the Easter Bunny, she decided.

At church, Lily felt awkward. When he spoke about the mite boxes, Mr. Paine didn't mention anything about Indians and Lily didn't know whether to feel special or left out. She fidgeted nervously throughout the service, not knowing whether she wanted him to say something about the Indians or whether she didn't want to be noticed until, finally, she dropped her mite box on the floor. It broke. Pennies went everywhere. It was remarkable how far those pennies managed to roll and what a lot of fuss it caused.

Parishioners all over the church scrambled around on the floor under their pews helping Lily gather up the pennies. It was wonderful. They were so kind to her. So kind that it might even have seemed like a good thing that she had dropped the box, if only her father hadn't been sitting there scowling at her.

Charley never could handle it when something happened to upset the appropriate and expected order of things. He could manage a blizzard or a hurricane without any trouble—things that followed a logical path from beginning to end—but here was his kid creating a circus in church and it turned him to stone. He looked down at his prayer book, drew his mouth into a straight line, and sat reading— like a good Christian. It wasn't his problem, he thought. After all, *he* hadn't dropped *his* mite box. Let that damn kid clean up her own mess. Let those damn people crawl around on the floor if they want to be so stupid. What on earth are they sending money to Japan for anyway? Only a few years ago...

Seven years ago. That was when Charley, a psychological wreck— malaria-ridden, but otherwise unwounded—had been transported from the Solomon Islands to a hospital in Massachusetts where he spent a year in a cloud—gray-opaque—not knowing—waiting for his mind to match up with his body again. It had been too much for a young man of that age. The war. The jungle. Death. Horror. Even survival. Living on wit and instinct and coconuts for weeks at a time. He was okay now. Doing just fine. Sitting in church on Easter Sunday, bursting with bodily health, and well on his way to spending the rest of his life not wanting to know. For a long time, in fact, he had been perfecting the art of closing his mind—battening the hatches against the storm of reality. Even so, things had a way of sneaking up on him unexpectedly. The mite boxes, for example. The pennies all over the floor.

Betsy too was mortified. She sat quietly, absorbed in putting the box together again—like a good mother—but she would never let Lily forget, if she lived to be a hundred. Years later she would suddenly remember. Again and again, she remembered, "I'll never forget the day you dropped your mite box. I was so embarrassed. You were always such an impossible child."

Privately, Lily wondered what had really happened. Just imagine it, she thought. Forty little mite boxes went to Japan that year and one little mite box went to Utah, or Idaho, or New Mexico. They must have been so impressed when it arrived. Or did Mr. Paine tell a lie? Did my mite box really go to Japan?

It was a thought that she would never have dared to speak aloud—at least not in the presence of her parents—but there was some justification for it. It always seemed to her, when she thought about it later, that the whole of that day had been a trick from beginning to end. She had no idea when she left the church that her Japanese experience was by no means over—that the day had only just begun, and the mite box episode was only a small part of it, but well before the day was done, she had begun to have doubts about Mr. Paine's promise. By the middle of the afternoon, in fact, it had become very clear to her that the Indians simply didn't have a leg to stand on.

At the end of the service, before Lily had a chance to notice how blue the sky was, Mrs. Lydia White came up to invite Betsy and Charley to an early afternoon tea. Mrs. Lydia White was an elderly woman of considerable importance in the church and she was inviting them to tea because she wished to introduce them to a visiting Englishman. Her purpose was self-evident. Betsy was an Australian—the war-bride of the photographs and Mrs. Lydia White was making the assumption, as many Americans do, that an Australian will of course always be delighted to meet a fellow Englishman.

This may have been true in those days. Indeed, at that time, many Australians, even those with the merest scraping of English blood in them, nearly always spoke of England as home, regardless of whether they had been there or not—people like Betsy, who was mainly German. Of course just after the war not many people wanted to claim a German connection in preference to an English one. And Betsy's family had long ago stamped out all traces of its Jewish grandfather. So what was left? And besides, wasn't it a fact that the English royal family was really German?

Betsy herself was of the unshakeable conviction that only she, amongst the entire American population, was capable of appreciating British humor. Alec Guinness was her avowed favorite, but anything British would do. She remained adamant about this even into her old age. On one occasion, after she had gone to an Anna Russell concert at Memorial Auditorium in Worcester, she had complained and preened simultaneously for hours. A man had sat next to her with a deadpan face throughout the whole thing. "Well of course I'm not surprised," she had boasted. "Americans have no sense of humor at all. No appreciation whatsoever. They are absolutely incapable of recognizing true wit when they see it."

Consequently, Betsy was especially eager to meet a visiting Englishman, and she made sure that nothing was going to spoil her pleasure. She stopped on the way up to Mrs. Lydia White's front door to tell the children to play outside, be quiet, don't go near the car, and don't let Matty go out into the street, you hear, Lily? They didn't need to be in the house with the grown-ups, Betsy told Mrs. Lydia White, who had suggested that the children might like to have a drink too. No. Definitely not!

Thus Lily and her little brother Matty were left outside with nothing to do. There was no place to sit in their Easter Sunday clothes. The ground was still wet from the last rain, even though the sun was shining. They looked at each other and wondered how long it would be.

They were still wondering when the door opened again with a crash and three children—two boys and a girl, all older than Lily—came bursting out over her and Matty like a tidal wave, seething and bubbling at them, talking all at once as though they were one. Hello, they said, I'm Robert. I'm Andrew. I'm Alice. What'll we play? Let's play war. Who wants to be the Japs? What's your name? Lily? Lily, you can be a Jap.

Oh no! Not Lily! She knew what her father would do if he caught her being a Jap. What sort of game was it anyway, she wanted to know. None of the kids in her street played Japs, she told them. In her street, they had Cowboys and Indians.

"Oh God! How corny!" Alice exclaimed. "Cowboys and Indians! Huh! That's for Americans. We play war," she insisted.

These were the Englishman's children and they wanted a game. It was, they believed, absolutely necessary to have a game. And their game was war, and they wanted Japs. Lily couldn't be a Jap, she said. Her father wouldn't let her. She would rather talk.

"Talk! What for?" Andrew wanted to know, stamping about, impatient to get going.

"About England," she said. "You are English, Mrs. White said. Is it nice to live in England?"

"Different," Robert answered.

"Are you going to stay here for awhile?" she wondered.

"Nah! We're going home," Andrew said.

"Oh, England! Oh, talk!" Robert bellowed, waving it all away with his hand. He picked up an imaginary machine gun, pointed it at Lily, and finished her off with a succession of staccato shots. "Eh-eh-eh-eh-eh-eh-eh-eh! Fall down! you're dead!

I can't," Lily said. "I have my Easter dress on. My mother will get mad."

"Oh bother! Girls!" Andrew exclaimed.

Robert shook his head in exasperation, clutched his invisible gun to him like they did in the movies and began running all over the yard shooting at random. "Kill the Japs," he yelled. "Kill the Japs."

Alice and Andrew followed suit. And it was very noisy.

The door opened and Betsy came out. "For heaven's sake, Lily!" she shouted, "You're making enough noise to wake the dead. Be quiet, can't you."

There was silence then. Matty stood with his shoulders all hunched up around his head. Lily was beginning to droop. Betsy glared at her for a moment and then went back inside, having settled the matter to her satisfaction—or so she thought. Noisy children, she always said, were intolerable—especially if they were her own. Indeed, in her frequently-repeated opinion, 'children should be seen and not heard' and, when there were visitors to be entertained, 'they should neither be seen nor heard.'

As the door shut, the English children rolled their eyes at Lily and grinned. And the noise started again. They were everywhere, killing people indiscriminately. Finishing off the enemy once and for all.

On that long, damp afternoon, while her mother was inside visiting an Englishman, Lily stood outside with Matty and watched, or tried not to get in the way, as the Englishman's children tore up Mrs. Lydia White's front yard in their game of war. Lily and Matty couldn't get the hang of it at all, and Lily felt like a stranger lost in some foreign land. She couldn't play the game and she couldn't stop the noise and the louder it was, the quieter she became. She remembered her Easter basket. The Easter bunny had left it in the night. It was on the chair near her door when she woke up. It had candy bananas in it, and jelly beans and chocolate eggs. It would be nice to have a candy banana, she thought. Did Robert and Alice and Andrew get a basket, she wondered. She didn't ask. Japs were their business, she decided. "Kill the Japs" was all around her.

All afternoon, Lily and Matty were surrounded by warriors. They were all over the yard, and out in the street, and around the car. They made Lily dizzy. They made Matty hunch his shoulders. And finally, they made themselves thirsty.

"Let's go inside and get a drink," they said then.

"We're not allowed," Lily told them.

"Oh! Not allowed!" they chorused. They shrugged at her, rolled their eyes, and disappeared into the house.

It was quiet again. Matty let his shoulders down. Lily stood watching a robin pecking at the ground beneath the great oak tree that occupied the greater portion of Mrs. Lydia White's front yard at the corner of Walnut and Prospect streets, where no other creature was to be seen at that moment and the oak, it seemed, was breathing a nearly audible sigh.

And then they were out again—more Japs.

Lily thought it would never end. It did. The adults appeared at last and she was surprised to find that the English children had a mother too. She had thought, since they had been invited to meet a visiting Englishman, that there was only a father.

She waited for them to say good-bye. It took a long time. And they did it so very well. All smiles. Charm. Manners. How nice! Delighted! A pleasure! Perhaps we shall see you again. Why yes! And how nice and how nice and how nice. And finally, Lily's family piled into their car.

She sank back into the seat and put herself together again, breathing deep and slow and thinking of the candy bananas in her basket at home. She looked straight ahead as they drove off, not bothering to wave good-bye. What obstreperous kids, she thought.

Betsy sat looking pleased with herself. Lily wondered what she would say. Her mother nearly always had something to say when they had been somewhere. Sometimes it was very interesting. What would she say this time? She looked so happy.

She didn't have to wait long. They had not even reached the end of the street before Betsy turned to Charley—her face still marked with traces of party manners—and exclaimed, "What a pity they are only passing through! He was such a nice chap! A really nice chap!"

Lily froze. "Jap," her mother had said. "A nice Jap!" There would be an explosion. She was certain of it. Her father would be so mad! She looked anxiously at Matty, who sat beside her shrugging his shoulders, up and down, up and down, and then at her father driving down the street with an absent look on his face, as if he were alone. Maybe he didn't hear, she thought. But there was no doubt in her mind that her mother had called the man a nice Jap.

"Such a nice chap, don't you think?" Betsy repeated.

Lily watched her father nervously.

Charley looked at Betsy and beamed an empty, angelic smile at her. "Mmm, yes," he answered. "A nice man... I was thinking, how about we have some beer with dinner?"

Betsy wasn't a beer drinker. Beer was a vulgar men's drink in her opinion. But just then she thought she really wouldn't mind having a beer. Yes! "A good idea," she agreed—and she put her little foot in its wedge-heeled sandal up on the dashboard—its dainty shape and her tiny ankle as always so pleasing to see. She smiled at it and allowed her mind to drift back over the afternoon. She was feeling more like herself than she had in several years.

Lily watched her father very carefully for a minute or so, then sank back into the seat once more, absolutely puzzled. She was having problems with language again. She ran it over and over in her mind as they drove home. A nice Jap! A nice Jap! Her mother had said he was a nice Jap and her father didn't get mad. Kill the Japs, she thought. All afternoon, those kids were killing Japs and in the house was their father, who was "such a nice Jap." How could it be?

It was all too difficult for her. She was very tired. She closed her eyes and thought of her candy bananas.

CHAPTER 4

1952

Aunt Agneta

They were at the farmhouse in Hubbardston waiting for lunch. Charley and his uncle Will were talking town talk. Betsy pushed in an extra word here or there. Matty was playing under the dinner table. Lily leaned back in her chair listening—her feet dangling just above Matty's head. Will's wife, Agneta, sat reading the newspaper at her own table in the bay window. The housekeeper, Eva, was in the kitchen getting the lunch ready.

The room was cheerful. The newspaper rattled occasionally. The conversation bounced about—loud or soft—as it pleased the men. They practiced wit, entertainment and serious business. Charley was a bit too loud—a little deaf even then perhaps—or too anxious to match his uncle Will, who was sitting so relaxed in his chair, smiling his tight, knowing smile. Will had the look of a man who owned it all. And why not? It was, after all, Will's house, Will's fields and Will's woods as far as he could see. It was the inheritance of the youngest of seven surviving children, and that was no small thing.

A stranger might have thought, from the way the talk was going, that the men were all that mattered in that room, but it would have been a mistake to focus exclusively on the noisy men—to forget Agneta, sitting there at her table in the bay window. The stranger would have been wrong. It was not possible to forget Agneta. She made sure of that, even when she seemed downright forgetful of others herself. At this very moment, in fact, Agneta made sure of it. Crumpling the edges of the newspaper in a sudden surprised fist and sucking in her breath with a gasp, she exclaimed, "Good gracious me! How dreadful!"

Everyone stopped talking and looked at her, waiting for the rest. Agneta went on reading her paper, oblivious to them. Absorbed? Or being theatrical, perhaps?

They waited, a long time it seemed until, finally, Will prompted, "Well, Agneta? We're waiting for you to tell us."

Agneta looked up then, over the top of her glasses, and said, "Fancy it! A Gardner man has been impaled by a deer."

There was a brief silence while they thought about this. Then Charley said laconically, "He must've been pretty stupid to do that."

"Well, you know," Will observed, "there are some pretty dumb people around these parts nowadays. When the hunting season starts, they come up from the city and think they're Daniel Boone once they get a gun in their hands."

"But he came from Gardner," Betsy said. "That's not a city."

"Well I don't know what you think it is if it's not a city!" Will snorted. "They got mills over there and parking lots for all the cars that drive around the streets these days. And the co-op. A supermarket even. I don't know what you think *this* is if Gardner's not a city. The boondocks, maybe!"

He sat back in his chair and smiled at Betsy, the same tight, knowing smile. He looked so comfortable sitting there in his favourite chair, in his blue plaid shirt. It was Will's mark—the blue plaid. Like some blazon, he wore it almost every day of the year, or so it seemed to Lily, who couldn't remember ever seeing her uncle in any other shirt.

Betsy puffed impatiently on her cigarette. It was fashionable to

52

smoke in those days. Useful too. A person could puff out his anger—blow smoke in someone's face. So she puffed. Puffed and seethed.

Damned New Englanders, she thought. So damned sure of themselves. You couldn't argue with them. They wouldn't know a city if they fell over one. She was the one who had grown up in a city—a real city. Oh yes! Gardner! Huh! Nobody would call Gardner a city unless they came from nowhere at all—like right here. Here is nowhere at all...

"Hell no!" Charley shouted at Will, bursting through Betsy's thoughts. "This sure as hell ain't the boondocks! Ya gotta go at least another fifty miles north for that. Jesus!"

"Don't swear in front of the children," Betsy reprimanded him.

"What I wanta know," he continued, not looking at her, "is how anyone could be so dumb as to get impaled by a deer?"

"Where is Boondocks?" Lily asked.

Agneta, who had been watching them, hawk-like, not moving, suddenly cleared her throat with a deep rumble and said, "Do you mind?"

Lily was startled. Aunt Agneta had such a strong, plain-speaking voice. Everyone listened when she spoke. Everyone. Even so, it was different for children, Lily knew. Children had to obey. All her aunt had to do was look at her. She could freeze Lily to silence every time with just a look. It was so embarrassing to be frozen like that—so embarrassing that every time she was in that room, she watched Agneta carefully. She believed that if only she was careful enough, she might see it in her aunt's face that she was about to do something wrong, and then she might stop herself in time. If only she could get it right, she thought, her aunt might be pleased with her and then she wouldn't be frozen.

Thus the watching had become a habit, except that today she had been distracted by all the talk and the words she didn't understand. She was listening, trying to figure them out, trying so hard that she forgot everything else until, all of a sudden, there was Aunt Agneta's voice so loud it made her jump in her seat.

Everyone looked at Agneta then, caught by that plain, loud voice and her sharp gaze. "You asked me what happened," she frowned. "If you want me to read it to you, you'll have to be quiet."

It was quiet in the room then. Outside, Lily could hear a snow plough at the bottom of the hill working its way up the road that went past the farm on its way to Westminster. It was some distance away, but the sound of it kept shifting back and forth, close one moment, distant and muffled the next, as if the wind was bringing the sound waves to them along some old winding Indian path instead of directly through the air—a tricky old wind.

Lily looked at her Aunt Agneta sitting at her table in front of the bay window. She always sat in the same spot, in her wheelchair. She hadn't been able to walk since she had broken her hip and that had happened before Lily was even born. So Lily had never seen her Aunt Agneta in any other way. For all she knew, Agneta was a fixture of the window as much as the braiding clamp was a fixture of her table. Lily believed that she never moved from there at all—slept there even. She had seen Agneta's fine big bedroom at the front of the house, of course, but it always looked exactly the same to her. Not even the wrinkles on the bedspread appeared to change. She thought that Agneta probably slept in her wheelchair instead because it was easier that way. She could see it for herself. Underneath the table, entirely covered with a large black and green plaid blanket, the bottom half of Agneta was already in bed.

Above the table was the real Agneta, the Agneta that Lily saw doing things, the person who could freeze you with a look. Lily knew that the bottom half of Agneta could move, but she had never seen it go anywhere and to her seeing was understanding. To her, seeing only in parts, her aunt's body was a puzzle—part blanket, part person. Cut off at the waist by a table, the person part was wrapped in a rose knitted shawl pinned at the neck with a brooch and to Lily, that half of Agneta seemed more alive than most of the other wholly functional people she knew. Above the table, Agneta was all motion. Plump arms and strong hands darted back and forth from under the shawl. Sharp eyes flashed through steel-rimmed glasses. And from the gray bun, pinned tight at the back of her head, soft, feathery wisps of hair escaped and danced about her forehead in merriment beyond the vision of the stern, busy woman, giving her a cheerful aspect in spite of herself.

At the table in front of the window, Agneta ate her meals, read the paper, had visitors, and braided rugs. For the last of these, she was famous in the district. They were exceptionally fine and beautiful rugs in all the shapes and sizes that you could make such a rug. And all of them were very much in demand. Lily loved those rugs. And she loved watching her Aunt Agneta making them. It seemed to her that Agneta was a magician of rugs—a very slow magician, of course. It took a long time to make a rug. Even so, it was nowhere near as mundane as whipping a rabbit or two out of a hat. Lily had seen a few people pulling rabbits out of hats, or turning one silk scarf into twenty scarves—all different colors and knotted together, or pulling money out of someone's ear. But she had only ever seen one person turning old rags into rugs.

Rags. The strips that were cut from the cast-off clothes that the ladies of the town brought to Agneta's house—the men's suits and the women's woolen skirts and dresses. When they came into Agneta's house, they were clothes. When they went out again, they were rugs. And they were brand new all over again. It was the most amazing trick—the transformation of old, tired-looking things into thick new rugs in all sorts of colours. All over the house, there were striped rugs in plain black with rainbows of colour woven in between. They were all over Hubbardston too—and at Barre and Westminster. And at her grandmother's house in Oxford. And other places that Lily didn't even know about.

When she wasn't at school and her mother allowed her to come over to the farmhouse for a visit, she sat and watched Agneta making the rugs. Putting people together in the most unexpected ways. Old friends, or old enemies. Regardless. Jim Harris's old gray suit, cut into strips dyed black by Eva, was being braided together with Lydia Erle's blue tweed skirt and Mary Ellis's old green dress. For all you knew, those three hadn't spoken to each other for years—some old broken love triangle perhaps—and now, here they were at one remove fashioned together into a rug for Rupe and Ellen Barton's front parlor. Most often, there was a big bag of clothes that the ladies had gathered and mixed in together, and you couldn't even guess the history of that rug. How many weddings and funerals had those suits and dresses attended?

"Whose dress was that?" Lily had once asked.

Agneta had looked over her glasses—always, she looked over her glasses—and said sternly, "Little girls shouldn't ask such questions."

But she never seemed to mind if Lily just sat quietly and watched. Lily had the impression, the longer she watched, that although Agneta herself never moved away from her spot, she really was moving in a sense—very slowly—every time she made another rug. It seemed to grow out of her, as if it were actually a part of her spreading out into the room beyond her table. It kept on moving like that until, finally— as children do when they have got big enough—it separated from her and left the house altogether and went out into the world.

The opposite also seemed to be true. Sitting there in the window— in the brightest spot in the house—Agneta seemed like a lamp placed to attract people—like moths. Without exception, each person who came into that long, low-ceilinged room flew at once to the end where Agneta was. The end with the light. The action. The no-nonsense talk. And the sharp wit.

Always, before meals, Agneta's braiding was put aside to clear a space for her tray. And while she waited, she found other things to do. Like reading a book or a newspaper. Catching up with the local news. Keeping an eye on things. Knowing what was going on. Out in the world, the rest of the family met people and gossiped. In the house, where no one ever stopped except at mealtimes, it was Agneta who owned the news. Like now. Sitting there with the newspaper in her hands, keeping everyone waiting to hear what had happened, she owned the story about the man from Gardner. And, as usual, she took her time adjusting the paper to suit herself, holding it up in order to catch the best light from the window behind her, turning it this way and that until she was satisfied. And Lily sat watching her and wondering about the word "impaled" that meant "dreadful." But how?

"Well," said Agneta, at last, "this is what it says:

Late Friday afternoon, Thomas Pike, aged 35, from Gardner, was killed when he was impaled by a deer. He had been hunting alone in the Barre woods. There were no witnesses. His wife, Mrs. Veronica Pike, reported him missing Friday evening. He was found on Saturday afternoon. According to the Barre Chief of Police, Mr. Bob Sanders, evidence found at the scene suggests that the deer had already been wounded and that it attacked Mr. Pike when he trapped it at the bottom of a gully. They think the deer must have charged at him in fright. Mr. Pike is believed to have shot the deer as it charged. Both were found dead.

"So, now you know all about it," Agneta concluded, punctuating her story with a tight, wry smile as she put the paper back on the table.

"Well, you know," Will said, after a moment's thought, "it's not the first time that's happened. I heard about a man up Monadnock way who got caught like that about twenty years back. You have to be pretty careful around deer. They don't like to feel there's nowheres else to go. And some of those big old bucks have mighty tough antlers."

"It might have been getting dark," Betsy suggested. "The paper said it was the afternoon. It gets dark so early. He might not have seen the deer."

"Well if he didn't see the deer, I'd darned sure like to know how it came to be wounded in the first place. Seems to me," Will said, "anyone that goes out in the woods when they can't see properly is a darned fool! A darned stupid city slicker."

Betsy puffed on her cigarette again. "I meant," she said, clipping her words short, "that he might not have noticed in the afternoon light that it had got trapped—or that it was so close." She sighed, stubbed out her cigarette on the ash tray, and picked up her knitting.

The conversation buzzed around the dinner table for some time—now that there was something to talk about in that otherwise empty winter world. A poet or a naturalist wouldn't have found it empty, of course. There is always something to be found, even in a desert. But for Lily—and possibly for Betsy as well—the winter landscape in this part of the state was empty in a way that was sometimes altogether too full. It might have been the fullness of nature breathing a sigh of relief in the absence of people, but to the lonely child, it was enormous and overpowering. After the storms, when the wind had died down, the earth lay smothered beneath such great piles of snow that at times it seemed to Lily as though, above the drifts, the air itself was held in suspension and everything had become so still and quiet that she felt she had gone deaf and then, suddenly, in the still, deaf silence, the suspension would snap and the sounds would multiply, so that it was as if the entire forest had awakened and was stretching itself—getting ready to do something. When it was like this, she would be doubly startled by the thud of a great clump of snow sliding off a branch into the drifts below—or a twig snapping somewhere in the woods, enormously loud, like a shot—or a squirrel skittering in the trees above, moving too fast to track.

The woods near the farm were so dense that even Lily's young eyes couldn't discern anything more than a few feet away in the heavy winter light. In the mornings, when she had to go to school before the sun had got up, she had to stand all alone at the corner of the Westminster road and wait for Mr. Carey to come with his car and get her. The town wouldn't send a school bus all the way out there for just one child— and her mother would never go down and wait with her. She couldn't leave Matty alone, she always said—it was too much trouble to have to dress him too at that time of day. So, every morning, Lily stood alone in the dark, unable to see anything clearly in the woods beyond the road and, as she waited, it felt as though the dark was actually touching her and the woods themselves were moving—closing in on her—like a monstrous, impenetrable army of giants.

"What's impaled?" Lily asked her mother.

"Shh!" Betsy said. "Be quiet!"

The talk around the table continued buzzing along. She was only a child after all, and children, as her mother always said, should be seen and not heard. Under the table, Matty was playing with his truck, making his own buzzing noises.

Inside the house, a certain coziness prevailed, although even this had a forced quality. It was as comfortable as any house could be that had no electricity or plumbing or heating other than that which came from the fireplaces, or the wood stove in the kitchen. Without any modern conveniences, the family—Will and the housekeeper Eva, that is—in an attempt to achieve a measure of comfort, were constantly engaged in a battle against the invasion of winter. Keeping the wood boxes filled. Keeping shovels handy for the next blizzard. Keeping the bucket of water ready in the kitchen to thaw the water-pump every morning, because every morning, without fail, even though it was inside the lean-to shed, the pump would be frozen. How funny it was, Lily thought—when she watched Eva pouring the water onto the pump, very carefully, a little at a time—you had to give water to get water. And the pump invariably came to life so slowly, and with such deep, unhappy groans that she was always surprised to see the water coming at last. Every time, she watched the process in utter suspense, leaning closer to it, wanting to see down into it to find out where the noises came from, wanting to discover how, deep in the ground, there could be water when everything on the surface was ice. "Don't touch the pump, now," Eva always warned, in her jolly, high-pitched voice. "Your fingers will stick to it and freeze. And you'll never get them loose until the spring."

There were a lot of old farmhouses in those days that hadn't yet reached out to meet the twentieth century, mostly because they had to wait for the wires to come to them, which they did—inevitably. The telephone wires had already come by the time Lily was there, but the nearest house was still a mile away. It must have been a very lonely place when Lily's great-great-grandfather lived there with just a wife and daughter, and a couple of farmhands.

It was still lonely when Lily's family was there nearly a century later, although, according to her father, when he was a boy, the place was sometimes full of people—Finns and Swedes who had come out for the apple harvest, or to dig potatoes in the big field below the house. There was no trace of them anywhere to be seen now, unless of course, the fruit pickers' cottage was a trace. Nevertheless, people always leave traces of some kind behind them, however faintly—some deed or witticism perhaps, to be recalled in subsequent generations as legend. The Finns, for example, had taught Charley how to say "son of a bitch" in Finnish, and now Lily—in keeping with the nature of oral tradition—knew it too, although she knew that her parents would be angry with her if they knew she knew.

In spite of its lack of modern conveniences, the old farmhouse was quite beautiful. It had been built in the nineteenth century, with some vision of the future, by Will's grandfather, who had come out from Sweden with his wife and daughter and bought six hundred and fifty acres of land. He must have thought he would have many children. He had placed his barn at the bottom of the hill and his house a little way down from the top, just below his apple orchard. He might have imagined that one day the place would be filled with grandchildren and great-grandchildren. If he had known, when he built the house with the big bay window, that someday the childless Agneta would be sitting there making rugs, he might have put the French doors between the dining room and parlor just so that she could keep an eye on Lily if she went in there—in case she touched something she wasn't supposed to. But what was there to touch in such a sparse and formal room, where not even the grown-ups went anymore? And what was the good of a front parlor, when no one ever came to knock on the front door?

In fact, what was there for Lily to do in that house except keep warm near the fire, or watch Agneta make rugs, or follow Eva about the kitchen, or play with her doll if she had remembered to bring it? But always, be good. And don't ask questions, her mother always said. Don't ask why Grandma never comes to visit. Aunt Agneta doesn't like her. Why doesn't Aunt Agneta like her? Don't ask questions! Why did Aunt Agneta marry a baby? Don't be absurd! Uncle Will isn't a baby. But you said she is eighteen years older than he is. And you were eighteen when I was a baby. Don't ask questions!

"Mom! What does that mean? Impaled?" Lily asked her mother again, leaning over as if to whisper, but speaking louder this time.

"Hush!" Betsy answered. "Don't interrupt! It's rude to interrupt your elders."

Lily sat back in the big, straight-backed wooden chair and looked at her Aunt Agneta. Was she very, very old, she wondered.

Agneta looked back at her—so stern over her glasses—as though she could see straight into Lily's mind. "Impaled," she said, "means that you get stabbed right through the middle with something sharp, like a spear—or a sharp pole. And then you die. The man from Gardner was impaled by the deer's antlers."

Lily's mouth opened wide and her eyes grew as big and dark as the inside of her mouth. Agneta sat watching her—looking right into her, until Eva, the irrepressibly cheerful Eva—who kept twenty or thirty or forty cats in and around the woodpile in the back lean-to shed between the water pump and the outhouse—Eva who complained incessantly but cheerfully— brought in a tray with muffins and jam and coffee. And Lily thought about the woods in the morning dark—and waiting for Mr. Carey. There might be a deer in those woods.

Years later when Lily was fifteen years old her Aunt Agneta would die and leave her an unusually large and exquisitely carved cameo with a fine gold setting and a thick gold chain. Lily would be astonished. She had never seen the cameo before. She had never thought that her Aunt Agneta liked her.

"You will certainly have to look after that," Betsy would tell her. "No one else got anything from Agneta. She wasn't even related to you. She was just your uncle's wife! Huh! Of course you wouldn't know anything about cameos, but that is a valuable museum piece. I hope you will appreciate it."

In the year that Lily turned seventeen, Eva who was diabetic, would go blind and move to an old people's home in Gardner. In the same year, her Uncle Will would be forced to retire from his job as town tax collector, the town having discovered that he had not paid his own taxes for more than twenty years. The family knew nothing of this. It would be weeks before they would hear that Will had gone to live with a brother in Chicago and that the farm and all it contained was gone. It had become the property of the town—nothing more than a family memory.

CHAPTER 5

1951

Creatures Great and Small

Lily had her first nightmare at Hubbardston, not long after Aunt Agneta had read in the paper about the man who was impaled by a deer—or at least it was the first nightmare she ever remembered—a dream so vivid and frightful that it returned to haunt her, both night and day. She woke from it into the absolute dark of her room, hot and sweaty with fear—hot, even under the crust of ice that had formed on the blanket beneath her nose.

In the moment of waking, she knew it had only been a dream. She felt the difference immediately. Even in the darkness of her nightmare, it had not been as dark, or as cold, as it was in her room. She was not happy to be awake, not certain that she had really escaped. She lay for a long time not moving—in fright—trying to see through the dark—trying to fix on some item, some piece of furniture, or toy that had not been in her dream—trying to hear something familiar beyond the utter silence of her room—to reassure herself that the dream had really ended—and lying there she was afraid. For a long time, in a darkness so total and unrelenting that she felt consumed by it, she was afraid, walled in by a darkness that she could not budge, no matter how hard she stared at it.

Her dream had been so real. The same place in Oxford town. The same people. Looking the same, doing the same things. Exactly the same and then not the same. Shifting in a flick, even as she recognized them, into something else no less real—and terrifying—concentrated entirely on her. She was the object of her own dream. In the dark of her dream, she was standing in the railway yard, all alone. Mr. Beauregard was coming towards her with his lantern, squinting at her in the night—and the sharp, black pebbles of the yard were cutting through her shoes. He was coming with the lantern—and she couldn't remember why she was standing there alone at night. There must be a reason. And then, in a flick, Mr. Dooby was coming instead—closer and closer—with the lantern in his hand and a horrible grin on his face. A manic and murderous grin. His eyes were crazy. Glinty. And then in another flick he had a knife. An enormous knife. He was going to kill her, she knew, and she ran and ran and ran, gasping for breath with the effort and the terror, and she heard Mr. Dooby snarling behind her, "I'll catch you girlie! I'll kill you. You can't get away! I'll kill you, girlie!" He thundered after her, waving the knife. Her legs were like lead. She was getting nowhere. She could hear him close behind her. Desperate, in slow motion, she turned towards the town—away from home. She couldn't get home. Not past Mr. Dooby. He would catch her. She was alone. Her father wouldn't come. He wouldn't know, wouldn't hear. She pushed, heavy and numb, towards the tracks. A train might come, she thought, and sweep Mr. Dooby away—and then a flick. Out of the darkness where the tracks should have been, a deer was pounding towards her with its head lowered, its huge antlers pointing at her. More deer were coming up behind it—and more still. A confused tapestry of deer shadows was spreading out to encircle her and she turned back in fright. The monstrous Mr. Dooby was there behind her, still grinning horribly and waving his knife. He lunged to grab her arm.

That was when she woke up. Every time. And every time, she knew immediately that she was not killed, that Mr. Dooby was gone, that the deer were gone, and yet she still did not feel safe lying there in that terrible room at the bottom of the house, in the corner of the orchard, next to woods that were so thick that the light of the moon could never find its way through them. This was Lily's nightmare. She would come to know it well. It occurred many times—not that night, but on other nights. It returned so often during the next year, and later still at odd times, that she spent half her waking time in a fright. Expecting something awful. The things in her dream were real, she knew. She had seen them before. She knew them all, straight or twisted. They were the things that scared her, all heaped together in a crazy jumble. They wouldn't leave her alone. To dream the same thing over and over, she was certain, was like being told: someday this will happen. That in itself was a nightmare—day or night.

She reached for her doll—for something soft to cuddle and hold close. It was gone. All the toys were gone. She remembered. Her father had taken them away. She had several dolls and soft toys—a bear and a rabbit. Only one of them really mattered to her—the doll, Fred. How absurd, her mother had said when she called it that. Fred! Why would you give a doll a boy's name she had wanted to know. It was silly, unless of course, she considered, you meant it for a nickname. If it was really Fredericka. Lily had nodded yes and said nothing. It was Fred. Not a nickname. Not even Fred actually, but dragged out a bit, more like 'frayed' and 'fred' mixed together. In Swedish, her grandmother had told her, it meant peace. Fred was the right name, Lily thought, but she never said so. Her mother would get mad if she knew. She hated Swedes, she always said. They were so stubborn.

Lily had taken Fred to bed with her every night since she had found her under the Christmas tree. A couple of years at least. The other toys had always spent the night on a shelf, but since the family had come to live in Hubbardston, she had started gathering them all into her bed every night—as security against the night perhaps, but against such nights, in the tacked-on room that wasn't even part of the real house, they were scarcely more than a drop of comfort measured out by a stingy hand. She had persuaded herself, nevertheless, that she would be safe, if only she could fill her bed with something. A doll or a bear even, was something—like a friend.

Lily wasn't entirely alone, in fact. Matty was there too in his crib, but he always slept—quiet and oblivious—a baby still really, although he was four now. He was always clinging to Betsy—or Betsy was always keeping him close. Matty would never hear it if something happened. No. Lily really was alone. Even so, there are degrees of aloneness. It was so much worse if Matty was sick and Betsy took him into the real house with them. It was so much worse to be alone then.

It had become a nightly ritual—Betsy tucking in the children—putting them away for the night. A neat dispatch. A little hurried—absent-minded. She had other things to do. So, every night, Lily gathered up her friends in a rush and pushed them in under the covers this way and that, making them comfortable. Making herself comfortable. And when it was done, Betsy went. She took the lantern with her. And there was no light

On the night of Lily's first nightmare, Betsy had a headache and Charley put the kids to bed. He was a true-blue Taurus. He went at everything like a bull. Cut the nonsense! No time to waste! Get moving! Don't stand next to the kerosene heater! Stupid child! You'll go up in flames. Move! Move! Move! There was no delicacy about Charley. He might have been out checking to see that the cows were properly fixed in their stalls. A chore. No more, no less. Get it over with. No stories. Never. Not even from Betsy. A little kiss from Betsy though. Most of the time. A little, distracted kiss. From Charley, nothing—

ever. And tonight Lily forgot her bear. She remembered after she was all tucked in and oh no! She scrambled out of her bed to get it before Charley could take the lantern away. It was the last straw. Charley in the doorway had had enough of this damned nonsense every night. She was too big for this kind of thing. It was the end. No more! Lily's entire ménage—cloth, plastic, stuffed and hollow—was removed from her bed. Forever. Not even Fred was allowed to stay. And Lily, in the unbearable emptiness of her bed and the overwhelming fullness of the night, cried herself to sleep.

When they had moved to Hubbardston at Thanksgiving, Lily thought it would be better. Mr. Dooby—the real Mr. Dooby—could never chase her again. It was only a joke everyone said. It wasn't, Lily knew. The first time maybe it was a whim—or the inspiration of a genuinely half-witted man. The first time, when Lily had wandered over to play with her friend Donald, not sure if he was home or if he wanted to play, his father, Mr. Dooby, was out in the yard, bent over cutting some rope. He had a big knife in his hand. She had come up so quietly that she startled him. He had jumped and the knife had flashed in the air. She had stepped back, hesitating, looking at the knife. At that moment—and it was possibly the only such moment in his life—Mr. Dooby was overtaken by a thought and carried along on the crest of it. Not knowing, but sensing the impression he would make, and enjoying the taste of it in his mind, he had pulled himself up to his full height—not very tall, but much bigger than Lily—and with a hideous grin, he had stamped towards her, waving the knife and snarling, "Come here, little girlie. Come here! Ha hah! I'm going to cut your ears off." Lily had fled in sheer terror.

From that time on, Mr. Dooby devoted himself to that thought. The one thought. It filled his mind. Gave him something to do.

Entertained him enormously. Every time he saw her coming, his eyes would light up. He would make his face go all hideous. He would reach for his knife. When he didn't have it, he pretended. Once he had got into the idea of his game as a permanent thing, he tried to remember the knife always, so that she wouldn't catch him without it. Even when he was inside the house, if he saw her coming down the street—on her way to school or the shops—he would wait until she was close enough, and then he would come running out with the knife, yelling, and getting ready to cut off her ears.

Always her ears. Lily's ears were the focal point—the place where his idea had fixed itself, like some spore settling at random and then growing into a great mushroom. And like a mushroom, the idea was a thing in itself. The limitations of Mr. Dooby's mind were manifest. There was no space in his head for two thoughts at a time. He could not vary his idea by even one degree and he replayed it endlessly. He became Lily's walking broad daylight nightmare.

Scaring Lily was just about the best fun Mr. Dooby had ever had in his life. It gave him a role to play. The entire street outside his house was his stage. And no one could stop him. Not his wife. Not Lily's parents. Not his son Donald. Not even when Donald complained that he had no one to play with anymore. In fact, Mr. Dooby enjoyed himself all the more when he had an audience—someone to stand and laugh at Lily's fright. A couple of neighbours were practically a full house to him.

Nobody, apart from Donald, ever really tried to stop Mr. Dooby, or took much notice, unless it was to laugh at the foolishness of it all. Betsy thought it was nonsense and scolded Lily when she came running home. Ignore him, she would say. On one occasion, after she had fled for home three times in the one day, Betsy went over and spoke to him about it. It was a joke, he had said, and, putting on his pantomime leer, he had waved his knife at Lily—and they had laughed about it—the two of them. But the knife was real, Lily knew. It was not a joke. And the face he made in front of Betsy was a different face. It was a joking funny scary face, not the really horrible face he always made. Betsy had never seen the other face.

"You are stupid," Betsy snapped at her when they were home again. "A silly coward. You should walk to school by yourself. Enough of this nonsense! I am tired of it."

And so Lily tiptoed past the Dooby house in terror every time, getting ready to run—trying not to disturb the man who might come running out like a dog. A couple of times, when Lily knew he had seen her coming, she had gone home again and begged, and not wanting her to be late for school, Betsy had walked her to the path on the other side of the Doobys' house. Even then, Lily had begged her to wait. "Wait till I get to the end," she had pleaded. "Then I'll be safe." And Mr. Dooby had stood there watching them go by, smiling like some harmless, frisky puppy. "There! You see," Betsy had told her, "he is nice. A very nice man really."

One day, Betsy told Lily that they were going to the Doobys after dinner to watch television—all of them, including her. She was aghast. She absolutely refused. "No! No! No! No! No!" she screamed. She would not go. But in those days, children did as they were told, and so she went.

It was practically an honor to be invited, Betsy had told her. The Doobys had just bought the first television set in the street, and now, said Betsy, "Here we are—the first family to be invited to watch it with them. We are so lucky. You should learn to be grateful."

Mr. Dooby behaved himself that night—or at least, confined himself to making faces at Lily when no one was looking. She sat close to her father all evening, pretending not to see and waiting to go home. On the television, some man with a mouthful of teeth kept laughing at his own jokes. She wasn't interested. She was a pest, Charley said, getting in his way all the time, bumping his glass of beer. Betsy frowned signals at him—indulging Lily for once—knowing that she wouldn't be there at all if she had a choice.

Ever since the day Mr. Dooby had become inspired by the theatrical possibilities of his knife, Lily didn't go there to play anymore. In fact, she never went there again of her own accord, except on one occasion not long before Charley decided to move away. Mr. Dooby was almost always at home during the day, but on that afternoon in the fall, when Donald came over to invite her to play, and Lily said no as usual, he insisted. His father had gone out for the whole afternoon, he told her, and he assured her that it would be okay.

It was the first afternoon in weeks that his father had gone out and Lily thought it must be a trap. After some hesitation, she agreed, but only if his mother said so. She went with him into his yard, where she could see that Mr. Dooby's car was gone. Even so, she stopped and refused to go any further. He had to go and get his mother, she told him—just to be sure. He went. She stood outside and waited. After a minute or so his mother appeared with a cheerful smile and told her that it was true. Mr. Dooby was gone and wouldn't be home again before dark. Lily would be perfectly safe, she said, and she smiled again—a bland, benevolent smile. "Would you like to come in and have a cookie," she asked, "a chocolate chip cookie?" No. Lily would not. She backed away in fright. "Would you like a cookie to eat outside?" she countered. "Yes ... please," Lily agreed—still hesitant.

A cookie outside was okay. How could you say no to a chocolate chip cookie? Nevertheless, she was as skittish as a wild animal and kept straying towards the street, getting ready to run home again. She liked Donald, but she couldn't help thinking that Mr. Dooby was lurking somewhere, waiting to surprise her. He had jumped out at her from behind bushes and trees and cars so many times. She ate her cookie slowly and stood back as Donald wandered about the yard. He was looking for something to do. She was searching for Mr. Dooby, checking nervously every few seconds to make sure that he wasn't sneaking up behind her. And seeing this, Donald became nervous at the thought that she would surely run off if he couldn't think of something pretty fast. The trouble was there really wasn't anything to do, not if Lily wouldn't play inside. It was fall. The leaves were falling and it was starting to get cold, and the outdoor toys had been put away for the winter, which, according to Donald's mother was "just around the corner."

There was no special rule about playing in those days. All the children played, without any real thought or plan, all over the neighborhood. It had been going on for years, until now. Now they played everywhere except Donald's house. It is true that some of the children still went to Donald's occasionally. They were not afraid. Mr. Dooby had never taken any interest in their ears. But from Donald's point of view, it was no fun at all to be playing in his yard if Lily wasn't there. It seemed to him a terrible thing and it had been going on for weeks. It wasn't his fault if his father behaved like a monster, but there was nothing he could do about it. His father became angry and yelled when he complained about it. Little boys, he was told, should know their proper place. They should know that children should "mind their own business." Donald had begun to think that the awful long season of his father's grand pantomime would never end and every day he became more unhappy. So now that he had a rare chance to have fun with Lily in his own yard, he wasn't about to let her go easily.

From Lily's point of view, this wandering around with nothing to do and Mr. Dooby lurking in her mind the whole time was no fun at all. She was becoming impatient. They had already wandered past the open garage three or four times. Donald had lingered uncertainly in front of it each time and now, here they were again, back in the same spot. She stopped and glared at him angrily.

71

"What are you looking at?" she asked, scowling. "What is there to do in the garage? Your father works in there."

Donald seemed puzzled for a moment and looked into the garage once more. Then, with the brightest of smiles, he turned to Lily and replied, "The windows!"

That's it, he thought, the thing to do! He would show Lily the windows.

"Look at the windows," he said. "My father has done all the storm windows for the winter."

She stood stolidly, looking from a distance.

"Oh, come on!" he said, "It's okay to have a look. Really, it is. My father won't come home. He's gone all the way to New Hampshire. Come on Lily!"

He pulled her into the garage to have a look at the windows. There were about twenty of them, all standing propped against the walls or leaning against saw horses—drying. Mr. Dooby had just finished putting new putty around the glass to hold it in place. The old putty, Donald told her, was all cracked and starting to come out, so his father had taken it out and put in new putty. Now the windows would be just like new. It had taken him a whole week to do it. "See how soft it is," he said, rubbing his finger along one of the window frames, feeling the putty. He took Lily's hand and pushed her finger into it to show her. It squashed flat, like play dough.

"It takes a long time to dry," he told her. "That's why they're all standing up. Look! I'll show you."

He pulled some putty off a window, rolled it into a little ball, and put it in her hand. It was soft and warm. She pushed it around on her hand. Rubbed it. Squashed it flat. Rolled it into a ball again.

Donald was pleased to see that she liked it. Now they had found something to do. He gave her some more. And some more. And then he took some putty for himself too, so they would both have a ball.

And then some more. And in a little while, Lily too took some putty from a window. And then some more.

Like Hansel and Gretel in the forest—forgetting where they were for a time—Donald and Lily munched and munched at those windows until their balls of putty were too big for their little hands. And seeing this, Donald quickly started a new ball so that Lily wouldn't hurry away too soon. It was great fun playing with Lily.

It took them a long time to get all the putty off those windows, but they managed it. Every last bit. By the time they pulled off the last piece, the sun had moved on in the sky. The shadows were getting bigger and Lily suddenly thought of Mr. Dooby with a shock. She had heard a car slow up out the front and she was in a fright all over again. The skittish look came across her face once more. In a hurry, she put her ball of putty in a corner out of the way, told Donald goodbye I have to go—and ran.

It wasn't Mr. Dooby's car. He was late getting home that day. He didn't get in until dark just as Mrs. Dooby had said, and then he wanted his dinner. He didn't discover what the children had been doing until late the next morning when he picked up one of the windows and the glass fell out and smashed. Pieces flew all over the place and Mr. Dooby, so suddenly and entirely surrounded by shards of glass in every possible size and shape, stood gazing at the floor in wonder. Having no idea how it happened or where to begin cleaning up the mess, he just stood and stared, until finally, he noticed that there was no putty on the window frame. He wondered how he could have been so careless as to put it up to dry without any putty on it. It had never happened before. He looked around at all the other frames, just to be sure, and one after another he saw that there was no putty on any of them. And then he saw the little piles of putty in the corner. He was still standing in the same spot, surrounded by shards, when his next great thought occurred to him. He would go into the house and get his wife to clean it up for him because, of course, it had to be her fault. If she had been paying attention while he was away, this couldn't have happened.

After that there was a lot of noise, and people up and down the street were talking about it. They couldn't help talking because the sounds they heard coming from the Dooby house that day were so loud that it seemed as though a new kind of theatre was emerging, much more dramatic than the one they had been watching all summer long—almost operatic, in fact.

Donald, who was only six years old, got a terrible beating. Lily wasn't punished at all. She waited all day for it and it never came. She would be in awful trouble, she knew, but she wasn't. Perhaps Donald never told. Her parents never said.

But at night, when she was in bed, she heard her mother saying to her father in the next room, "Silly fool! He had it coming, didn't he!" She heard them laughing together.

Charley roared about it. "What a joke!" he yelled. "Jesus! I sure would've liked to be a fly on the wall when he picked up that window. Jeez! What a mess! Glass all over the place! Holy Cow!"

Charley was winding himself up just picturing it. His laughter seemed to come rumbling out of him from somewhere in the depths of his stomach, rising in pitch as it went until it ended with a squeal just above his ears. "And the putty!" he gasped. "What a mess! Wrecked! Hooo! Whatta joke! All over again! He's gotta do it all over again! Hah! It'll be snowing before he's done. Jesus! ..."

"Ssshh!" Betsy said, "You'll wake the children."

Lily heard no more. Mr. Dooby never came out with his knife again. He never even bothered to look at her when she went past. He might have been too busy fixing his windows, or maybe, while he was thinking about his windows, the other thought—his one and only original thought—had flown out of his small head and he had forgotten it.

She had no idea what Mr. Dooby thought that day. The only

certain thing was that she would remember him for a long time to come and there was no comfort to be had in such a memory. But as she was soon to discover, nothing else was certain. Her whole world was about to change, quite suddenly, without any warning, and her HerHHHHhhkkk=er nightmares were lurking just around the corner, rather like Mr. Dooby himself. It would not take much to bring them forth. All they needed was a trigger, unhappiness perhaps, or something seemingly innocuous, like a very dark night without her doll or soft toys of any kind.

CHAPTER 6

1951

Roller Coaster

They would be moving to Hubbardston. They had sold the Oxford house. Just like that! It had all happened much more quickly than expected and for Lily it was altogether too much. One minute Mr. Dooby was leering at her with his knife and the next the whole family was leaving town—and the time in between had seemed a mere flick. It was as though she had been strolling along, humming happily to herself, thinking what a beautiful day it was, when all of a sudden the earth had fallen out from under and she was careening wildly down a hill, with nothing to hang on to. The dark nights at the back of the fruit pickers' cottage and the nightmares that went with them were yet to come. The world was unraveling in fits and starts, it seemed.

That was how it appeared to her. It didn't make sense. It all seemed just minutes. In fact, nearly four weeks had gone by since the windows incident, but minutes or days were all the same to her. How could anyone tell the difference between a minute or an hour or a week if the same awful thing happened every day for weeks on end? How could she even ask such a question? She was just a child—a very nervous child—although her mother preferred to call her silly, as in 'just plain silly.'

Perhaps it was a good thing that, for all her perspicacity, Betsy couldn't see inside Lily's mind. What would she have made of it when, just a few weeks later, a whole new world would be unfolding before them—like a kaleidoscope, packed with an ever-changing series of scenes and events, and each day so full that to Lily two months seemed like a whole year? But that was yet to come and neither of them could have guessed what Charley would decide to do next. The move to Hubbardston would come first. It was always one thing after another.

For Lily, this move was a difficult thing. It wasn't just a question of how things seemed in minutes or hours. It was about knowing what would happen next. Mr. Dooby no longer chased her with his knife, but the damage had been done. Although her nightmares had not yet begun, she was still not able to walk down the street without feeling anxious. If you asked her where her favourite place was in the whole world, she would tell you it was the kitchen in her own house, where it was warm and safe and there was corn chowder cooking on the stove and music on the radio and sometimes her mother would sing along with it.

She had only just begun to feel comfortable in that small world outside the kitchen—her street, her neighbourhood—when late one Saturday afternoon, just before the sun went down, Charley had come barreling into that kitchen, grinning like the cat. He had been grinning for miles—grinning so hard that when he drove up the street, he didn't even see Mr. Dooby up the ladder pushing a storm window into place. Into the kitchen he came and, still grinning, he took Lily's favourite place away from her.

"We're moving to Hubbardston," he had announced, "as soon as I can get the fruit pickers' cottage ready."

Within two weeks they had sold the house. After that, it seemed to

Lily that the whole world was spinning around her. Her mother was rushing about all day, every day, "busy, terribly busy," "getting things ready" and telling her to keep out of the way, which she did. She sat on the front step most of the time, thinking about the day when her father had come home grinning. She thought about it so much that she was sure she could remember every bit of it. She could see it in her mind—*exactly*. Her father had said that they would be moving to Hubbardston as soon as he could get the fruit pickers' cottage ready.

She had stood very still, wondering how it had happened, and wondering also what she would do without her friends from school. It was such a long way to Hubbardston. She would never be able to play with them. Did her mother know about this, she wondered? It was such a small house they lived in, yet she had never once heard her parents talking about moving, and if they had been talking, she would surely have heard. Didn't her mother tell her almost every day that she had big ears? She thought her father had gone out to buy some wood! Didn't her mother say he had gone to buy some wood? Didn't her mother say, "I wonder what's keeping him so long?" So how did it happen that a person went out to buy wood and decided instead to move to another place? Did her mother know about this?

Lily had looked at her, puzzled.

For a moment Betsy had also looked puzzled. Then she squawked, "What? Whatever are you talking about?"

"What? What? Are you deaf?" Charley had replied. "You heard me! I said we're moving!" I went to see Uncle Will. He agreed. As long as we aren't any trouble to them, he doesn't mind, and we can live there for *nothing*. Well ... you know what he's like—cantankerous old devil! Ya wanna know what he said? 'I sure as hell ain't gonna be held responsible if you freeze to death in the winter, but if you can manage, and if it ain't gonna cost me anything, it's okay with me!' That's *exactly* what he said. So it's okay. We're moving."

"I can't believe you," Betsy had said, as she put down the dish she had been drying—slowly and carefully so that she might not break it. And when she spoke it was in the same slow, quiet way: "How on earth do you think we'll manage? It's a dump. Nobody in their right mind would dream of it. Not even fruit pickers would stay there these days. You must be crazy."

"Ah you're always finding fault! You never can see the good of anything. You don't even know what it'll be like. I'm gonna fix it up. You won't recognize it when I'm done!"

"God, Charley! I can't believe this! For heaven's sake, winter's coming!" She spoke a little louder this time.

"It's only October. There's plenty of time. We'll manage."

"You lied to me! You said you needed to get some wood. Don't tell me you weren't planning this the whole time! You went straight to Hubbardston, didn't you?"

"It's time."

"Damn it, Charley! What do you think we're going to do? Manage! You say we can manage! What are we supposed to do with this house? Burn it? You think someone's just going to come walking in here tomorrow and buy it? You need money, you know. Even if it's a piece of junk you want to fix, you still need money to do it. And you can't do that if we can't sell the house. "God help us, Charley, it's only a year since you built the workshop so you would have more space to do your carpentry work. How are you going to do that at Hubbardston? There is no workshop—nothing like it—just an old broken down barn crammed full of junk—whole generations of junk. If your uncle ever managed to get in there, he'd never be able to find his way out again. How many years do you think it took him to make that mess? Time, you say! Time for what? Did you ever think of consulting me? Did you ever think I might have some say in the things we do?"

"It's time to move," Charley said. "This street is getting to be a jungle. And I know a jungle when I see one!"

Oh yes, Betsy had thought. If anyone knew enough to keep out of the jungle, it surely was Charley!

Lily, on the other hand, had no idea what he meant. Jungles had millions of trees with long swinging ropes, and snakes, crocodiles, tigers, monkeys, parrots. Little Black Sambo lived in a jungle and melted a tiger for butter! She certainly knew that. They had told her so at Sunday school. They had even shown her the pictures in the book. How could a street be a jungle? It was full of people. In fact, Lily thought it was more like a parade. If you sat on the front step for a while, just about everybody would go by. But you had to sit there to see it. The trouble with her father was that he never sat on the step. He was always somewhere else—out in his workshop or driving his car. She liked sitting on the front step—as long as the door was open so she could hurry back inside if someone scared her. Grown-ups would wave at her and call out as they walked past and she would smile and wave and breathe in deeply through her nose and smell the leaves falling red at her feet.

Their house was in a straggly, run-down street on the unfashionable side of the tracks off the main thoroughfare, where the houses were mostly small and the trees were mostly big. Great old oaks and maples rambled out over the neighbourhood, bowed lazily to passers-by, scraped at upstairs windows, dropped their leaves, and creaked and groaned with regret at the passing of summer. Lawns wandered out to the road, unhindered by sidewalks or fences. People took short cuts across lawns, vacant lots and other people's yards. Only visitors and delivery men walked up the paths.

The ice man came every week with a truckload of ice. Children from all the houses ran out the moment they saw him coming so they could get a chip of ice to suck on. And every time he would say with a great big laugh, "Hey! I know these kids! It's that Lily again, and Donald, come to get my ice." And he would hand each of them a small chip—Lily, Donald, Matty, Alan, Peggy and all the others who came running. He knew them all and every time he came, he would tell them to mind his truck while he took the blocks of ice wrapped in hessian bags into the houses where he would put the ice in the ice boxes. And the children would stand at the back of the truck juggling their ice chips from one hand to the other, freezing both hands and tongues and enjoying every minute of it. It was fun to go to the ice truck, Lily thought. Mr. Dooby never went there. It was safe.

Her mother had told her that it wouldn't be long before the ice man stopped coming, because everyone would soon have one of the new electric refrigerators, and you didn't need blocks of ice for those, she said. Lily couldn't believe it. Indeed, when she stood next to the truck, sucking on an ice chip, she refused to believe it. She thought her mother must be teasing. She often said things like that when she knew that Lily really liked something. It can't be true, she thought. But that is exactly what happened. In no time almost everyone seemed to have a refrigerator. Even her parents had bought one—just a week ago. They thought it was a wonderful thing—so modern, so up-to-date! Her mother especially loved it. She no longer had to mop up the water from the melted ice, because no matter how careful she was she always managed to spill some on the floor somewhere between the ice box and the sink. For her the refrigerator was a godsend. From Lily's point of view, the best thing about it was the word: refrigerator. She would roll it around on her tongue and make it sound like alli-gate-or. "There was an alli-gate-or," she would say, "in the re-fridjer-ate-or." And the ice man stopped coming.

The coal man, on the other hand, continued to come for much longer, even though he was never as friendly as the ice man. Whenever a child got in the way he fussed and growled. "Hey kid," he would yell, Ya wanna get your head knocked off! Stand in the way like that and when it all comes pouring down the chute, bam! Your mother'll kill me!"

He said the same thing every time and the boys invariably got in

82

the way on purpose, to see if he would make a mistake and let the coal go before it was safe. Lily always stood a good way back, while the boys laughed their heads off at the coal man and went closer. She didn't think it was a bit funny to see him glaring like a monster with a coal-smudged face, his mouth turned down and eyes squinted up. Sometimes the mothers came out and told the boys off. "Just you wait till I tell your mother," they would say, shaking their finger at them, and the boys would scramble. But Lily knew to be polite, because her mother had told her, "We need that coal. If you don't want to freeze to death in the winter, you had better be good!"

Her grandmother and grandfather also needed the coal. She had seen it pouring down the chute at their house too, from inside— down in the cellar, where she stood with her grandfather, watching as it tumbled with a great loud rattling noise, shiny and black, into a big wooden bin with a gate which could be opened when the bin was nearly empty. Just about every house in the town had a coal chute in those days and everywhere she went, it seemed, there would be that truck and the man with the coal-smudged face.

Sometimes she thought that some interesting thing was happening just about every minute of the day in that street, and she could tell you all about it, if only you would stop and listen. But most of the time people were in a hurry, though they would always smile and wave. Sometimes they would say something like, "My goodness! What do you know about that!" and they would walk a little faster so she would know how busy they were. Sometimes they would stop for a while and ask how her mother was, or tell her what a good girl she was, or what a pretty sweater she was wearing, and, when they were gone, she would always think what nice people they were.

One thing was sure, in those days it didn't take much to bring people out to see what was going on in the street. On warm days, even her mother would sit on the front doorstep—shelling peas and watching the world go by, or at least the small portion of it which frequented her street. And they in turn would watch her sitting there, doing something different from everybody else—knitting—or shelling peas.

None of the other mothers bothered with shelling peas any more. "What for," they would ask. "Don'tcha know you can buy 'em frozen at the A & P? You must be crazy making more work for yourself." But Betsy always said she liked having fresh peas—and perhaps she also liked seeing and being seen. She was small and cute in her calico apron with the rick-rack trim, and her unusually nice legs looked good propped up at an angle to steady the pot with the peas. Sometimes she let Lily help, but only for a moment or so because Lily would upset her rhythm, or get in the way, or forget herself and eat a pea. One way or another she was bound to cause trouble for herself even if it was a perfectly beautiful day to be sitting on the front step.

Betsy was shelling peas on the day when the organ grinder came by. He had a small, brown monkey, dressed in a little red jacket trimmed with gold braid, and a station master's hat to match. He stopped in front of their house, smiled at Betsy and bowed. Then he moved closer to the front step and began turning the handle on the organ, which was inside a wonderfully decorated box. It had a leather strap attached to each side and he wore it around his neck to keep it from falling when he turned the handle. It also had a stick attached underneath to keep it steady at the right height.

Lily thought it was the most beautiful thing to see because it had such pretty red flowers on it, but she had no idea until the man began to turn the handle that music would come out of it. She was so amazed that she jumped up to get a better look. She wanted to see how it worked. And in the same instant the little monkey started dancing to the music. It danced until its owner stopped turning the handle, then it stepped up to Betsy, bowed politely, took off its hat and held it out for money. Betsy pulled a penny out of her apron pocket and dropped it into the hat. The monkey bowed again, then, clutching the coin in its hand, it scrambled up onto the organ grinder's shoulder and dropped it into the bag he held out. Lily saw how quick the man was when he put the money bag into his pocket and was surprised when he winked at her as he started the music again. Once more, the monkey jumped down and danced, and the organ grinder watched it, even as he smiled at the gathering crowd. It was as though he could control the monkey just by looking at it—and it seemed anxious to please him.

Lily wasn't sure about the man, but she loved the monkey. In fact, she was enchanted by him. She had never seen such a clever and polite little animal. She wanted him to keep dancing all day long, but the next time he held out his hat, Betsy shook her head. Her apron pocket was empty, she said.

Oh no, Lily thought! And she rushed into the house to get her piggy bank, hurrying the whole while—afraid that he would be gone before she got back. She knew she had enough pennies in her piggy bank to keep the monkey dancing for a long time, if only he would stay long enough. She could easily understand the connection between the monkey and the money, but she never thought of the man at all. She had no idea how many apron-pocket pennies it would take to make a full meal for a man or a monkey.

The monkey was still there when she returned, standing patiently with its hat in its hand. Betsy and the man were talking. Lily put five coins into the hat before Betsy stopped her, frowning at her for giving away her own good money, when there was already a crowd of neighbours standing there. They should be the ones filling the hat. Not that Betsy said so out loud; she just looked the words, and Lily understood.

The organ grinder, who had seen the frown, also understood and stayed just long enough for another dance or two and a few more coins from the neighbours. Then both man and monkey tipped their hats, bowed to the crowd, smiled, and went on their way down the street, where they disappeared from view behind the trees! For an all-too-brief time, they had been a small sensation. Not part of something big like a circus—they were more like a small piece of a circus left behind and finding its way somehow. The little crowd went home again and, Lily who had never been to a circus or seen a real monkey, or such a music box, was bereft, but she did not cry. Her mother would not have liked it.

For days afterwards she couldn't stop thinking about the monkey. It was the best, most wonderful thing she had ever seen. She sat on the front step every day, thinking about it—about how small it was, and polite. She remembered how it had run up onto the man's shoulder so fast and how it had done it so easily and she wondered whether they might come back again.

While she sat on the front step, thinking about the monkey, she realized that lots of unusual things had been happening recently—almost every day. In all the time that Mr. Dooby had been scaring her, she had never really noticed anything but him and his knife and now, suddenly it seemed, the whole street was alive and sparkling. So she sat there wondering what would happen next.

No sooner did she think about it than a shiny green convertible with a rumble seat drove up the street and stopped outside the Curtis house—which was opposite the Doobys'. By the time the driver stepped out, half the kids in the neighborhood, including Lily, had come running to see this wonderful car. The driver was young man with shiny black curly hair, shiny black shoes, shiny black trousers and a creamy shirt, loose at the neck—and he was looking immensely pleased with himself.

That's Jack," she heard one of the boys whisper. "He's a real cool cat. He goes with Betty!"

Jack, who had come to get Betty, honked the horn three times, then leaned against the car and puffed on a cigarette while she kept him waiting—which, according to the custom of the time, was the proper thing to do if you were a girl like Betty and you had dark curly hair and sparkling brown eyes and you were the best baton twirler in town—and you looked great in a short skirt. Jack, who leaned against his car and puffed, was thoroughly enjoying the admiration of the little crowd around him, especially from the boys, who jostled and bumped each other just to get a close-up glimpse of his rumble seat.

"It's the only car with a rumble seat for miles and miles around! It's FAMOUS! My dad told me," exclaimed one boy, who wanted people to know that *he* knew all about it!

It should perhaps be said here that although Betty was nowhere to be seen at that moment, she too was part of the interesting things that happened in Lily's street, particularly when she practiced twirling her baton outside in the yard where everyone could see her and say "Ahhh!" when she threw her baton high up in the air, twirled around in her short skirt, and caught it again, with a beautiful white-toothed smile.

"You can see for yourself," Lily once heard an old lady saying to another old lady, "she almost never drops it." And one of the boys had told her that Betty was getting ready for the state baton twirling championship. "That's why she's outside all the time," he said. "She can't throw it in the house. The ceiling's not high enough."

A street that had champions was a good place to be, Lily thought—especially if it brought cars with rumble seats that you could get a ride in.

And so it happened. On the day that Betty kept the young man waiting so long that he had to waste time showing off for half the neighbourhood, men included—all of whom had come out to see the car with the rumble seat—Jack, with a great flourish, suddenly grabbed a bunch of kids, including Lily, and dumped them into the rumble seat. Then he opened the driver's door, hopped in and, with a flick of his hand started the motor and they were off! What an adventure that was! Down the street they drove for about fifty yards—or until they could hear the men behind them yelling, Hey Jack! Stop! Jack! Here's Betty.

Back they went again. Out of the rumble seat went all the kids and into the front went Betty and off Jack drove to a grand round of applause. And Lily was bursting with pride to know that *she* had ridden in a rumble seat, in a car driven by a genuine "Cool Cat". What's more, she had added something new to her vocabulary!

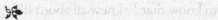

There was no doubt in Lily's mind that things were happening which made her street a very exciting place to live, and she liked it, but just as she and Donald, with never a thought about the consequences, had found pulling putty off windows utterly satisfying, she was not yet able to see that in the midst of all that excitement there was also a disorder which, in the end, threatened to topple into chaos. Not even Mr. Dooby had managed to put that thought into her head.

Betty wasn't the only one in the Curtis family to attract attention. The whole family was a magnet for attention that summer. The big Curtis boys, Sonny and Paul, who would have been at least seventeen or eighteen years old, were building a roller coaster in the vacant lot which stretched across the backyard of their own house and three others as well. It was, everyone thought, a tremendously audacious and exciting project and it attracted a great deal of attention—nearly all day every day and often into the evenings. Perhaps this is what made the street begin to seem like a jungle to Charley. There was always someone coming around to see what was happening, and they left their cars higgledy-piggledy, wherever there was space. Big kids were everywhere, trying to help, or getting in the way, hoping they would be remembered when it came time to get a ride.

It was an extraordinary thing to see a roller coaster, stretching out over most of a vacant lot in that run-down back street in a small country town. It was at least half as big around as a real roller coaster and almost as high, or so it seemed to Lily, who could see it from her own backyard. She had seen a real roller coaster once—from a distance. It was awfully high. This one, she thought, looked awfully high too, especially when she was standing near it. It would surely be right, she thought, because Mr. Curtis was a builder, so his boys would know how to put things together, and everyone could see that they were taking great trouble to get it right. They were also looking seriously important in the way they went about it. All of them, Sonny and Paul, and the friends of their inner circle—Bud and Jim and Gus—strode in every morning and went straight to work like professionals—eyes squinting under their baseball caps—measuring everything, mouths full of nails. They left piles of sawdust everywhere.

All that summer, in every spare minute they could manage in the daytime, they worked on the main structure and at night they were busy building the cars in the garage. It was getting to be the most impressive thing in town and it had a thoroughly authentic look about it, even to the rails for the cars. It was built of wood, with bits of bent metal hammered onto corners "to create a brace". Wooden planks had been hammered into place—hundreds, it seemed, in all directions: vertical, horizontal, diagonal, long or short, depending on the angle, or the bend, until it had begun to look like a giant puzzle. It was very high at one end and very low at the other and the angle was so steep that anyone who sat in the car going down would surely be getting a very fast ride.

On the day they decided to test the car on the rails for the first time, less than half the roller coaster had been built. There was still a big gap between one end of it and the other on the side away from the houses, and it looked as though the two ends wouldn't be meeting anytime before the next summer, but one of the cars was ready and the big boys couldn't wait to see it go. Everyone knew it was happening. Word had got around as fast and mysteriously as it always did in that neighbourhood and kids came pouring in from all directions to have a look, and get in the way.

It happened that Betsy had already chosen that day to make a new dress for Lily's doll Fred, and Lily learned the meaning of the word 'dilemma' when she discovered how difficult it was to want to do two things at once, especially if you wanted to do both of them equally. She knew that she couldn't ask her mother to make Fred's new dress the next day instead, because if she did that, her mother probably wouldn't make it at all. She also knew that she couldn't go off and watch the roller coaster ride while her mother was sewing, because, if she wasn't there to watch, her mother might just decide not to finish it. So she spent the morning fidgeting impatiently—dashing out the back door and craning her neck to see past the Whitney's backyard, trying to get a look beyond the crowd which was waiting on the edge of the vacant lot, then hurrying back into the kitchen to see if Fred's dress was nearly done.

Every time she ran out to see what was happening with the roller coaster, she could hear Sonny shouting at the kids to get out of the way or he'd give them a good swat, and if they didn't move back, he told them, he would take the car back inside and nothing would happen. There was a deep authority in his voice. They were 'hampering his preparations,' he said, and it could be 'dangerous'. Lily would rush back inside again to tell her mother what was happening—or not happening. She tried very hard to make her mother think that the most important thing was Fred's dress, but she was so afraid she was going to miss out on seeing the car's maiden journey that she was generally making a pest of herself, so finally, Betsy, who had already remarked in a rather wry way that it was indeed a dilemma, gave in and put the unfinished dress on Fred, saying, "Go. I'll do the buttons later. Go on! Go have a look. Don't get in the way. And watch out for that Larry!"

Lily ran off carrying Fred in the new dress, which she hoped someone would notice. It was such a wonderful thing, she thought.

Her doll had a new dress, and she and Fred would both get to watch the new roller coaster in action. She arrived just in time to discover that nothing would be happening that day. Someone had measured wrong. The rails were too wide for the car. It didn't fit. She heard someone saying that they would have to build all the cars again 'from scratch'.

The atmosphere in the vacant lot had turned sour all at once. Kids groaned, shrugged their shoulders, loitered a while longer, or left, depending on their instincts, or curiosity. Sonny and Paul were dark and smoldering. Bud and Gus and Jim looked embarrassed. Nobody was sure who had got it wrong, but all of them were wondering why they hadn't checked more carefully. "Who measured this anyway?" Sonny asked. And Larry, who was thirteen, but still the little brother in the Curtis family, was showing off again. Never allowed to help and always wanting to be noticed, he was skidding his bicycle all over the place and being a pain.

Lily left in a hurry. Larry was making her nervous. She took the short cut through the Whitney's yard, knowing that he wouldn't follow her there and it gave her an excuse to tell Mama Whitney the news about the roller coaster. She could also show her Fred's new dress and explain about the buttons.

The Whitney house had become like a second home to her ever since the last winter, when her mother had got sick with rheumatic fever and gone to hospital. Lily and Matty had stayed with Mama Whitney and her family because Charley couldn't manage work and the children by himself, and Betsy, who was mad at Charley's mother, refused to let her have them. She had told people that it was all Linnea Stearns's fault that she had got sick with rheumatic fever. "If she hadn't been out gallivanting at one of her Ladies' Aid meetings, I wouldn't have got so sick," she said. "It was just a bad cold to begin with. She could have been helping me—minding my children—but what can you expect from a *Malmqvist!*" And Lily would explain to people, in case they might be confused, that her grandmother had only been a Malmqvist until she married Charley's father, William Stearns.

Thus it happened that during all the weeks when her mother was away Mama Whitney had become like a second grandmother to her. She was never once allowed to see her real grandmother, who lived only a mile away. It was difficult for her because she dearly loved her grandmother, but she also knew that it was a hard thing to love her because her mother didn't like her at all—and her mother had told her what 'loyalty' meant. She had learned so many interesting words in her short life, soaked them up by the dozen, eager to understand what they meant so that she could use them herself—but she didn't like the word 'loyalty'. The sound of it when her mother said it made her feel uncomfortable.

The Whitney house had been a busy, crowded one to stay in. All the Whitney children lived there, even though they were grown up, so all the days of the week had been like the special days when an aunt or uncle had come to visit and made a fuss over her. She liked it so much that even after her mother came home again, she spent a lot of time at the Whitney's. She had become so accustomed to being there that sometimes they had to remind her to go home again, like today, when she had so many things to talk about and Mama Whitney said, "Go home, Lily. Can't you hear your mother calling you? It's lunchtime."

Fred's dress was still waiting for its buttons after lunch. Betsy had got tired of sewing. "It would be nice," she said, "if we all went for a little walk together, down to the end of the street, past the Dooby's and the Curtis's."

Lily would have preferred to stay home and watch her mother putting the buttons on Fred's dress, but she knew that "it would be nice" meant that she had no choice. So she ran on ahead, thinking that if she ran they would get home again faster and then her mother would get those buttons done. It was nice to be running, she thought. It felt good. The street was clear and—with her mother behind her—she knew that nobody would bother her.

How was she to know that Larry Curtis was just around the corner on his bicycle? The setback in the progress of the roller coaster had made the big boys bad-tempered and preoccupied. A major revision of plans was required. One thing or the other would have to be rebuilt and none of them wanted to be distracted by a noxious little brother, so they had locked him out. And Larry, furious, had jumped on his bicycle and gone racing all over the neighborhood menacing smaller kids, skidding in front of people, spreading his rage wherever he went. He had been seething and raging for the past half hour at least. He was still seething when he raced down the path that led past the Beauregard's and skidded out into the street just as Lily ran past the Whitney house. He saw her coming, narrowed his eyes, and rode straight at her very fast. She stopped the moment she saw him and stood frozen. She had no idea which way to go, but she was certain that he meant to smash right into her. He came so fast and so close that she could see the hate on his face.

Two things happened in that last second: she closed her eyes so she wouldn't see it when he hit her, and Larry swerved so sharply away from her that he skidded, wobbled dangerously and dragged his foot on the road as he went past. He did this because he had seen Betsy coming out of her yard—and she had seen him. The business might have fizzled altogether except that Matty, who had let go of his mother's hand in that same instant, ran out into the middle of the road, straight into the path of Larry's bicycle. Thus Larry hit Matty instead.

Lily saw it happen. She had turned to watch Larry, afraid that he would come back at her again. She could see that her mother was just feet from Matty when it happened. She wasn't sure whether Larry had run into Matty or Matty had run in front of the bicycle, but it certainly did knock him down. Larry stopped for a moment, not sure what to do, while Betsy ran over and picked him up. He wasn't badly hurt—just a bit bruised and scraped. Larry hadn't been going very fast by then. There was nothing to worry about, but Matty was shrieking his head off—probably more from fright than pain. All might have been okay within a minute or so, except that Larry, who had shown no concern for Matty, rode off again, making rude remarks to Betsy, which in turn left her standing in the middle of the road, patting Matty and shaking with a frightful rage of her own, a rage which she immediately turned on Lily, screaming. "Why didn't you stop him? Why? You were right there! You horrible child! You hate your brother! You didn't even try to stop him! You mean, jealous, hateful child! You didn't even try..."

"But I wasn't there," Lily cried. "I was near Larry's house. You saw me. I wasn't near at all. He rode at *me*. He was going to hit me on purpose."

"You should have stopped him!" Betsy shouted, patting and dusting Matty—kissing him better.

Lily, who had scarcely moved from the spot where she had nearly been run down, was stricken. It had all happened so fast and she was so small and Larry was so big and he nearly hit *her*, and it wasn't fair. And she burst into tears and sobbed her pitiful and overwhelming grief in a flood that soaked her face and dripped all over her shirt.

Betsy, relentless, continued her attack. "You are such a stupid little coward," she snapped. "You don't care about your little brother. You could have stopped that boy. You didn't even try. You are such an awful child."

"I couldn't," Lily sobbed, gasping for breath by then. "It's not true."

Betsy gathered Matty up and stormed into the house, where she fussed over him, and ignored Lily—all afternoon. She entirely forgot about Fred's dress. She never did put buttons on it.

And rage, it seemed, was threatening to become an epidemic.

❦

That night Charley strode over to the Curtis house to deal with Larry—his mouth clamped shut, clenching his fists—getting ready to explode. Lily went with him, although he seemed not to be aware of her presence. She knew the face that approached Larry's father. It was a tight-jawed, no funny business face, a 'my kids can walk down the street without your kid running them down' kind of face. A 'you better deal with that boy of yours' face. A tough man, Charley. A killer of Japs. A jungle fighter. A sniper scout.

But in front of Mr. Curtis, Lily was amazed to see him suddenly put on a face she had never seen before. It was a good-neighbour face, a smiling, let's-not-have-trouble-in-our-street face. It was a face which seemed to have turned a corner and taken a different path from the one it had started on—a face that smiled nervously and said, "I know you are a fine and respectable man and boys at that age, well you know! But my Matt..."

Charley had been working as a laborer for Mr. Curtis not long before. He didn't want trouble. Mr. Curtis not only owned his building company, he also owned the biggest house in the street—and a driveway that was always filled with cars and trucks. He was, in that respect, the biggest man in the neighbourhood, although he was actually quite skinny, and only an inch or so taller than Charley.

"There's one thing you can be sure of," Mr. Curtis told him, with his own smile—an inherently superior, good-neighbour smile, "Larry won't bother Matty again."

They talked for a minute or two after that, as if they were friends and it was important to talk about things. Who knows what they said? Lily could never remember. The banality of it stunned her, even though 'banality' was not yet a word in her vocabulary. The weather perhaps! Or so she thought years later, when she was old enough to consider the possibilities of banal conversation. It never ceased to infuriate her that her father had let him get away with it. But he did and that was that! Everything would be okay, or so they had agreed.

All the same, Charley went around smoldering for days afterwards until, finally, he punched Earl Whitney in the jaw and knocked him out cold—in his front yard—right in front of his mother and his big brother Emery and his sister Essie. And the whole bunch of people who were standing around watching—the whole baseball team which had been playing happily in the street outside Lily's house, just a couple of minutes earlier, before Charley had got mad at them.

Every evening for a whole week, after work had ended for the day, Earl had the baseball team around to practice batting. Although summer had been over for some time, the weather was still good and they wanted to make the most of it. They practiced in the middle of the street outside Lily's house. And every night Earl had told Lily and Matty to "move on up the yard now, out of the way." It was necessary, he told them. He didn't want them to get hurt, because they thought it was such good fun to watch the baseball and they always got too close.

No one knew exactly how it happened, but it seemed that Charley or Betsy had got mad about it and Charley had been just inside the front door, waiting for Earl to say it again, because there was no time at all between the moment Earl told the children to "move on up now" and the crash of the door when Charley came tearing out of the house in a fury—so fast that he put the fear of God into every one of them.

The whole team scattered when they saw him coming—glowering like a berserk. But Charley was focused on Earl. He chased Earl into his own yard yelling "nobody tells my kids in their yard" and he punched him in the face right there in front of everybody.

Lily looked at Earl lying on the ground so unexpectedly and it seemed that the earth had tilted all of a sudden and thrown everything off balance. She felt a bit off balance herself. She stood stone still, holding her breath, and holding it…watching and waiting and wondering what next! Nothing. Nothing was next. Except that it seemed that something had broken. Not in Earl, but in the family. In Mama Whitney and Emery and Essie—who had all turned white, and Papa Whitney—who had come running out when it happened. That family. The one she had stayed with last winter when her mother was so sick.

Lily looked at her father—at the grim look on his face, the one he wore so often. Brooding or angry or preoccupied, it was all the same look. It wasn't in essence much different from his laughter—the roaring, over-the-top laughter—the laughing-double laughter that was like having a second helping at dinner. The extremes were like the two sides of the one thing—and both were dangerous. Laughing excessively. Exploding with anger.

She knew this and was always watchful in her father's presence. Beware of quiet unpredictability. The Beauregard's dog had taught her that when it bit her. Beware of the man who is absorbed in his thoughts is what her father had taught her, although he didn't actually bite. She could be interested in what he was doing. She could watch him making wood shavings down in the cellar, when he was practicing to be a carpenter. She could watch him learning the trade. He was proud of his workmanship. He even liked to show off sometimes and if she didn't get in his way, she might get a few shavings to play with. But she couldn't stay too long. He would get bored with showing off, tired of the questions she asked, of her wanting to know how and why. 'Off you go now,' he would say. 'It's time for bed.' Or 'your mother wants you upstairs.' And she went, or she got big trouble.

Once, at bedtime, as Lily was crossing the room to the stairs, Charley suddenly swooped on her and lifted her high into the air, tossed her up, caught her, spun her around, and held her upside down. It was so unexpected—going from bedtime routine to carnival in an instant—that it gave her a fright. All in a tumble she was, thinking she was going to be killed, that he was mad at her, that she had done something wrong. She was so surprised and so delighted when she realized that it was a game and, laughing and squealing like an ordinary kid, she wanted more.

At that moment Charley put her down so abruptly that she nearly fell over. She had looked at him eagerly, jumping up and down and begging, "Please do it again!" But his face had gone back to its usual no-funny-business look. The look he always had when it was time for bed. "Go on now! Upstairs!" he said.

She lay in bed and thought about the game for a long time. It had been so sudden and unexpected—flying through the air—dizzyspinning upside-down—and then THE END! "That's enough! Go to bed now!" She just couldn't understand it. Her father had never played with her like that before. He hardly ever laughed like that—really, really laughed—just like a kid. And then he had stopped—so suddenly that she wondered if he had forgotten how the game was meant to go. But perhaps it was because her mother had frowned. She remembered. Her mother had said, "It's time for Lily to go to bed." And, "You shouldn't be getting the children excited at bedtime."

Lying in bed, wondering, Lily thought of the wood shavings—piles of them curled up on the floor in the cellar where her father was working—a few feet from the coal bin at the bottom of the shoot. Wood curls smelled warm and piney. What she would like most, she thought, was for her fine, straight hair to curl up and stay that way. Just like the wood.

She had known for a long time that she had to be wary of her father, because she never knew how he would react to anything, but this terrible thing he had just done to Earl she couldn't understand at all—especially now, when it had been so much better and happier in their house. Knowing her father as she did, she could understand the suddenness of it, but she could not fathom the 'Why?'

For several years after the war, Charley had been working as a laborer on building projects. His family had become accustomed to seeing him come home with a long face because he had been laid off again. Sometimes, it was only for the rest of the day, or for a couple of days. Sometimes, it was for several weeks. But the reasons had become so repetitious that he stopped bothering to explain. It happened when supplies hadn't been delivered—timber or bricks or concrete or pipes or shingles. It happened because the weather turned bad and the job had to be cancelled for that day—or week. Sometimes the supplies were already there, but it was an indoor job and the carpenters or plumbers didn't need a laborer for that. Sometimes it happened because of a strike—not because the supplies couldn't be delivered, but because striking workers blocked the deliveries. It was a very restless time—not long after the war and the Great Depression before that—and there were an unprecedented number of strikes, all over the country. Whatever the reason, it was hard when her father was laid off. They had to "tighten their belts," he said, and eat less because the electricity bill was more important than their stomachs. And Betsy made corn chowder, because corn and potatoes and milk were cheap.

Lily, who was only three when they moved to the little house in Park Street, couldn't remember a time when it was different. There had been so many days when her father drove into the yard early, and sat for a time in his car. He was hunched and sad-looking when he came into the house. This happened again and again, until one day, when he came into the house looking sad, Betsy put a cup of coffee on the table in front of him and a small bag and some papers. "We need to talk." she said. "This can't go on."

Charley opened the bag and found that it was full of money—mostly coins and one-dollar notes.

"I have been saving this for months now," Betsy said. "I hope there will be enough, but if there isn't, perhaps the government can help. There's the GI Bill. You are a veteran, after all."

Charley looked at the papers. They had names and phone numbers on them. He seemed confused. He may have been wondering where all that money had come from, when they scarcely had enough to pay their bills.

Betsy, who always seemed able to read his face, jumped in before any contrary thought had a chance to settle in his mind and explained what she had in mind. She had thought it all out in advance. Laborers, she told him, were dispensable. Bosses could always send them home. They were not respected and, no matter how hard they worked or for how long, the pay would always be bad. Other workers could keep on working regardless of the conditions—carpenters, for example. "If you were a carpenter," she said, "and you were a good one, you could work every day and be paid more money."

Then, keeping the thought moving, she reminded him of the beautiful sideboard his Swedish grandfather had made—and suggested that he might have inherited the same talent. "You have always liked wood. You could train to be a carpenter yourself."

And when Charley frowned, as she had expected he would, she reminded him that the same grandfather had built the house at the top of Green Hill for his family. "It was such a fine house," she said. "It still is." She also reminded him (although he didn't need reminding) that he had lived there himself when he was a child. It was where he had learned to skate and ski. It was also one of three houses his grandfather had built there, and various members of the family had lived in them all at one time or another.

She pointed to the papers and told him that he only needed to call one of the numbers, and the money was to create a buffer, because it could be difficult to manage while he trained. But wasn't it already hard, she asked? The difference, she said, was that there would be money at the end of it.

And so the conversation went, in a one-sided fashion. Charley scarcely said a word. He sat so still, in fact, and for so long—staring at the bag of money—that it was impossible to guess what he might do next. What he did next was walk out the door, get in his car and drive away. The house was very quiet after he left, and Betsy made sure that the bag was hidden again in a safe place.

Early the next morning Charley called one of the numbers. He had returned before dinner the day before and never said a word about money or carpentry or any other thing. He just ate in silence. Lily, who had already gone to school when he made the call that morning, heard nothing of the conversation, but her mother told her later that they had said yes, he could train with them. Carpenters were needed, they had told him. Recent hurricanes had done so much damage that they didn't have enough men to keep up with it all.

Her mother was smiling when she told her that everything would be better soon. And they would have a very nice dinner that night to celebrate.

That is how it happened that Charley learned to be a carpenter. And it was true. Almost as soon as he was awarded his certificate saying he was a qualified carpenter, he was hired full-time by J.C. Danvers, a big firm in the city nearby—and he was never out of work again.

To Lily, who was standing there looking down at Earl, it was entirely incomprehensible. There were so many 'whys' in her head. Why wasn't everything better? Why was her father so angry? Why had he smiled at Mr. Curtis? He didn't even need to work for him anymore. He had a much better job now. Why had he hit Earl, who was a good friend? Earl, who was the youngest in the family, was her favourite. He was funny and he laughed a lot, and he played games with her and made her laugh. He was the only grown-up who ever did that.

Earl was conscious again and Mama Whitney was there to help him. As mothers always do, she wanted to pick him up, dust him off, and inspect the damage. She wanted to see if he was okay, but he pushed her away, more embarrassed than befuddled. He didn't want anyone thinking he was a weakling. Blood trickled over the edge of his lip and he swayed a little as he got to his feet. Charley stood expectantly—clenching his fists, waiting. For someone to say something? For something to do? He was waiting to finish the business.

Emery, who was Charley's age, was getting ready for a fight, but Mama Whitney stopped him. "Enough," she said. Then she gestured towards Charley, as if she meant to make some repairs—stitch up a torn friendship and make it wearable again. She was sorry, she said. "Perhaps Earl shouldn't have..." She nodded at Charley then and put her arm around her son to help him walk to the house. Charley looked tired.

No one said anything as Mama Whitney gathered Earl up. His friends hovered over him, ignoring Charley. Earl himself looked for just a moment as if he wanted to say something to him, but he seemed confused—the way that people look when they have mistaken someone's identity. Perhaps it seemed to him that it wasn't really Charley standing in front of him but some stranger. He turned and walked into the house, hunched and tired-looking himself.

Betsy also looked confused—standing halfway between Charley and Mama Whitney and not knowing which way to turn. Charley glared at her, clenched his jaw tight, turned his back and strode off to his own yard, expecting Betsy to follow, which she did. That business is finished now, his back said. We have other things to do. He opened the door to hurry them into the house and saw that Lily wasn't there.

"That damned kid! I'll fix her," he growled, and he thundered back across the lawn.

Lily was still standing at the front of the Whitney place, gazing into the empty yard.

"Lily!" her father barked. "Get over here RIGHT NOW! You'll be staying in your own yard from now on!"

That was when Charley drove up to see his Uncle Will—the very next day. And every weekend afterwards, right up to Thanksgiving, the family went to Hubbardston, where Charley worked at getting the fruit pickers' cottage ready for them to live in.

It was about a hundred feet or so from the farmhouse, just inside the orchard on the other side of the stone wall, in the corner by the woods. It had been built many years earlier for the apple pickers who came in the fall and stayed a few days. It was a light-framed, one-room shack—suitable for the Indian summer at worst. It had a wood-burning stove at one end, and a bench that passed for a kitchen at the other. The stove was for both cooking and heating. It was enough for some fruit pickers to pass a few warm nights in. Now Charley had decided it was going to be a house for a whole family to spend the winter in.

He knew just what to do. He was a carpenter now. He knocked a hole in the wall at the end past the wood stove, and built a good-sized room onto the existing exterior wall. This would be Lily's and Matty's room, he said. Then he made a tiny room, scarcely bigger than a closet, that you had to walk through to get to their bedroom, and in it he put a toilet with a pail which would have to be emptied every day down in the woods. He built the addition on a light wooden frame with boards nailed over it horizontally, and on the outside of that he nailed black tar paper to keep out the drafts. The ground sloped away beneath it and the end where Lily's bed would be was much higher off the ground than the rest of the house. There was nothing underneath it except the stumps that held the building up.

Lily wondered about this. "Won't it be cold?" she asked. It got so cold in the winter, even in Park Street, she thought.

Charley glared at her. "It will be just fine," he said. And he went on working, according to his own private plan.

She shouldn't ask so many questions, she knew. Hadn't he told her many times? He knew about building now, he had said. You had to trust him. It would be okay. She stopped asking questions, but she kept on looking and wondering. When it was finished, there would be more, she thought. There had to be more, if it was going to be okay like he said.

But there was no more. That was all there was.

Just before Thanksgiving, Charley announced that the place was ready. He had measured everything perfectly and it all fit. And he saw that it was good. And they moved into it.

And still Lily worried about it. It was getting very cold and there were no inner walls. No cupboards or shelves. No storm windows. No electricity. No plumbing. No bath. No sink. No place to wash clothes. No water, except in the pump at the big house—a hundred feet away.

And then it snowed. It snowed until it reached the roof of the cottage.

And then it froze inside and out and it was hard.

CHAPTER 7

1952

Charley Flies South

They were arguing. On their way to the drive-in restaurant in Houston, Texas, where they had eaten dinner every day for several weeks, Betsy and Charley argued. It was the same argument and the same dinner every day. They argued at other times too, but on the way to the restaurant was when it seemed the worst. Perhaps it was because they were all so hungry by then, or tired, or bored after another day in which Betsy and Lily and Matty had nothing to do except hang around the trailer park waiting for Charley to get home from work, and maybe wash some clothes in the disinfectant-smelling concrete laundry that was adjacent to the disinfectant-smelling concrete toilet block that was next to the showers where no matter how hard you scrubbed yourself you could never come out feeling really clean, or if you did feel clean, it was only for a minute or so, because by the time you'd got to the door on your way out, that smell would be clinging to you all over again. Or maybe it was just that being packed all together in a small car space and driving around a city that wasn't home, the argument seemed more concentrated. It was louder when they were in the car, and more troublesome, so that it seemed at times as if it was following them, like some dog. It kept on hounding them all over Houston, and down into Galveston where they sometimes went to watch the ships coming in. The arguments got to be such a regular thing, in fact, and so exactly in time with the music they played on the radio every time they were in the car, that, finally, it began to seem as if life itself had got stuck. Like the needle on a record player, it kept on repeating itself. The song. The argument. Life.

Almost every day, just when they were getting near the restaurant, there would be that song on the radio, "Shrimp boats is a-comin'." The same jiggy voices would be singing in the same jolly way, as if the singers assumed that the whole world was just as happy as they were or at least if everybody in the world wasn't happy to begin with, they surely would be once they'd heard that song. There was such conviction in it—such wholehearted persuasion. There could be no doubt about it. Those shrimp boats certainly were a-comin'. Their sails were in sight. And Lily began to believe that she would look back one day as they turned into the parking lot and there would be the boats coming in right behind them. And maybe, just for once, when Betsy and Charley stopped their arguing, they would find they were having shrimps for dinner instead of hamburgers, except that Betsy would never eat anything that had a shell on it, unless it was a nut. Lily certainly knew that.

This was what she had come to expect since they had arrived in Houston. Even before she could see the restaurant at the end of the street, she would start humming that tune in her head, without ever noticing that it had got into her head before it had got onto the radio. One good thing about that song, it usually brought the argument to an end—if Charley started to sing along with it, or if they just got out and went into the restaurant. Either way, it was a delaying action. Like the bell at the end of round two.

This time it was different. It started out exactly the same way. That song. That street. But Betsy went quiet all of a sudden in the middle of the argument, as if she had just given up. They drove along for a minute or two without anyone saying a word and it seemed like a pretty good thing until Betsy turned to Charley and said, "I think it would be a good idea if we got a divorce."

She said it so quietly—so matter-of-factly—as if the children weren't sitting there in the back seat to hear it, or wouldn't understand anyway, or it wasn't really any concern of theirs. Putting it like that— sliding it in sideways across the song—gave it immense power. It was the angle from which it came—sideways. Like an earthquake, it fractured the pattern they had been weaving for weeks. So quiet that it magnified the moment enormously, set it apart and made it the absolute and only truly real thing in the world. So quiet, and yet it was louder in Lily's ears than all the shrimp boats in Texas.

She went cold inside with panic. She knew what a divorce was. And she believed her mother really meant it. She sat forward on her seat urgently and held her breath. Her parents would surely notice her sitting there stiff with fright. They would tell her it was just a joke. But they didn't notice her at all. There seemed to be some invisible division between the front seat and the back, and Lily thought the air inside the car had gone fuzzy all of a sudden. They were playing that song again so loud it got scrambled inside her head. If they got a divorce, she thought, she would never find her way home again. Home was weeks away. She would be lost forever at a drive-in restaurant in Houston where they didn't even sell shrimps, and no one would ever find her again. Her grandmother wouldn't know where she was.

For a long time, she had felt that she belonged to her parents only because she had got into the habit of keeping an eye on them. Sometimes they had just gone off without her. Once, at a country fair, she hadn't noticed that they had gone and she'd had troubles finding them. Another time, a year or so earlier, she had fallen out of the car as they drove down a country road in Massachusetts. She had been squashed into the back seat alongside her grandmother and grandfather and Matty. Betsy had insisted that Matty sit in the middle between his grandparents. "So he'll be safe," she had said, and they were making a fuss of him. Lily—crushed up against the door—was feeling slighted. She had squirmed and twisted herself around in her seat until finally she had managed to turn her back to them. Then she had propped her chin on the window ledge and looked out at nothing in particular. She wanted them to see that there were other things to look at besides Matty. All of a sudden, the door had popped open and out she went. She had crashed down onto the gravel and tumbled over into the grass at the side of the road, and then she was up again without taking a second to think about her injuries. She was running after the car. 'Wait for me,' she yelled. She was so sure they would forget all about her. They were already stopping by then, but the thought was in her head nevertheless. They might have kept on going without her.

She looked at them now across the invisible division and she could see that they had already forgotten her. If they got a divorce, neither one of them would want me, she thought. She looked at Matty. He had his shoulders hunched up again. Did he know what a divorce was? He knew something was the matter. She could tell from his shoulders. It was awfully quiet in the car, except for that song. "Why don't you hurry, hurry, hurry home," it sang. Her mother would never leave Matty in a restaurant, she thought.

She tried to think about the arguments her parents had been having. What was it that made them worse than usual? It seemed to her that ever since the day they had moved to Hubbardston—or the day her father had punched Earl—or the day he had resigned from his new job... She couldn't find the beginning of it—only that her mother had started sounding more querulous and the further south they went the more they argued. It seemed that her mother couldn't be pleased with anything, and her father could never get things right. He was jumpy and restless the whole time, wherever they went. Nervous. A going-going-keep-on-going kind of nervousness that kept interrupting things all the time so that they always seemed to be doing things by halves.

Like the night they drove into a trailer park in Georgia after driving all day. They were all so tired and ready to sleep. They had only just got tucked into bed when a bunch of locals started rocking their trailer and yelling at them to go back where they came from. Charley shouted at them out of the window to go away and leave them alone, but they just kept on rocking and yelling. He pulled on his trousers and went out to get the owner of the trailer park to do something, but the man just laughed and spat. "Yankees!" he said with a sneer.

Charley came back with a face like stone and told them to get in the car "on the double" and he hitched up the trailer in a tremendous hurry while Betsy pushed Lily and Matty into the car, still in their pajamas. Hitching things together, he moved frantically, belying his stone tough Yankee face, and the men, still pushing the trailer and jeering and hooting weren't fooled for a minute. He was so anxious to get away before those men had a chance to do anything more that he drove off like a madman the minute they were hitched. He would have driven over one of them rather than stop.

"Don't look back!" he ordered. "Those guys don't need any encouragement! Jesus! Bloody bastards! Southerners! Damned southerners! I knew there would be trouble driving through Georgia with a Massachusetts number plate."

He mopped his face and looked in the side view mirror to see if they were being followed. Then, seeing Betsy's puzzled look, he added, "They've never forgiven us for winning the war."

"What do you mean, 'winning the war'? What war?" she asked.

"The Civil War," he said, still peering at his mirrors.

"Oh for heaven's sake, surely not!" she exclaimed. "That was over long ago—long before you were born even. Golly! They weren't much more than kids being a bit silly. If we had ignored them..."

"It's not worth taking the risk of ending up dead in Georgia," he said. "And anyway, you could see for yourself, the owner wasn't going to do anything. Not for us anyway. The bastard!"

"Maybe it was your fault."

"What do you mean? How could it be my fault? We'd only just got there!"

"I know, but—well—it seemed to me that—when we were arriving... Oh I don't know! I just thought..."

"What? What did you think?"

Charley's mood was changing from nervous to just plain mad, and Betsy was backing off. She was too tired to make a fuss and he was ready for a fight. His adrenalin was kicking him into action still, even though he was almost safe—or at least, there didn't seem to be anyone following them. And he certainly wasn't scared of the little woman sitting alongside him. It would be a whole lot easier to deal with her than half a dozen Georgians. He looked in the side view mirror again.

Betsy was nervous too. She felt that she had set a trap for herself, suggesting that Charley might have been the cause of the trouble. She knew he would be cross with her no matter what she said. She looked at him. He was waiting for an answer—working on his anger as he waited—setting his face in a scowl that turned into a grin, which at the very point of it being fixed, became awful. She turned away and stared into the night. It was so dark—so very dark.

She sighed when she answered him—a deep, unhappy sigh. "I remember," she said, "that when we drove through the gate, one of the men who was standing there spoke to you. Remember? He only said 'Hello.' He was quite friendly really and you ignored him—as if you didn't hear him. Maybe you didn't, but he seemed ... oh, I don't know—I thought maybe it made him angry. Perhaps that's why they bothered us."

"Bastards!" he boomed. "Of course I didn't answer! They hate Yankees! If I'd answered, they'd have picked a fight. They were just looking for an excuse."

They didn't continue arguing that night. Betsy was tired and Charley was busy looking in his mirror to see if they were being followed. And he was mad. Real mad! They had got something for nothing, those guys. He had paid for the night in advance. They probably did it all the time, he complained to Betsy. Robbing suckers like him, who were dumb enough to pay in advance.

Charley was a dyed-in-the-wool New Englander. He never paid a cent for anything he didn't have to. It made him even madder when Betsy told him what a good thing it was he had paid in advance. Otherwise, they might have had the whole state of Georgia following them. And besides, they had to pay in advance. Didn't he know? How else could they make any money in trailer parks? If they let people stay without paying first, they would all be driving out before daylight every day!

Sometimes, Betsy thought, Charley could be so stupid. But it was a thought that she kept to herself—hidden behind her eyes and her down-turned mouth, as she pressed her face against the window, and the privacy of the night.

They drove all night. Charley was determined to get safely into Florida. Betsy stayed awake because she didn't trust him not to fall asleep at the wheel—or do some other foolish thing as long as they were still in Georgia. They had another argument when he told her he meant to keep on driving all the next day as well.

Charley went on like that for days, moving frenetically, doing things unexpectedly, always with an air of extreme urgency. Once, in Florida, after driving for miles on an old, narrow highway, looking for a suitable place to stop and have lunch, where there wasn't swamp right up to the road on both sides, hunger finally got to be more insistent than whatever it was Charley was worried about. They stopped then.

"Stay near the car!" he barked at the children as Betsy made boloney sandwiches. He was nervous and impatient, eyes darting here and there, ears tuned on alert. He looked like a wild animal that was being tracked.

"Whatta ya wanta waste time putting mustard on them for?" he complained to Betsy. "You're taking too long."

"For heaven's sake Charley, there's nobody for miles. You'll get indigestion if you eat too fast. And you need to rest awhile," she told him as she handed him the first sandwich.

"Stay near the car!" he barked again.

Lily and Matty hadn't moved at all. There was nowhere to go. There was just a narrow road and miles of swamp. There wasn't even a place to sit. They stood next to the car to eat, managing at best a bite or two before Charley suddenly yelled at them in a panic, "Get in the car, on the double!"

"On the double" meant faster than lightning or you'll get a bruise—and don't ask questions. You had to take it on faith that there was some good reason for it when Charley barked military orders.

"Jesus!" he shouted as they drove off. "Jesus!" He was shuddering and squirming in his seat. "Holy cow! Shit! That was a close call!" He went on twitching and squirming.

Lily tried to see back past the trailer to find out what the trouble was, but she couldn't. It was too wide.

"What are you going on about?" Betsy demanded. "Jeepers, Charley! We were eating lunch. There was nobody there. Not for miles. You are so jumpy these days, it's driving me crazy."

"A rattlesnake," he said. "There was a rattlesnake. Right next to us. Two feet away! Whew!"

He shuddered again.

"There was nothing there," Betsy said.

She looked at Charley as if he might be dangerous and she had to be very careful with him.

112

"There wasn't anything on the road," she insisted. "Not even a stick. I looked around myself when we stopped."

"Of course not," Charley argued. "It wasn't right there where you could see it. If you'd seen it, you'd be dead by now. But I heard it. It was real close."

"I didn't hear anything."

"Sure you did! That buzzing noise. You must've heard it. It was a rattler—sure as death! If you can hear it, you're practically dead already. It's just as well for you that I'm around to hear these things. You need someone to protect you."

Betsy closed her eyes. When she opened them again, she saw that she was still holding her boloney sandwich. She saw that a corner of it had already been eaten. It seemed odd—she couldn't remember. She looked at it for a whole minute then squeezed it tight with both her hands. She was pleased to find that she had altered the shape of it—left the marks of her hands on it. She looked out the window and licked the mustard off her fingers as she watched the swamp slide past. It seemed such a long time—so much swamp. She lost track of it—forgot herself—until, finally, not looking at Charley, but remembering, she repeated, "I didn't hear anything."

Nobody except Charley had heard anything. They finished their sandwiches in the car. It would be two more hours at least before they were able to stop for a drink.

Even without snakes or Georgians, Charley was impossible. He couldn't relax for a minute. They drove all the way to Sarasota to visit his aunts, Ruth and Katrina. He hadn't let them know they were coming. Just drove up to the house and knocked on the door. They weren't home. "No point in wasting time," he announced, shrugging his shoulders. He took some grapefruit from the tree at the back and left a note: "Thanks for the grapefruit. Sorry to have missed you. Charley."

He and Betsy argued. She wanted to stay awhile. He wouldn't wait. They had to be on their way again. And so they drove on leaving Sarasota behind in a blur. They headed north towards Pensacola.

Why were they in such a hurry? Where were they going? They had never told Lily where they were going. Maybe they didn't know themselves. They were just going. Incessantly. Restlessly. Charley did all the driving. He knew the whole country backwards, he said. When he was a kid—about fifteen—he had run away from home and gone everywhere. Rode the rails. Hitched rides. Got odd jobs. Ended up in a jail or two. A kind policeman perhaps was giving him a bed for the night—and a meal. Who knows? But as Charley said at every turn along the way, he knew it all—good and bad—and he could show it to them. And yet here he was pushing his way through it as though it was just a bad dream coming back to haunt him. It didn't seem that he really wanted to see it all again. He kept on rushing by, taking wrong turns, ending up in strange places. Like the day they got lost in the back blocks along the Mississippi River, where the people kept their washing machines and television sets on their front porch, and the men came out with guns and narrowed eyes when Charley finally had to stop to ask for directions. He was sweating all over. It must be the heat. Or it was that license plate again.

In New Orleans, people told them it was much too early for the Mardi Gras. "You would have liked it," he told Betsy as they drove on into Texas. They stayed five days in Houston, while he worked to get some money. And then they were off again, across the mountains and the desert to El Paso and Tucson. They went into Mexico twice—over the border to Nogales and Juárez, where they hurried in the same nervous, impatient way that they did everything. In Mexico, Charley told the children not to speak to anyone. "Don't even look at them," he said. "Down here they'll put you in jail if you look cross-eyed at a person, and they won't let you out again until your hair is gray."

Lily walked through the streets of Juárez not speaking to anyone—not even looking. She was concentrating on not looking cross-eyed. Staring intently at the end of her nose, she started to get dizzy from trying not to look cross-eyed.

The shops were bright and beautiful, and the children of the town were free to roam. They roamed everywhere, surrounding the tourists like gypsies. "Please mister, give us a penny!" they shouted. Charley set his face tight and waved them away. It was dangerous to talk to children in Mexico, he believed.

Lily sneaked a look at them. They were beautiful. And happy. She would have liked it if she didn't have to obey her father. "Please mister, give us a penny!" she would have shouted.

It had been like this for weeks. Everything they saw or did was stamped with hurry and fear and impatience and jumpiness. Lily couldn't understand why they had gone into Mexico at all if it was so dangerous. Charley wanted Betsy to see it, but only in a hurry, without really stopping. It was as if he had become so accustomed to seeing the whole world in a rush that he might have felt dizzy if he stopped going, going—even for a moment. When Betsy stopped to buy a little silver bracelet with turquoise stones on it for Lily, Charley stood guard—even though there was no one else in the shop.

They visited Mexico for about two hours, which was more than some of the places they had been. After a few weeks of travelling like this, Lily had a fruit salad of images in her head of blurred roadside stalls that sold cross-eyed black mammy coconut-head dolls with kerchiefs. Alligators and flamingos in a St. Petersburg park were confused in her mind with little ballerinas—glimpsed in passing from some courtyard in Sarasota—dressed in pink and leggy as flamingos themselves. Orange groves and cactuses mingled in her head and way back, in the deep recesses of her mind, behind the groves and cactuses, the Suwannee River kept on disappearing in the distance in exactly the same way it had the day they drove past it without ever stopping. It was an important place, she knew, because her father had sung a song about it—even though he couldn't find the time to stop.

Boloney and mustard sandwiches were the only consistent items in all the places they had been, from one end of the country to the other. They were eating boloney sandwiches when they met a cowboy riding up El Capitan on his horse. It was a great moment. If you had a map and a bag of miniature boloney sandwich pins, you could use them to mark all the places where something interesting had happened that later on got mixed up in the one great blur of travelling on forever—or so it seemed.

And there was the schoolwork. That too was part of the salad, or maybe it was the real cause of the blur—seeing things in parts, from book to landscape to book—reading, writing and arithmetic. All the way down the east coast, across the gulf and up into the mountains of the southwest, past swamps and plains, flatlands, lowlands, mossy trees, and countless hundreds of billboards, Lily worked on the "instructional materials" that Betsy and Charley had bought at the place in Annapolis—the place they had to go out of their way to get to because the principal of the school in Hubbardston had told them about it.

From the day they bought the materials, Lily had to study as they drove. Matty was too young for school and could do whatever he liked. He sat in the front with Betsy a lot of the time. And Lily in the back hurried, not frantically like Charley, but eagerly. They wouldn't let her watch where they were going until she had finished her work, so she hurried.

The "instructional materials" came in a thoroughly organized folder, filled with work to be completed each day. Betsy had an "instructors" booklet, which had the answers and an estimated completion time for the work. There were numerous addition and subtraction exercises, which Lily could easily figure out on her fingers, if she didn't already know the answer. There were small books to be read—all of which were about Dick and Jane and their pets Spot and Fluff—walking, skipping, running, hopping, jumping. It was the same characters every day, although the story was different in each of them. They were walking to school in one book, skipping rope in another, running down the lane after the dog in the third, and so on—one little book after another. Lily could read one in no time. There were also writing exercises, which consisted of simple sentences to be copied on the paper provided especially for that purpose.

She had been pleased to start her new schoolwork. She was always happy to be learning something new, but she also knew that she would be in a school again somewhere, sometime, and it would be embarrassing to be a long way behind the others. The trouble was that the work was so easy that her mind would wander and then she would write the wrong answer. And there were so many distractions. Even when she really tried to pay attention to the page in front of her, the passing world would intrude on her peripheral vision. A billboard that was different from all the others would catch her eye, or a beautiful bird with a red head and speckled wings, or a wondrous blue mountain wrapped in pink clouds, or Live Oaks drooping with Spanish moss or a scarecrow with beady black eyes and a ragged hat, shaking its fist at the corn. She would forget for a time what she was supposed to be doing and soak up each new scene for as long as it remained in view— or until her parents told her to get back to her work.

Only once did the "instructional materials" capture her so entirely that she lost track of the passing world. It was a writing exercise. All she had to do was read and copy onto the paper the simple sentence: "I see said the blind man to his deaf wife." And Lily, who had her pen ready to write, in a hurry as usual, stopped. She read it again—and then again.

"How can this be!" she exclaimed. "How can she hear him, if she is deaf? How can he see her, if he is blind?"

"What is the matter with you? Let me see that," Betsy said, as she reached over the seat and grabbed Lily's writing page.

She looked at it for a minute or so and then said, "Hmmph! There is nothing wrong with this. What is the problem? You just have to write it."

"How can he see her if he is blind," Lily asked?

"I suppose it is meant to make you think," she replied. "Go on. Write it out, and remember to be neat." She turned around and went back to the little chat she was having with Matty.

Lily sat back and thought about it. She thought and thought until she ceased to see the landscape passing by, but no matter which way she thought about it she couldn't see how it made sense. She knew that it *had* to make sense, because someone clever had written it, and it was surely meant to teach her something. And that thought made her sit up straight with an anxious look on her face. It had just occurred to her that in all the time she had been looking at the landscapes flying past her window, she might have missed a whole lot of important things—sentences she hadn't thought about at all when she wrote them out. So she turned back to the beginning of the writing exercises and read them all again—carefully. They were all very simple and as clear as could be—sentences like, "Tom's mother baked a cake," and, "The old man raked the leaves." All of them made sense, all except for the one about the blind man and his deaf wife. She looked at it many times and every time she asked herself, "How could she hear him if she was deaf?"

From all of those weeks of learning during that going, going time in the back seat of the car, it was the only thing she never understood. She would think about it many times over the years without ever knowing quite what it meant until one day—perhaps twenty years later—in answer to a question, she heard herself saying, "I see said the blind man to his deaf wife," and she knew exactly what it meant.

In the meantime, the child Lily, sitting in a car with a pile of papers on her lap and unable to fathom the meaning of that sentence, wrote it out just as her mother had told her to do. And then she went on as usual—hurrying because she liked to see the world go by. If she really hurried, she could get through a whole day's work in an hour or two.

Charley couldn't see the sense of that. It was another of the things that he and Betsy argued about. "There must be something wrong with the materials," he told Betsy in the voice he always used when he was being unarguably logical and clear-headed. "It says on the instructions that it is designed to be the equivalent of a whole day's work. So if she finishes it in an hour and a half, there either has to be something wrong with it, or she is cheating."

"She can't be cheating," Betsy argued. "I have the answers in a separate book. She can't know them in advance. Besides, what does it matter if she finishes early? She can learn something from seeing the landscape. As long as she gets the answers right, what does it matter?"

"School is from nine to three-thirty," Charley insisted. "That's six and a half hours. She needs to do five more."

"Even at school they don't work the whole time," Betsy reminded him. "They have recess and lunch. And they do other things, like singing."

"Oh, I like singing!" Lily chimed in.

"Not in this car, you don't!" Betsy told her. "You always sing flat. It's awful! Just don't you sing, I'm telling you. You'll get on okay in this world as long as you don't sing."

Lily sat back again, a little bruised by her mother's remark. Then, testing to see if it was true, she began humming very softly to herself, while Charley figured out what to do with the extra five hours.

The answer came to him all at once with brilliant clarity.

Multiplication tables! "When I was your age," he told Lily, "I knew them all from one to twelve."

"Nonsense," Betsy snorted. "You never did. She's only seven. They don't even start teaching them until the end of grade three."

"They've got lazy since I was a kid," Charley insisted. "When I was a kid, I knew them all."

"Sure! When you were eleven."

"When I was her age. If I could do it, she can."

"If you could do it! Ha! Tell me Einstein, when did they teach you to spell awful, 'o-r-p-h-u-l'?"

"What's a multiplication table?" Lily asked.

"You don't need to know that. You just have to learn it," said Charley.

"It's so you'll know how to work out how many things you'll need if you're having a party or something," Betsy explained, ignoring Charley. "If you have ten people coming and you want to know how many hot dogs to buy if they're going to have two each—or if you want to give five pieces of candy to each child. You can also work out how to divide things equally if you know the tables. Like how many pieces of cake you'll need."

"If you cut the cake in small pieces, you get more," Lily told her.

"You're confusing her," Charley interrupted. "Just write one out and make her learn it."

And so it went. One times one and two times two and so on in order, and then out of order, seven times six and nine times seven—one table after another to take up the correct amount of time that was left after Dick and Jane and Spot and Fluff were finished for the day. It took up the time and blurred the view from one end of the country to the other—every day. No days off. Saturday and Sunday included. She would get ahead, Charley argued. And he stressed that learning was a moral responsibility. What's more, he thoroughly enjoyed quizzing her in the trickiest ways he could think of—for hours.

✤

Across the country they went—one small family—or miniature classroom—disconnected from the world at large—in a black 1950 Ford, towing the twenty-three foot trailer in which Betsy had stored the things the children had got for Christmas. Presents admired on the day, and not yet removed from the boxes they came in. Put away too soon. "You'll have to wait," she had told them, "for a little while, till we're settled." But since Christmas, the only time they had ever settled for more than a few days was in the last few weeks when they had stayed in Houston, after they got back from Tucson, so that Charley could work to earn some more money. Betsy wouldn't let them have the presents then either. They weren't settled yet. Not yet, she had said, and she had looked away with a strange lost look in her eyes as if she was trying to remember something far away and dim.

Charley had come home with the trailer one night just before Christmas, so pleased with himself you could have thought he was Santa Claus himself on an early round. They would be going again, he had told them. He had given up his job and they would be moving on. Taking the house with them this time, or some of it at least, he had laughed.

His cousin Dagmar had shown up at the farm unexpectedly a few days earlier with her husband George and their two little daughters, all of them wrapped in warm affluence. Fur jackets, fur hats, collars, muffs. They were just up from New York City where they had been for their vacation.

"Delighted to see you again, Charley. And how are you keeping?" Dagmar asked.

She smiled. Gracious. Well-groomed. Blue-eyed. Clear-skinned. A real smooth woman.

Betsy's chin went up. She smiled with her mouth, but in her eyes there was a trapped look. It was the worst possible time and the worst possible place. The fruit pickers' cottage, savaged by the snows of winter, was no place to be inviting guests.

Charley's attempt to turn it into a home had been a dismal failure. The impossibility of it had been obvious from the start. There was just too much work for one man to do in his spare time. Three or four Saturdays and Sundays were all the time he had before they had to vacate the house in Park Street and he must have known, even before he began, that it was already too late in the season for such work. Yet he had insisted on bringing his family there to live for what seemed to them no good reason at all—or at least it was not a reason he could articulate. It was a reflex more than a thought. Thoughts always worried him. If someone had asked him outright, he would probably have refused to answer, or if he did answer, he might have said something about a jungle, but he would never have admitted that it was because he had knocked his neighbour's son Earl out cold for no reason other than that Earl was young and free and Charley, who worked more hours than he had ever thought anyone should, just to put frankfurts and beans on the table, couldn't bear the sight of any young man playing baseball in the street outside *his* house.

By the first week in December, it was almost unbearably cold in the cottage. Everyone suffered—except possibly Charley, who would rather freeze in the cottage than have Earl living next door to him—or Earl's mother, whose eyes had become so cold since the day he had punched her son that she seemed blinded by the ice in them—she, who had always been so kind to Betsy and the children. It seemed to him that since then the whole world—even Betsy—had turned cold on him. It was as if a horrible winter storm had swept in out of nowhere in the middle of a warm summer day and frozen all the beans and tomatoes on their stems, and turned them black. It seemed to him that everything good had been killed all at once, and it was more than he could bear. In comparison with that, a small, cold cottage was nothing. He was tough. He was an ex-marine. A survivor of Guadalcanal.

"You must come in and have a cup of coffee," Betsy said, smiling at Dagmar and George.

Dagmar looked past her to the cottage and summed it all up in an instant. She declined, so very graciously. "How kind of you, my dear, but no, we really can't. I am so sorry, but we've run out of time. We were just passing through and it seemed like a good idea to drop in—but then you know we got lost getting here. And we really wanted to let you know that we'll be practically neighbours soon. We'll be moving east from Ohio next month. We've bought a house in Connecticut—or, actually, we're having it built. It's almost finished. Mother and Dad will be moving up from New York soon after us, and then we'll all be together again. It will be so lovely," she said, bending over and putting her arms around her little girls—three pretty blonde heads coming together for a moment, "It will be so lovely for my girls to get together with yours."

"One of mine is a boy," Betsy corrected her.

"Well, of course! I just meant—Well! We really must be going! ... Oh, how silly of me," she remembered—a little awkward by this time, "not to introduce my little darlings properly. Lily should have a chance to get to know Ellen and Kitty-Sue right now. It will be so much nicer later if they know each other already."

Ellen and Kitty-Sue stared at Lily—expressionless.

"Well," Charley interrupted, "I don't know if we'll be seeing you then. We'll be moving on ourselves. We're going south."

Betsy looked startled.

"Florida maybe. Or Texas. Yep. We'll be moving on for sure," Charley told her.

Betsy said nothing. She was beginning to think that this nowhere world of hers had no firm center at all. Nevertheless, she smiled. You have to keep smiling, she thought. They had come all the way up to see them and then couldn't stay for coffee. No time! But the present was all there was—that and the fruit pickers' cottage. She didn't need to look behind her to see what it was that had taken Dagmar's time away all of a sudden. Sometimes it did the same thing to her.

"Well," Charley said after they had gone, answering her unasked question, "I've been thinking. It's warmer down south. And I've heard there are lots of jobs in Texas."

"You have a job here," Betsy reminded him. "It's the first steady job you've ever had."

"Yeah, but..."

"Yeah but Dagmar! Nice fur. Very nice, don't you think? And a Cadillac too," she sighed. "And so, we go south next."

"You'll like it there," Charley assured her. "It's warm. No snow."

A divorce, Lily thought. They might really do it. She remembered a night a few weeks earlier in some other trailer park somewhere in Louisiana. Her parents were fighting then too. It was big. They were yelling and Betsy had walked out. She wouldn't ever come back, she said as she slammed the door behind her. They could all go to hell. No one had moved after she left—or spoken. It was a strange city and her mother was gone. Lily and Matty sat looking at their father, who just sat and looked at the floor, and Lily wondered if her mother might get lost.

Not knowing what to do, they waited—all of them. The radio was on. Even that seemed quiet, muffled by the waiting, and the suspense, until finally, the voice on the radio got to be more insistent. Without any other sound in the room, it pushed its way into Lily's mind and the droning voice began to separate inside her head and form itself into distinct words. A woman was speaking, but she didn't make any sense. "Those burby old switches," Lily heard her say.

She wondered what it meant. She thought she must have misheard, yet when she tried to iron it out in her mind, it stayed the same no matter what. She kept hearing those words exactly, and she couldn't make them into anything that didn't sound hilarious to her. "Did you hear that?" she asked her father. "That lady said 'burby old switches'!"

He didn't answer, but one corner of his mouth twitched just a little, with a hint of the beginning of a smile. It was enough to give her a license. It was just the thing she needed. She exploded. She laughed herself into a fit. She was so nervous just then she could laugh at anything—anything at all. And she got carried away with it, laughing all over the place, up and down the scales, digging deep inside herself to get every bit of laughing out of her that she could find. She had to hold her sides to keep herself from falling apart.

It was infectious. Matty caught it too. "Burby old switches!" he shrieked. "The lady said it." He was laughing too.

And then Charley caught it. But his was a peculiar laugh, funny and sad all at once, and a bit too loud.

Betsy came back in then, and stood glaring at them with a tight angry face. They went on laughing, more nervous than ever with her standing there. It was the wrong time to be laughing and they knew it. And knowing it made it all the harder to stop.

It was Matty who stopped them finally. "The lady said switches!" he explained.

All at once they were sober. Betsy might have been standing outside the whole time—and they were laughing. She might have thought they didn't care if she went away.

Lily thought of this as they drove up to the drive-in restaurant. She leaned forward again urgently, and this time she pushed her way through the invisible division. "Ma!" she called, her voice thin with tension, "You won't get a divorce, will you?"

"I guess so," Betsy answered. "I think I will have to. I can't stand this any longer. Don't you agree?"

"No," Lily urged. "No. Not a divorce. I need a mother and a father. Or else I might get lost."

"Me too," Matty said.

Charley fixed Betsy with his silly grin. "You heard 'em," he said. "There's gotta be two of us. So how about some shrimps? The shrimp boats are comin'. Their sails are in sight."

"You're in the wrong place, Charley," Betsy sighed. "It's hamburgers here. Greasy mustard relish ketchup hamburgers."

"Why don't you hurry, hurry, hurry home?" sang the voice on the radio.

"It's too far away. Too damned far," Betsy told the voice. "A whole ocean away."

"Wake up America!" Charley shouted, flinging open his door. "This is the land of the free! Out! Out! On the double. Let's eat!"

It was what he always said when he wanted to make a big impact on things. "Wake up America! This is the land of the free!"

The next day Charley came home from work grinning again. "Tomorrow!" he said. "We're heading home! I've quit again."

"When we get home, will I be able to play with my Christmas presents?" Lily wanted to know.

"You betcha!" Charley shouted, spinning her around, her feet hitting the cupboards inside the trailer.

Betsy said nothing. What could she say? Home? Home was not Houston, or Galveston, or Tucson, or El Paso, or a fruit pickers' cottage. Or Charley? All that driving all over again, she thought.

Seeing her standing there looking so forlorn, Charley hesitated. He was having a lot of trouble getting things right these days. "You name it, Bets," he said. "We'll do whatever you like. I thought we might head straight on up through the centre. It'll save us a couple of days at least."

They were off again the next day, just as Charley had promised. Somewhere in Oklahoma, they fled in advance of a blizzard. Blizzards in the south, he told them, were worse than anything. Nobody down south knew anything about plowing snow, he said.

They stopped on their way through Ohio to visit Dagmar and George. No one was there, so they kept on going. They had forgotten that Dagmar had said they were moving in a month and it was more than a month since then. It had got bitterly cold by then and they were in a hurry again. They had to have another argument before Charley agreed to stop so that Betsy could get into the trailer and find them some winter clothes. It had been so long since they needed them that she had trouble remembering where she had put them. Things could get lost it seemed even in the smallest spaces.

By the time they drove up the hill to the farm and the fruit pickers' cottage, Lily knew the whole twelve multiplication tables in all directions. It was only February and the snow was deeper than ever.

CHAPTER 8

1952

To School in the Back Seat

Maybe it wasn't such a long time. Maybe she had just forgotten how long it took to drive out from town, but the shadows had begun to gather themselves into recognizable shapes and a touch of colour emerged here and there from out of the dark.

Mr. Carey was taking an awfully long time, Lily thought. She was beginning to see real things in the woods—branches—rocks—a bit of green princess pine poking up through the snow at the foot of a rock—yet it was still dark. She remembered the deer and stood listening. It was quiet. The drifts were much higher than when she had last stood there. The snow plough had pushed the snow into banks as high as it could go and then, when there was more snow, if it hadn't frozen solid, it had slipped down over the edges of the bank and pushed its way back into the road again and the road was getting narrower with every storm.

She waited on the Westminster side of the bank—away from town and as close as she could get to the road without actually being in it. She didn't want to be seen standing there alone by anyone other than Mr. Carey. They had told her at the farmhouse that he would come, but she wasn't sure. They had met some gypsies in Virginia and her father had told her to stay away from them. "You can never trust a gypsy," he had said. Her mother had said that a little girl should never talk to strangers at all. She wondered if Mr. Carey knew she was back. How would he know? She had been away so long—and now she had been waiting so long—and she was beginning to ache with the cold. Her legs hurt, and her back hurt. She stamped her feet and jumped up and down to get warm and then she stopped because she had given herself a fright with her own noise. A deer might hear her, she thought. Someone...

At that moment, Mr. Carey's car came to a stop in front of her. She jumped at the suddenness of it—coming up behind her like that—from the wrong direction. Even so, she ran across the road in great excitement. She had so many things to tell him, but just as she reached the door, she saw that there was another girl sitting in the front seat, and two boys in the back.

"You will have to sit in the back seat," Mr. Carey told her, "because Ellen likes sitting in the front."

He seemed to think it was a great joke to have a full carload. "Fancy that!" he said with a peculiar sort of laugh—not quite funny, "I'm almost a proper bus driver now!"

"These are the Miller kids," he told her, once they'd got going. "Those devils in the back with you are Marty and Jerry. Jerry is the one sitting next to you. They live a mile or so further up the Westminster road. I guess you and Ellen will be in the same class. I expect that you won't be finding it so lonely now that there's someone your own age nearby."

Mr. Carey had nodded in the direction of Ellen and she had looked away. From where she sat in the back seat, Lily could just see Ellen's nose, pointing upwards, not quite touching the window. Marty and Jerry started poking and pushing at each other—giggling. Marty leaned over and whispered something to Jerry, who laughed and sneaked a look at Lily. She watched them for a moment then decided that she too would look out the window. Jerry poked her in the ribs. She turned to look at him and saw that he was chipmunk-faced and cross-eyed for just a fraction of a second before he transformed himself into a portrait of innocence, hands folded on his lap. He was clearly an experienced rib poker.

Lily looked at Mr. Carey and saw that he was watching her in his rear view mirror.

"So how was Texas?" he asked with a wink.

Marty whooped, "Texas! Ha! We've been to Germany."

"Yeah," Jerry said, "We lived there for five years. Our father's in the army. e'He's an officer. Yeah! We can speak German, can you? Heh? Sprechen sie Deutsche? Yeah, I'll bet you can't."

Lily frowned. She could see that Mr. Carey was still looking at her in the mirror.

"*Was* in the army," he said. "A sergeant. Now he's driving a truck."

"Ellen's the best," Marty said. "She started talking German when she was practically a baby. She can say anything."

Ellen had nothing to say. Her nose was still pointing at the window. Lily wondered if she should say something to her, but she couldn't think what. She had a cousin named Ellen. She was blonde too, but she was nice. This Ellen was like a stone wall. No—more like a snow bank—cold—very cold—and blank. A blank white blonde cold bank with a pale stuck-up nose—a pale nose that had a bad smell under it—a smell like a bucket from the toilet. When her mother went out to empty the bucket, she would say, "Hold your nose if you don't like the smell!" Maybe she thinks I might get to sit in the front seat sometime. Maybe she thinks those boys are silly. Maybe she's shy...

Lily continued to wonder about Ellen the whole way into Hubbardston. She was inventing and speculating—filling the gaps left by the silence of the real Ellen. Feeling the possibilities—imagining the bad—crossing it out—imagining the good. It would be awfully nice to have a friend in her class, she thought—a real friend.

Ellen stepped out of the car as it stopped at the school and strode up the path without a word of thanks or a backward glance. The boys scrambled over each other and tumbled into the snow as the door opened. Within seconds they were gathering up handfuls of snow and pelting each other with snowballs. Ellen had already been surrounded by a flock of admirers who took her off arm-in-arm to the playground at the back. They would get a few minutes at least before the bell rang, Lily thought.

Except for Ellen, she knew all of those girls. They were the popular ones in her class and the leader, as always, was Irene Prentiss—the teacher's pet. Two months had gone by since Lily had left the school and still she remembered that whenever she raised her hand to answer a question, Miss Maddock always chose Irene. She stood for a moment watching them walk away and then she sighed. She wasn't at all sure that this was preferable to shrimp boats in Texas.

Mr. Carey called out to her, "You forgot to close the door Lily!"

She turned back to the car, embarrassed. He must have seen that no one had noticed her. Perhaps after all those weeks they had forgotten her, but she had remembered them, and she felt awkward standing there alone.

"I'm sorry," she said.

He smiled at her and said, "You have a nice day Lily. I'll see you this evening and don't you forget that you'll have to tell me all about Texas sometime."

"In Galveston they have shrimp boats," she said.

Mr. Carey laughed, and waved as he drove off.

A snowball hit her in the back of her head and broke up into small pieces, which for the most part slipped down into the crack between her neck and her jacket.

The next three weeks were bad for Lily. Ellen Miller never spoke to her at school or in the car and Ellen's daily welcome into the inner circle made Lily feel more isolated than ever—and somehow bedraggled.

I must be ugly, she thought. The mirrors at school told her so. Whenever she washed her hands at school, there she would be, staring back at herself—at her straight brown hair, her big eyes and full lips and thin face. Looking in the mirror like that was like being in a crowd of one. There were no mirrors at home and it was the most company she ever had at school in those weeks. The girl in the mirror—herself—what was it about her? Lily didn't like that girl either. She could see it in the mirror. She could see that she was a girl without friends. It was the lips, she thought, and her mouth. They were too big. Much too big! She pulled her mouth tight and bit on her lower lip to hold it in place. Yes, that was better. All of the most popular girls had small mouths and small teeth. But there was nothing she could do about her teeth. She had lost her front teeth early and the new ones had already come in. They were huge, she thought. They made her look like a beaver. In the mirror, it was plain as could be. She was all teeth and all mouth and it made her miserable.

Irene went around with no front teeth at all and everyone said she was cute. Yes she was, but it was the same with all of the popular girls—small mouths and small teeth. She remembered her mother making a remark about, "birds of a feather!" She had said it in a scornful way and made it clear that she was talking about people who were all of a kind. She had even wrinkled her nose so that Lily would see that she didn't approve of such people. Lily could understand what she said, and she could also see how the girls at school were very much alike, but it didn't make any difference at all. One way or the other, she was miserable.

Every morning in the car it was the same. Lily had to sit in the back with the boys, who seemed to get worse every day—except when Mr. Carey told them to 'cut it out.' Only twice did she get to sit in the front seat, both times because she was earlier than usual getting down to the corner and Mr. Carey had stopped and picked her up on his way to the Miller house. They could talk a bit then, like they used to before Lily went to Texas, but she soon learned that it wasn't worth it to get the front seat ahead of Ellen. On those days, Ellen's nose was more stuck-up than ever—and at school she found that she was the object of more than usual attention. When she saw Ellen whispering to her friends, she knew that they were talking about her. She knew because they all looked at her and giggled—or looked disgusted.

In class, when Miss Maddock wasn't looking, a whole row of girls on Ellen's side were staring at her with poker faces and when Lily noticed them they smirked and ducked behind their books, where they snickered and sneaked sideways glances to see if their fellow conspirators were doing the same.

It was easy to put Lily out of her stride in that classroom. Miss Maddock had arranged the desks in a U-shape, with herself in the centre of the U so that one row of pupils sat facing the other. Lily sat in the exact middle of the *far* side. *Far* is how she saw it, because Irene sat directly opposite her, and she was sure that Irene would never be on the far side of anything. She was Miss Maddock's favourite.

Sometimes Lily thought that Miss Maddock was as bad as the children—snooty and mean. But then she wondered if the children were snooty and mean because Miss Maddock was. She had no idea why Miss Maddock hated her. She was just sure that she did. Was it because she had moved to Hubbardston in the middle of a semester? Or that she was an outsider in a very small town? A far out outsider! Yes, the Millers lived much further out, but they had always lived in Hubbardston. Aunt Agneta had said so, and she knew about everything and everybody in town. She had been there forever, longer even than the Millers.

How could Lily know why Miss Maddock was so horrible to her? She was only seven years old. Once, when she raised her hand to answer a question, Miss Maddock had called on three other children instead and they all got it wrong, at which point Lily called out, "I know it!"

Miss Maddock had stared at her then—for a minute it seemed— then marched her out into the corridor and made her stand in the corner behind the door. People kept walking by and she ducked down every time so they wouldn't see her standing there in disgrace. She didn't want anyone to know that she had been bad. She had no idea how long she stood there, but when the bell rang to go home, she knew that she must have been there for a long time—more than an hour, maybe almost two hours. She was very tired by then and didn't know what to do. She was still standing when all the children went running past on their way home. And Miss Maddock didn't come. And she was worried that Mr. Carey might go without her. And, thinking that, she stepped out a little way into the corridor. She thought that if Miss Maddock saw her standing there, she would let her go.

At that moment, the Principal, Mr. Pearce, came along. He seemed surprised to see her there. "What are you doing standing there, little lady?" he asked. "You should be going home now. Have you lost something?"

"Miss Maddock told me I have to stay here," she said.

"Oh! Why was that?"

"She said I was naughty."

"Were you?"

"I guess so. I don't know." She looked down at her shoes, feeling embarrassed.

"Well, I guess you'd better stay here while I go and ask Miss Maddock."

Mr. Pearce was back in just a minute. "You can go home now," he said, "but first you will want to clean up the things on your desk." And he smiled at her—a real smile, it seemed.

She was surprised. He didn't seem to be angry at all. In fact, he stood and watched as she put her things away, as if he was making sure that she would be okay. Miss Maddock didn't pay her any attention at all. She was very busy at her desk. Lily thanked Mr. Pearce when she left and then called out good-bye to Miss Maddock as well. It felt good to do that with Mr. Pearce standing there. He would know that she was grateful—and polite.

CHAPTER 9

1952

Home

It was a few days later. Lily hadn't come home from school. It was a whole hour later than her usual time for getting home and it was dark and snowing heavily. Betsy would have to dress herself and Matty to go out in it. It was the most inconvenient time of day—time to be getting the dinner ready. Charley would be home soon and there was plenty to do. It made her angry. It worried her too, which made her angrier. She didn't have time for this sort of thing and she hated leaving the stingy warmth of the cottage on days like this. She hated getting wet, making a mess every time she came back inside, tracking in snow and the dirt that went with it. She would much rather be inside sitting near the fire where she could be warm. She could close her eyes then and think of home.

This was what she did every day—sat in her chair near the fire and thought of home. There was nothing else to do. Town was four miles away and she had no car. She couldn't drive a car, anyway. In all the time she had been at the cottage she had never met a soul from the town. All she had for company during the day were Agneta and Eva over at the farmhouse—and Matty. Every day she walked over to the

137

house to get some water, pick up the mail if there was any, and say hello. She stayed for an hour or less and talked the same talk. Then she went back to the cottage and sat near the stove and tried to keep warm. She filled the stove with wood. She knitted. She played the same games over and over with Matty.

What else could she do? Without electricity she couldn't even listen to a radio. The house was so small you could clean it in an hour—but then it was so dingy it looked exactly the same, clean or not. Why bother? She looked around the room—dark as its wood-gray walls—at the sticks called furniture crammed into it—one bed, a table, four chairs and a cupboard—hardly anything, and yet it took up all the space. She amused herself sometimes trying to think up names for it. Call it what you like, it wasn't a house—or a home. You could joke about it if you were in a good mood, and call it something like "Renovator's Windfall" or "Kozy Kastle". But in the end, what stuck in her mind was "Charley's Disaster". She couldn't get past that one. No matter which way she twisted it, it always flicked back into the same shape, which was one big mess. Whatever you might choose to call it, it all added up to Charley. She looked around the room and dreamed of the place where she had grown up.

She dreamed of the wattles and hibiscuses, the gum trees and loquats, the river below the house and the Skipping Girl Vinegar sign perched high above the building across the river. She could see it from her room all lit up with coloured lights that flashed on and off and raced around in a circle so fast it made it seem that the girl really was skipping. The lights flashed twenty-four hours a day, every day of the year. She thought too of the Chinese market garden across the street from the Skipping Girl, just below the house.

From their house up on the hill overlooking the river, Betsy could see them both. They were her landmarks—the girl and the garden. In the garden, all the vegetables were set out in perfect rows. The Chinese family who owned it worked hard in that garden—always. Their father had a pigtail. She could see that from the house too—from the large front room with the marble mantelpiece and the beautiful French clock. She remembered the day when the man had come running out after her brother Max waving his big knife at him—yelling. The next time he saw him, he shouted, he was going to cut Max's head off!

Poor Max. It scared him half to death. Max had tried to persuade his father to send the police down there right away to deal with that man. What right did a Chinaman have yelling at him like that, he wanted to know? What he'd got instead was being marched right up to the man's front gate and made to go in and apologize for his rudeness, because there was no doubt in his father's mind that Max must have been rude. Max was overcome with terror. It made him shake so badly that his apology had come out in staccato bumps. Poor Max.

"I am a good man," the Chinese man had told his father. "I work hard—but those boys!"

He had had enough of the rude faces and the taunts and the pranks. He wanted to know how he could make this clear. He could barely speak English and when he was upset it was worse. His words got all mixed up then. He had only picked up his knife to show them what he meant. 'Stop bothering me' is what he meant.

With his father looking on, Max and the Chinese man had made peace. After that, at least once a week when Max walked past, the man would come running out with a bag of vegetables for him to give to his "nice father."

Sitting in the cottage near the fire Betsy thought of her father. How could she compare him, or the life she had lived in Australia, with this—*now*? Would it always be like this, she asked herself.

They had spent weeks racing all over the country like maniacs—she and Charley, towing that trailer everywhere. Unsettled. Going nowhere in all the dirt and dust. She had hated it. She had felt that wherever they went in the whole of this country, which seemed so pleased with itself, there was nothing but overwhelming squalor or insurmountable wealth and in the midst of it, she was just some small foreign woman dragged about from one dirty camping spot to another. A nobody without a home. No landmark. It had made her feel even smaller, and insignificant.

At home in Australia she had felt as big as the house she lived in. Here, she was living in a place so small that it pinched. It was worse than being in the trailer, although that too had pinched. Everything pinched these days, she thought. The whole country pinched. Even so, the cottage was the worst. Worse even than going nowhere in a hurry.

In Houston at least there had been other women—in the trailer park laundry washing clothes—hanging around chatting under mossy trees. She had held her head high and felt superior when the Texas women waved goodbye. She would soon be living in a real house, she had thought, while they would still be washing their clothes in that stinking laundry. "Y'all come back sometime, ya hear?" they had called out as she and Charley drove off. She knew she would never see them again and it had made her feel good. She was leaving. She was going to live in a house. She, at least, could speak proper English. Her family had class—real class. How could those yawling women ever know that? You had to know a thing to recognize it, she thought. And she knew it—she surely did. Underneath her floral-printed, rick-rack-trimmed apron, she knew she was a person of class.

Every day she sat in the cottage, waited for letters from home and was unhappy when they didn't arrive. Charley went out to work. He had got his old job back again. He had friends there. He brought their jokes home and laughed that big laugh of his. Lily went to school. And Betsy sat by the fire with Matty in a place so cold and ugly it made her grow a little smaller each day and she remembered what it was like to live in a real home.

"That awful child!" she snapped as she pulled Matty's jacket off the peg behind the door. "She is such a nuisance."

It was always a bother getting Matty ready to go out in that weather, even for so short a distance, and the whole time she was dressing him—tugging at the zipper on his jacket, fumbling with his mittens, thumping his feet into his boots, she fumed and bumped and rocked him so violently that he had trouble staying on his feet. "She is the most unreliable child!" she complained as she pulled his hat down over his ears and steadied him back into place with a pat.

Lily is going to get hit, Matty thought. His mother was mad because she didn't come home from school. His mother had said it was time to get the dinner ready and he had asked where Lily was. "It's dark out," he had said and now she was mad.

A look of alarm had skittered across Betsy's face at Matty's question. She had shrugged her shoulders as it went—pushed the thought away before it had a chance to settle. Nevertheless, she had stood up abruptly and gone to the window. It was covered with ice, its dull gray frosting the color of night. Beyond was the dark—and it was snowing heavily. Lily hadn't come home from school and she hadn't even noticed until that moment. She had been so busy remembering.

"She must be over talking to Eva," she said to Matty. "She should know better than to keep Lily there at this time of day."

She stood staring at the blank window and willed the door to open. "Surely she will be here any moment now," she said. "She's afraid of the dark."

She opened the door to get a better look at the weather. The wind was getting up and the snow was coming down on a slant. There was ice in it. She called out. There was no answer. She listened hard. "You can never hear anything in this damned snow," she grumbled. The house was getting cold as she stood there calling and that too made her angry. And all at once her anger grew large and encompassed the whole world around her—Lily, who should have come straight home—the dark, which could swallow her up—Eva, who should have sent her

141

home by now—Charley, who would be impatient if his dinner wasn't ready on time—Matty...

If I could just dash over without Matty, she thought, as she pushed him into his clothes, it would be so much easier. But I can't leave him. He would be afraid ... he might hurt himself. The stove is so hot...

She muttered as she pulled Matty through the snow. It seemed such a long way to the big house when the snow was deep—and Matty kept falling over. I'm going to give that kid such a beating when I get her home, she told herself. She will learn not to do this again

Betsy was right about that. Whenever she or Charley hit her, Lily certainly did learn not to do that thing again—whatever it was they had hit her for. But there would always be some other thing that she could never have guessed would be wrong. She tried her very best to remember them all, but it was hard. She never meant to be naughty; it just happened, and she couldn't understand how she did so many bad things without meaning to. It embarrassed her too because she knew that Matty was always good. So she tried even harder, so that her mother would think she was good too.

She had learned all sorts of things. To be quiet mostly. Not to fight with Matty. Not to make a noise when Betsy was talking to her friends. When Betsy was reading a book. When Betsy and Charley were talking. And she had learned what things not to say—like *hell*. Betsy had washed her mouth out with soap and water for saying that. One day last spring in Oxford, when she was out in the yard playing with her doll after Sunday school, she had said *hell*, just to see how it would sound to say it out loud. All morning at Sunday school the boys had been saying *hell* and every time they said it, they giggled and looked to see if the teachers had heard them. Lily knew they were being very naughty, but she couldn't understand why it was naughty. Grown-ups said it—even her parents. She had heard them lots of times. Just that morning the Sunday school teacher had talked to them about going to hell. She had said it was in the Bible. It might be the sound of it when you say it, she had thought—if you are a child. "Hell!" she had said to herself very quietly.

It was barely more than a whisper, but Betsy had heard it. She had been standing right there behind her. She had come up so quietly that Lily didn't know she was there. It gave her an awful fright. Betsy had yelled at her and dragged her into the house—into the bathroom— and pushed soap into her mouth, and splashed water all over her face, and banged her face on the sink, and hit her and yelled the whole time, telling her what a bad bad bad girl she was.

At least a dozen years would pass before Lily would think of saying *hell* again. There is no doubt that she learned when she was hit, but it was a real shame she couldn't learn to do the right thing all the time so they wouldn't need to hit her—or that she couldn't understand how very aggravating she was most of the time and remember to be quiet in time. If only she could learn to behave herself.

Betsy too asked herself questions like: What can you do with a child like that? Why is she always doing some stupid thing to make you mad—going from the sublime to the ridiculous? Talking and talking until you want to wring her neck to shut her up. Or else she goes into a great black silence—disappears right into herself. The more you yell at her, the more she disappears. It's as if she isn't there at all. Oh you can see her all right—standing perfectly still staring at you with those big eyes—nodding her head if you demand an answer. But she doesn't say a word. Not a single word! What goes on in her head? Who knows what she thinks? If only she weren't so stubborn! She's just like her grandmother! Sometimes I can't stand the sight of her standing there looking like a Malmqvist. It makes me want to hit her ... I wouldn't ever hit her for that reason of course! No! ... But what am I to do when she does such bizarre things—like that day—riding her tricycle all the way down to her grandmother's. She wasn't even four years old ...

over the railroad tracks and all. A mile and a half ... and across Route 12 too! She could have been killed! Why? Because she wanted to visit her grandmother! Oh she's a Malmqvist all right! She sulks—forgets her manners—tells lies! Oh lord! I'll never forget that time with Ellie Beauregard. It was so embarrassing having to tell that awful woman that Lily was a liar... How else can I make her pay attention—so she'll learn? If only she didn't look like that...

It was perfectly reasonable that Betsy had lost track of the time and forgotten Lily. Lily was always late these days and she had got used to it. Mr. Carey was renovating the Willett's house—kitchen, dining room, the whole works—even putting new bedrooms into the attic. The entire town knew he would be late getting to the school, even though he always said he would try to be there on time. The Willetts were in Virginia visiting relatives and Mr. Carey was working overtime to get the job done before spring.

Betsy, of course, had never met the Willetts, but she knew all about them. Everyone talked. Agneta did, at least. Agneta said people just couldn't figure out where all that money had come from all of a sudden. "Fancy doing up a whole house all at once!" she had exclaimed. "No one in these parts ever does a thing like that!" Betsy wondered if someone had died and left them some money. "Maybe they won it," Eva had suggested. "There's a lottery over at Gardner, you know."

Whatever it was, Betsy thought it was a whole lot more interesting to be thinking about where the Willetts had got that money than it was to be worrying about whether Mr. Carey was a bit late. It didn't really matter anyway. There were only two families who needed him to drive their children, and they had already got used to it. Lily had been at least half an hour late every night for the past three weeks and she had often stopped on her way past the big house to talk with Eva and Agneta. After a few days, Betsy had stopped noticing.

Lily was not at the big house.

"Oh my goodness," Eva gasped when Betsy asked about Lily. "What do you suppose can have happened to her? Oh my! Oh ... my! What will we do? Oh, my..."

Eva was a slow-witted but cheerful woman or, as some people thought, a cheerful and complaining woman—a well-blended mixture of a person—like one of her recipes. She had spent so many years creating delicious smells in her kitchen and looking after Agneta— moving Agneta back and forth between her bedroom and the bay window, bringing her food, washing her clothes and dying the strips for her rugs. Plain black. She needed so many in black. It was the black that set the colors off so well, Agneta always said, and Eva made it so. She dyed the strips and cooked the food and cleaned everything. She had bustled about the kitchen and stepped over so many cats in the lean-to shed every time she went out to the clothesline, or the well, or the outhouse—humming and complaining to herself all the while— that, finally she had mixed herself into a person who was cheerful and complaining all at once.

She didn't need to be anything more. All she ever did was work for Will and Agneta, and go to Gardner once a week on the bus to visit her sister and do some shopping. She had never attempted anything more ambitious than that, not since the time she and Lily's grandmother had gone to Boston to see a show and then, on the way home, had accidentally taken the train to Albany in upstate New York instead of Worcester in central Massachusetts.

Lily's grandmother, not the Malmqvist one but the Australian one (Betsy's mother, Tilly Bolle), was not unaccustomed to having such adventures. She even found them quite amusing. But for Eva once was enough and she had made up her mind never to leave the farm again except to go to Gardner once a week.

Lily's Grandma Tilly was an opaque, fading image in her mind, stuck in the past tense. She knew her in the present only by the letters and parcels which came from Australia occasionally, nowhere near often enough for her mother. Whenever they arrived, she would dip into her mind and fish out the memory of her grandmother as she had been at the time when she came to visit. She was only three years old then and it had been such a messy visit—such a here-and-there, coming-and-going visit, that all Lily had left of it was a dusty old memory, which she kept tucked away as a picture in her mind, no less real than her other small treasures. Sometimes, even when there wasn't a letter or parcel to remind her, she would take it out to have a look at it—but it had become hard to see. It had faded so much. She would close her eyes tight and concentrate with all her might on her grandmother and how it had been when she came, but by the time she was seven, the most she was ever able to find inside her mind was a small dark shadow in a hat who had once bought her fish and chips.

"Impossible!" her mother had said, when Lily spoke of it once some years later. "My mother would *never* have bought fish and chips!"

But Lily remembered it well. She and her grandmother had taken the bus to Worcester that day—just the two of them. They had shopped all morning long. There had been so many errands to do, and they *had* to do them, her grandmother told her. Lily's mother had a new baby and was too sick to do errands, she had said. Lily remembered the shop, and how hungry she had been. They had walked such a long way that morning.

Her mother, who wouldn't believe a word of it, argued that she must have forgotten where they had eaten lunch, because, of course, she was so little at the time. "Children," she insisted, "never remember anything of their earliest years. It couldn't possibly have happened."

Lily had argued in turn, "It happened. I know it did."

But in the face of Betsy's assertions, she began to doubt herself. She decided to let it go, knowing that she could never win an argument against her mother. Nevertheless, she wondered how her mother could be so sure, when she hadn't even been there. So, once again she reached into her mind for her memory. She was pleased to find that, after all those years, there was still a glimmer of it left. She could just make out the tables and the wide seats along the wall, and the window looking onto the street. Of course it's true, she told herself. How could you forget fish and chips if it was the one and only time in your childhood when you'd had them? How could you forget if it was your grandmother who had bought them?

The shop had been long and thin with tables down the side, and benches with high backs like they had in ice cream parlors. It was in a side street somewhere. They had walked and walked until she was tired, and then they had stopped. Her grandmother had stood and looked through the window of the fish and chip shop for a minute and then she had said, "This is the place." They had gone into the shop and her grandmother had walked up to the man at the counter and spoken to him just as though she did it every day. Lily had thought her grandmother must already know the man. They had sat down at one of the tables. She had sat on the side of the table opposite her grandmother, just like grown-ups did. She could see out of the window into the street.

"Ah!" her grandmother sighed as she sat. "Now doesn't that feel better already? It's a good thing to take the weight off your feet for a bit!" And she asked, "Are you very hungry, Lily?"

Lily had nodded. She remembered that too.

"It's just as well if you are," her grandmother had said, "because they always give you so much in this country. Do you like fish and chips?" she had asked.

Lily didn't know. She had never had them.

"You will," her grandmother had said. "Everyone likes fish and chips. You will have some orange juice too, and I will have coffee. A cup of coffee will be a good thing—just about as good as resting my weary feet. ... Of course, I already know better than to ask for a cup of tea in America, but the coffee will be all right, I expect. They make good coffee in this country—usually. And there is always plenty of it. Bottomless coffee. Now that's funny, don't you think Lily?"

She had smiled then. Lily remembered. It was *her* mother who would never buy fish and chips.

Her grandmother remembered her too, a long time after she had gone home again. When she was seven years old, her grandmother had sent her a doll for Christmas. It was very small—only eight inches tall, but it had a complete outfit: underpants, undershirt, dress, jacket, bonnet and bootees—all hand-knitted in a blue and white lacy pattern, in the finest Australian yarn. Her mother had told her several times how fine it was, and that her grandmother had knitted it all especially for her. She wanted Lily to know this and "appreciate" it.

Grandma Tilly had come all the way from Australia on a ship, just so that she would be there to help when Matty was born, because Betsy had nearly died when she gave birth to Lily. But then, after only three weeks, she had moved up to the farm to live with Uncle Will and Aunt Agneta. Late one afternoon she had called Will from some place in Rutland. She had been walking, carrying her bags the whole way, and she was tired out. She told him that she couldn't stand staying with Betsy and Charley any longer, although she didn't mind if they drove up to Hubbardston occasionally to visit her. Will had driven down from Hubbardston to get her, and that was that.

Betsy and Charley had been arguing when she left. She had packed her bags and walked out the door. No one had tried to stop her. Lily had no memory of her grandmother's sudden departure, but she did have a memory of visiting her in Hubbardston, although it was faint and smothered in shadows—and no amount of searching could draw it out. It wasn't until years later, long after Tilly had died and Lily was grown up, that Betsy told her about it.

"We thought she would be back in a few minutes," she said. "And then, when we realized she really had gone, we didn't know where to look for her. It seemed for a time that she had just vanished. Your father drove all over town looking for her, but she was nowhere to be seen. We had no idea—not until Will called us."

She stopped for a moment or so and it seemed that she too was searching for a memory. Finally, she said, "It was probably for the best. She was happy there."

When Lily argued that her grandmother couldn't possibly have walked all the way to Rutland carrying heavy suitcases—it was at least twenty miles, Betsy looked offended and dug her toes in. No one ever questioned her version of a story.

"My mother got on just fine with the folks on the farm," she went on, "which was a good thing since she had a six months' ticket. They rather liked having such a lady staying with them. They told me they liked hearing her talk about her friends and relations "down-under." It gave them something to talk about. She bustled about and did things in the house. She chattered about this and that. She had so much to say. She told them all about her adventures and made them laugh. 'Isn't it funny,' she exclaimed to them once, 'how my adventures always seem to last about six months!' I can just imagine her saying it: *Why it seems like just yesterday that I spent six months in New Zealand with my husband's cousin, who was married to the Lord Mayor of Wellington.* I can almost hear

her laughing at that point, and explaining to the folks on the farm that of course it was exactly the opposite to her coming to stay with them, because she had only gone to New Zealand for two weeks on that occasion and finished up staying six months because of a shipping strike. According to Agneta, my mother was 'philosophical', although somewhat repetitive. *Life is like that, isn't it?* she would say, always tossing it off with a bit of a chuckle, followed by something like, *You just never know how long you will be spending anywhere. But one thing is certain: it is so nice not having to dress for dinner every night here on the farm like they did at the Lord Mayor's house.*

"Yes," Betsy said, "The folks on the farm were happy to agree to that, especially now that they had my mother staying with them so unexpectedly for five more months. Imagine them having to dress for dinner every night! It sure was amazing, they told me, how adventurous a short, dumpy woman, who always wore a hat and gloves when she went out, could be! Travelling all over the place in that fashion must be really something, Will said to me once—and I had the impression that he might have liked to do the same thing himself. But nobody ever asked me what I thought of it all. Maybe they thought I had enough to do looking after my children."

On the night that Eva and Tilly went to the show in Boston. Eva had thought that Tilly, being a city woman and a great world traveler, would surely know how to get the right train home, and Tilly had thought that Eva, being a native of Massachusetts, would of course be familiar with the Boston transport system. Neither of them had looked at the signs. It was just so easy, they had thought, as they jumped onto the first train they saw that was the same color as the one they had come on. They were well on their way before they discovered that they were on an express to Albany instead of Worcester. It took them another two days to find their way back to Worcester.

It is true that Eva was slow-witted, but after nearly sixty years of living in that part of the state, she knew what could happen to a small child lost in a big snow storm, and for a moment all she could see in her mind was that dear little girl, buried somewhere under a mountain of snow. If only Will hadn't gone to that meeting over in Westminster, she thought. He could have been out looking for her in his truck. And that thought was enough to make her see what needed to be done. Yes! The first thing to do, she decided, was to go out and look for Lily.

"You go straight down to the corner and see if something has happened to her," she said to Betsy in a firm and purposeful tone, quite unlike her usual one. "We'll mind Matty while you're gone. You hurry. Quick! But wait—I'll get you a flashlight! And then I'll ring Mr. Carey and see what he knows"

"No," Betsy said. "I'll call Mr. Carey. That way we'll know what happened."

"How will we know? Well, if you think... Yes, maybe you should... Oh my goodness!"

She sat on a chair—confused all over again. She felt helpless and rather weak. She had just figured out what to do, and now what? What should she do? That Betsy is such a spiky person, she thought to herself. If I tell her to do a sensible thing, she decides to do the opposite. She could be halfway down to the corner by now. It's so hard dealing with her, it gets my head in a muddle and I can't think straight.... What can have happened to that dear little girl?

Not knowing what to do, Eva began to take off Matty's things. He would surely be staying with them for a while, she thought.

Betsy was already on the phone to Mr. Carey. "Have you seen Lily this afternoon?" she was asking. "She didn't come home from school today and we don't know where she is."

There was a moment's silence before Mr. Carey replied. "No," he said. "I haven't seen her since this morning. I thought she must've gone to visit a friend after school... although it was a bit unusual, but then I guessed there must be some reason if..."

"I don't understand," Betsy interrupted. "How can that be? She was supposed to come home as usual."

"She wasn't there when I came by this afternoon. It was just the Miller kids and they didn't say anything, so I assumed..."

There was silence again as Betsy and Mr. Carey at opposite ends of the line realized that Lily really had disappeared. Betsy's face changed color as she thought about it. The rosy patches on her cheeks were suddenly rimmed with white. White lines appeared at the sides of her nose and around her mouth, giving her a pinched look. She swallowed and clutched the phone tighter. She couldn't think where Lily might be. The town was so small and all the people knew each other...

"I just thought she must've gone to play with a friend," Mr. Carey repeated.

"Who?"

"Well I don't know. I mean, I thought she must've forgotten to tell me, that's all."

"No. She knows she is supposed to come straight home. She wouldn't have. She's supposed to ask first. She never goes anywhere anyway. Oh dear! Where is she...?"

An edge of panic was creeping over her. She cast her mind back over the past few weeks searching for a clue, and found nothing—no hint at all. She couldn't remember Lily ever mentioning any children she liked, or wanted to play with after school. Now that she thought about it, she realized that she couldn't remember Lily ever saying anything about school. Was it because she hadn't really been listening to her—or because she just didn't say much? She was beginning to feel hollow—and a bit dizzy. Mr. Carey was talking again. He sounded far away.

"It's funny," he was saying, "now that I think of it, how quiet those kids were on the way home. They're usually a bag of trouble. Not that I ever complain about them, mind you, but they aren't exactly a quiet bunch, those Miller kids. It's Lily that's the quiet one. She's as good as gold. It's a pleasure to be driving her. She's a real polite little girl. I'd sure like to know where she is."

"So would I," Betsy said. "That's why I rang you."

Surely Mr. Carey could be more helpful, she thought. She had spent so little time in the town since they'd moved to Hubbardston, she couldn't even remember what it was like near the school, or what the school looked like... It looked like...a school...red bricks...just a school.

"I'm thinking about the Miller kids," Mr. Carey went on, after another pause. "I have a hunch they'll know where she is. It's a pity they don't have a telephone, but if you could just drive on down to their place, I'm sure you could find out from them where she is. They're pretty close to you really—only about a mile further on."

"I can't," Betsy said, her voice shaking by now. "I don't have a car. My husband is still at work and Uncle Will is over at Westminster. It's much too far to walk in this weather. I just can't do it... I don't know what to do."

She felt dizzy again.

"Now don't you worry," Mr. Carey said. He was calm. "I'll come and get you myself. I've got a truck. It's no trouble at all for me to drive in this snow. I'll leave here right this minute. You just go down to the corner in about ten minutes and wait for me. I'll pick you up and we'll go straight on to the Miller place. Don't you worry! We'll have your Lily back in no time. You can be sure there's a perfectly good reason for it. She'll be just fine, you'll see. I'll be right there, quick as a wink..."

Betsy nodded, put the phone down, and burst into tears. "Don't you worry, he said! What a dumb thing to say! That stupid kid!" she sobbed at Eva.

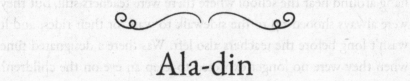

CHAPTER 10

Ala-din

The second time Lily got to sit in the front seat of Mr. Carey's car the whole row of girls who sat opposite her at school spent the entire day staring her down. Ellen was having a powerful effect on people, it seemed. And her brothers had also turned nasty. They had been a bit of a nuisance before, but now, what had been bothersome or just plain silly

behaviour had become truly nasty—and physical. It seemed that they were determined to inflict pain on her whenever they could. On one day that week, Jerry had pushed her over hard and twisted her arm at the same time. A teacher had seen him do it and told him off. The next time Jerry wanted to hurt her, he looked first to see if there was a teacher nearby.

By the middle of the week, Lily was dreading the afternoon wait for Mr. Carey. He had a new job in the daytime. He had told them that he was working on a house. 'Renovations' she had heard him say. He had also said he would try to be at the school on time, but he was late nearly every day.

Before that, even when the Miller boys were bothering Lily, they weren't especially bad, but now Mr. Carey's delays made space for more mischief and when Jerry and Marty joined the toughest boys in the fifth and sixth grades in some scuffle or full-blown snowball fight, they always packed the snow hard and they meant to hurt.

Lily and Ellen—keeping a distance between each other, tried to hang around near the school where there were teachers still, but they were always shooed up to the sidewalk to wait for their rides, and it wasn't long before the teachers also left. Was there a designated time when they were no longer expected to keep an eye on the children? Lily didn't know, but it always seemed much worse when they were gone.

For several days Lily stood on the sidewalk, watching the boys with one eye and the school with the other. It was funny, she thought, how you had to be inside that building for so many hours every day and you weren't allowed to go anywhere else, but when you wanted a safe place to be at the end of the day, you were absolutely not allowed to be inside that building.

On the one particular more than usually miserable day, inside a building was where she wanted to be. Mr. Carey was awfully late and she was awfully cold and the boys were horrible and all the teachers were gone and she looked around again, still hunting for a safe place. The town library was next door. She saw it every day but had never been inside it. She knew what a library was, but she was certain that seven-year-olds didn't go into them. They were still reading Dick and Jane and Spot and Fluff and they didn't need a library for that. She saw a woman go into the library and it occurred to her that she had never seen a child go in there. Maybe, she thought, it was only for grown-ups.

The boys were being horrible—throwing snowballs at some of the younger boys. There was a scuffle and Lily saw Jerry hit one of them, who kicked at him in turn, then ran off up the hill. And suddenly she was in the middle of it—boys on both sides of her and a hard snowball hit her in the middle of her back, and the merest whisper of a thought flew right through her, like a bird—a very light bird—like a sparrow. She looked around for it and it was gone, and she remembered that it had come once before and danced about her—an uncatchable thought that had hovered for scarcely a moment then disappeared. It had happened, she remembered, when there were no teachers and the building was locked and Ellen stood aloof and Mr. Carey wasn't there and a snowball hit her again and in that thought was a whisper of an idea—a door could open.

Knowledge was the key to mobility and power. Knowing what she could do could also enable her to do it. It was the inscrutability of grown-ups that was paralysing. Not knowing if she could go through a door, or if she would be allowed—not knowing what would be on the other side. What Lily knew was that she had to do as she was told. Stand on the sidewalk and wait. Stand, sit, do, don't. A man had come to the school to take pictures of everyone and she had refused to smile because the proof of her ugliness would be sent home and her mother wouldn't like it. A snowball hit her on the back of her leg and she seemed to be walking through a puzzle and trying to put the pieces together. Ever since they had come back from Houston, it seemed, she had been disconnected from the world around her and from the day she had found Ellen sitting in the front seat of Mr. Carey's car she hadn't been able to find herself again.

She was standing in the library. A snowball had hit her on the back of her leg. She had turned around. Jerry was grinning at her. She had stooped to pick up some snow—to hit back—and a snowball had hit her in the face and the pain was spreading across her nose and cheeks and mouth and her eyes watered and she was standing in the library.

Between the snowball and the library was a black spot. She could not remember how she came to be standing in front of a desk and a young woman was asking her what she wanted.

She didn't know what to say. She wanted to stay there and be safe, but libraries were for books, not people, she thought, and she was afraid that the woman would make her go away. She said nothing. She was trying to think what to say. She had never been inside a library before.

The young woman walked over to the window, where there was another woman standing, looking out. They were talking, nodding their heads yes, nodding again no. Lily looked around her. It wasn't a very big room, but it was full of books on shelves—rows and rows of shelves. Shelves filled the whole room so that you could scarcely see anything beyond the first row, except that there were more shelves.

"Would you like to read a book?" the young woman asked.

Lily was startled. She hadn't seen her come back to the desk, but now she was there and smiling—a real smile it seemed, not just a smirk.

She nodded yes, even though she didn't want to read a book just then. She wanted a warm and safe place to be, but in libraries, she thought, you read books. That's what libraries were for—and she was beginning to feel warm again—and not afraid—and the woman was so kind. Yes, she said, she would like to read a book. And she wondered if they would have a book for someone like her.

The woman was smiling at her. "Come with me," she said. "I will show you where the books for you are."

She led Lily past all the rows of shelves to the side wall, and then they turned left, where at the end of still more shelves there were tables and chairs tucked into a corner to create a quiet reading area. The young woman—who Lily thought of as 'the Lady' stopped just short of this area and pointed to the shelves lining the walls on her right.

"This is where we keep the books for children," she said. "How old are you? Seven?"

Lily nodded yes, and when the woman asked if she could read, she nodded again more vigorously. That was the most important thing, she knew. If she couldn't read, she had no business being there—and then she would be out in the street again—and another snowball would hit her smack in the face. She wondered if the lady could see where she had been hit. Was there a mark?

The woman smiled and said, "The bottom four shelves are for seven-year-olds. You can choose any book you like. And if these are too easy for you, you will find the eight-year-old books on the shelves above. Then, on this side," she said, pointing towards the street, "there are books for older children. You might want to look at those too sometime. And here," she said, "is a little stool for you to stand on if can't reach what you want."

Lily thought the lady was being very kind, but she knew that grown-ups could be impatient, and there were so many books and they all looked the same and she was afraid that the lady wouldn't let her stay if she took too long, and all that she could see of the books on the shelves were the spines in various shades of red and blue and green and black, their names printed in small letters.

She stood still for a moment, casting her eyes this way and that, looking for a book that stood out from the others. And just as she was getting confused and nervous, there it was, on a different shelf, higher up—the book she wanted to read. It was the only one on the entire wall of shelves that was standing with its cover facing her, and it was beautiful. In green and yellow and blue and brown there was a picture of a man in an enormous hat, sitting and reading to a boy and a girl.

She could see that it was on a shelf too high for her to reach, so she turned to the stool and, in the same moment, the Lady said, "Ah yes, it is a beautiful book, but it's in the section for ten and eleven year-olds and I don't think you will be able to read it. Perhaps you might like to read one of these," she said, pulling off the shelf directly in front of her two or three perfectly respectable books with perfectly nice pictures.

Lily looked at them for a minute or so and then, like a magnet, her eyes went back to the book with the man in the hat. It wasn't just the picture that drew her to it. It was that she wanted to see what was inside it.

"It's not allowed?" Lily asked.

"Of course it's allowed," the Lady said, "if you can read it. But there's no point in just looking at the pictures if you can't read the story."

And then, seeing how forlorn Lily looked, she said, "I will let you have it if you can read it to me."

She reached up and took the book from the shelf very carefully, as if it was made of glass and she handed it to Lily, who sat down on the stool and opened it just as carefully. On the first page she saw a small ink picture of two men carrying great heavy bundles on their backs—bundles tied up with ropes—and she wondered what was inside them. And then she saw the first page, and the next and the next and it was all words. She had never seen a children's book with so many words. A wave of heat went through her at the sight of all those words on the one page.

The lady was looking down at her and Lily felt stupid. All she had wanted was a safe place to sit until Mr. Carey came to get her—and she wouldn't be allowed to sit there if she couldn't read. But then, as she looked down at the first page again, she saw words that she already knew and she thought she could sound out the others. It might not be as hard as it seemed. She began at the top of the page with the word "ALADDIN".

"Ala – *din*", she read out loud. It was the heading on the first story. And then she began at the beginning. "*In one of the large and rich cities of China, there once lived a tailor named Mustapha.*"

She knew all of those words except for 'Mustapha,' which she sounded out slowly, and then looked at the lady in surprise. She had already learned some of those words in school, but there were others, like 'tailor', which she had learned from walking past the shop window on Main Street in Oxford, and, although she couldn't say it properly, she knew that 'Mustapha' was a name for a man, because he was the tailor.

As she read more, she discovered that Mustapha, *"could hardly, by his daily labour, maintain himself and his family, which consisted only of his wife and a son."*

And in the next paragraph she read, *"His son, who was called Aladdin, was a very careless and idle fellow. He was disobedient to his father and mother, and would go out early in the morning, and stay out all day, playing in the streets and public places with idle children of his own age."*

The wonderful book had already begun to light up for Lily like no other book she had ever been given to read. It was not only beautiful to look at with its glorious pictures it was also exciting to read it. She knew that Aladdin was a son and a son was a boy. And even the word disobedient, which looked hard, was very clear when she sounded it out. Her mother said it to her almost every day, so she knew immediately that Aladdin was a naughty child—just like herself.

The Lady lingered for a while, looking down at her, and Lily read on, moving her finger down the page to show that she was making progress. It was very important to get it right, she thought, and she didn't stop reading until she came to the bottom of the page. She looked up then, feeling quite pleased with herself, and she saw that the Lady had gone back to her work at the desk. She could hear the two women talking quietly, but she couldn't hear what they were saying. She only knew it must be okay for her to keep on reading.

And so she read quietly to herself and for a long time she forgot where she was, and the words no longer challenged her. It was a story—a wonderful story—and she knew what it was saying to her. There was an African magician, who claimed to be Aladdin's uncle. He came to make Aladdin rich, he said. And the story went on...

"'I am your uncle,' the magician said. 'Your worthy father was my own brother. I knew you at first sight, you are so like him.' Then he gave Aladdin a handful of small money, saying, 'Go my son, to your mother,

give my love to her, and tell her that I will visit her tomorrow, that I may
see where my good brother lived so long.'

"And Aladdin ran to his mother, overjoyed at the money his uncle
had given him. 'Mother,' said he, 'have I an uncle?' 'No, child,' replied
his mother, 'you have no uncle by your father's side nor mine.' 'I am just
now come," said Aladdin, "from a man who says he is my uncle and my
father's brother. He cried and kissed me when I told him my father was
dead and gave me money, sending his love to you, and promising to come
and pay you a visit, that he may see the house my father lived and died
in.' 'Indeed, child'" replied the mother, 'your father had no brother, nor
have you an uncle.'

"The next day the magician found Aladdin playing in another part
of town..."

Lily had been reading for a long time and had forgotten where she
was until she heard voices in the other room—loud, noisy voices. She
stopped to listen and heard Mr. Carey talking to the librarian and she
thought he had come to take her home. She had no idea how long
she had been reading, but she was sure that the boys and Ellen must
be outside waiting, and she wanted to cry because she hadn't finished
reading the book.

And then she heard her mother talking—and it was awfully
confusing. She couldn't understand how her mother could be there
with Mr. Carey—unless he had gone without knowing that Lily was
in the library. But why didn't the Miller children tell him? And how
did her mother know?

And that thought led to more thoughts, piling up on her all at
once, one after another. It must be very late now, she thought—and
there is so much snow—and it is so difficult to drive in it—and I will
be in trouble...

She looked down at the book on her lap, then clutched it very tight
as she walked into the other room, wondering what would happen
next. And there was her mother looking happy, and Mr. Carey looking

happy, and the Lady was smiling at her—and she wanted to cry because she would have to give her the book.

"I haven't finished reading it," she said as she handed it to her.

"Ah!" said the Lady, smiling at Lily as if she was the only person in the room who mattered, which was an entirely new experience for her. "Would you like to join the library?" she asked. "If you join the library, you can take the book home and bring it back when you are finished with it. And then you can get another book whenever you want."

Lily looked at her mother, just to be sure before she said yes. Having never been in a library before, she had no idea that she could take a book home, but here she was, all of a sudden, standing like Alice in Wonderland on Christmas Day in a whole new world. Even her mother, who was the most awfully impatient person she knew, was suddenly transformed into a fairy godmother—cheerfully agreeing to wait a few minutes more, while the librarian conjured up a brand new library card for her. Mr. Carey, who always seemed to be the most cheerful and patient person on earth, just smiled. And when it was done, the Lady put both the splendid library card and the wonderful book into a bag, saying to Lily that it was to keep it all safe and dry in the snowy weather.

And after that they all went home.

That's how it was. Her father had already come home. Eva and Matty at the farmhouse had been waiting to tell him what had happened—and all was okay, because, said Eva, "Betsy and Mr. Carey went off in the car to find Lily and that's a good thing because they went to the Miller's house and Mr. Carey has a truck."

It all made perfect sense to Eva. And she was right. All was well. Approximately forty-five minutes later, Mr. Carey drove up to the farmhouse with Charley's wife and daughter. Charley had already lit a fire in the stove at the fruit picker's cottage, and had managed to put a meal together. And when all was done, he heard the story of how his wife and daughter came to be in Mr. Carey's truck at that time of day. But not a word was said about Marty and Jerry and the snowballs. That must have come later, after Lily was in bed.

It wasn't until after dinner that Lily was allowed to show her father the book. "Look," she said, "it has two stories in it—and beautiful pictures. The first story is called Ala-*din* or The Wonderful Lamp."

"You've got it wrong," Betsy said. "It's A-**ladd**-in. And you won't be reading any of it tonight. It's already too late. You can read it tomorrow after school."

It wasn't until the next day, when Mr. Carey was driving his usual carload of children to school, that Lily heard what had happened after she went into the library.

Focussing on the Miller children in his rear-view mirror—all three of them in the back this time—he said most seriously, "You all know what happened yesterday, and you know how your failure to tell me that Lily was in the library caused much worry and trouble. I don't need to say more about that. We dealt with it at your house last night, and your parents weren't pleased with you. I also called the Principal last night and told him what happened. All of the bus drivers must tell the Principal when something bad happens—and leaving a child behind on a cold winter night is bad. I don't know what he will say to you, but I think you will be told that there will be no more hard-packed snowballs. And now I am telling you that Lily can go to the library any night after school, and when I come to pick you up, if she isn't already waiting, you Jerry will go in and get her—and you will be polite."

There was unprecedented silence all the way to school. And even when they arrived at school, all of the Miller children seemed awfully quiet when they left the car. Lily hung back, just in case, and Mr. Carey said, "That's quite a bruise you've got on your face Lily. It will go away, but right now it's a useful piece of evidence. You have a good day, Lily."

She smiled and, for the first time since her family came back from Texas, she was happy. No one else said anything to her about her bruise, but Mr. Pearce smiled at her once when he walked by, and even Miss Maddock seemed nicer—for a minute or two. Sometime during the day, Lily went to the girls' toilets just to see what her bruise looked like and she was surprised to find that it looked just like Mr. Carey sounded when he talked about it. Evidence, she thought, was a lovely new word to remember.

At the end of the day, she clutched the bag with the wonderful book close to her and went straight to the library where the Lady smiled and said how nice it was to see her again.

By the time Mr. Carey arrived to pick up the children, Lily was deep into the history of the magician as given by himself: "*my good sister,*" said he, "*do not be surprised at your never having seen me in all the time you have been married to my brother Mustapha. I have been forty years absent from this country, which is my native place, as well as my late brother's; and during that time have travelled into the Indies, Persia, Arabia, Syria and Egypt, and afterward crossed over into Africa, where I took up my abode. At last, as it is natural for a man, I was desirous of seeing my native country again, and of embracing my dear brother...*"

And suddenly there was Jerry, standing in the doorway, looking like a gentleman, which was no less surprising to Lily than the discovery of *Ala-din*. And that is how it would be for the rest of the school year. Mr. Carey and the Lady said so. It was okay to smile.

Quotes from:

Aladdin or The Wonderful Lamp and Ali Baba and the Forty Thieves.

The Mackenzie Edition

With color reproductions from the original paintings

T. Blakeley Mackenzie

Albert Whitman & Co., Chicago, 1929

CHAPTER 11

1953

Moving Again

In the library time disappeared and Lily, who spent most of that time slipping across borders into an entirely different world, scarcely noticed the real world outside her. The snow had melted by degrees and the newspaper deer that had frightened her so had vanished, because, in her mind there were no deer in the land of Ali Baba.

The world went on nevertheless. With or without her, things were happening all around and Lily, who was oblivious as long as she had a book in her hand, never noticed that other words had been attached to her—spoken words. "She is exasperating," Betsy would say, and "such a bother." But for the most part, as Betsy saw it, Lily was quite simply, "That awful child!" It was a thing that she said again and again, as if it was a refrain.

Betsy, whose life was about to change for the third time in one year, was not certain what would come next, but considering Charlie's track record she was not at all sure what he would do. She knew from experience that being at his mercy was a nerve-racking thing and she had no idea where they would end up this time. It was much easier to grumble about Lily, who lived in a book.

167

But how could Lily hear what her mother was saying when she was somewhere in Arabia with *Ali Baba and the Forty Thieves*? She had finished *Aladdin* weeks ago and was halfway through Ali Baba when her parents decided to spend whole weekends looking for a real house to live in—and once again they drove everywhere.

Every weekend they went from one house to another—three or four houses every time—and Betsy always frowned and said no. There was only one house that captured Lily's imagination. It was big and in the brown of a never-painted house outside, and inside it was like a fairy tale with lots of small rooms and even smaller closets, and every room seemed to turn in all directions. It was nothing like all the other houses they had looked at and it would be so much fun to play there, Lily thought. They could play hide and seek all day long and never find anybody. It would be such fun!

And again Betsy said no. It was her loudest 'no' ever. "It is the most ridiculous house I have ever seen," she exclaimed. "It must have been built by a madman."

That was when Lily began to wonder if the right house would ever be found. And every time her mother said no, she thought of being at the same school again, with the same teacher for another year, and she began to feel miserable. That was all she could think of until finally they went home to the fruit pickers' cottage, which even she knew was nothing like a cottage—or a home.

A week later Charley, who was looking very pleased with himself, hurried them all into the car to look for yet another house. "It's going to be a good day," he said to Betsy. "I have a hunch that we will find our house today."

Had he noticed that Betsy's frown was getting deeper every time he mentioned another house?

On that day they drove and drove and drove, until Lily began to wonder whether they would end up in Texas again, but just when she thought they would never get there, they went over a small bridge and turned to the right, and to her astonishment she saw that they were in the town where they used to live—the town where her grandparents still lived—where her old friends from school also lived. She wondered if they were going back to their old house, but just as she was about to ask her father, he turned abruptly to the left and drove up four hills before he stopped in front of a big red house. And she saw that there were fields all around it to run in, and there were woods beyond the fields, and there was a front porch with two great Colorado blue spruce trees in front of it. Of course she didn't know that they were spruce trees. She just thought they were beautiful, and she held her breath and hoped that her parents would say yes this time.

It wasn't a really big house, but after the fruit pickers' cottage it seemed like a mansion to her, and she kept her fingers crossed and didn't dare to speak the whole time they walked through it, upstairs and down, with Betsy exclaiming at how large the closets were, and how nice it was to see such lovely big fields and pastures through the windows, and how nice it was to see that it had everything they needed—although she did say that the stove was "inadequate" and they would need to get another one. And when they went down into the cellar, she could see at one glance that there was plenty of room for both Charley's workshop and her laundry, and she was most impressed. But most of all, Betsy thought it wonderful to see the great empty spaces on each side of the house. "What a gift it would be," she said, "to have only one neighbour on each side, and with a good long distance between us all."

And then when the inspection was done, Lily and Matty were sent to the car to wait while Betsy and Charley spoke with the man who had opened the door for them. Did he own the house or was he an agent? Lily didn't know, but she certainly knew that they had a lot to talk about because they stood outside and talked and talked and talked... It seemed like forever to be waiting so long. When finally her parents were back in the car again, after all that talking, neither of them said a single word. They just hopped into the car and off they went, and when they turned to the right at the bottom of the hill, she knew that they were going back to Hubbardston without stopping to see her grandparents, not even for a minute.

She couldn't understand it. It was nearly nine months since they had last seen them. She looked at Matty, who was shrugging his shoulders again. She decided not to ask any questions and once again she pressed her face against the window and looked towards the back of the car so that her parents wouldn't see how sad she was. It had been so long and she had missed them so much.

In the week or so after seeing the red house, nothing was said about it—not in Lily's hearing at least. It was as though it had never happened. School went on as usual, and although it was getting close to the end of the school year—and she would be having a birthday soon—not a single word was said about anything that might happen next.

As predicted, her birthday came. It was her eighth and it seemed to her that there was something really special about turning eight, even though she wasn't expecting anything. They lived a long way from any stores and her mother didn't have a car, so she was truly surprised when she was given a beautiful birthday card with happy birthday wishes on it. She was even more surprised when her father, who had disappeared for a bit, came back with a large bag in his hand. It was her birthday present, he said, but she couldn't open it yet. They would have to go outside and she would have to watch carefully so that she would learn 'how to do it.'

It wasn't until they were standing at the top of the long sloping hill—a short distance from the driveway—that her father opened the bag and showed her that it was a kite. It was much bigger than any kite she had ever seen, and it was beautiful. It was shaped like a diamond and it was red and yellow and green and purple, and all the colours were reaching for the point at the top, and there was a thin black border that went all around it. Every bit of it seemed to be reaching for the sky and she thought it was beautiful.

Although it was still on the ground, it shifted at the least movement, as if it was in a hurry to fly and although her father had said that it was hers, she was not really sure, because she wasn't allowed to touch it—not yet. She had to learn how to hold it first, he said, because it was very important to get it right.

Lily had seen kites before, but never so beautiful, and it made her nervous, not knowing what would happen next, not knowing whether she would be able to pay proper attention to how to hold it, but she thought that if she really paid attention, she might even be able to hold it on that day—her very special eighth birthday.

Charley, who knew exactly what to do, opened the kite to its full size and began to work his way along the line slowly so that it could rise off the ground bit by bit, and all the while he was telling Lily exactly how it should be done —so that she would know how when it was her turn. And she watched every tiny bit of it as it moved upwards.

There was a wind from behind, Charley said, so it was a perfect day for flying a kite, and she watched as he let it go up so slow, higher and higher, and the higher it went, the harder the wind blew and the kite began to fly about, leaping and diving in all directions, so that it seemed as if it was alive—as if it was flying with the wind, all of its own accord.

And then it really was flying of its own accord, because the line broke and the kite flew off on its own without any help from Charley. It happened so suddenly that all that he had in his hand was the bit of line that was left behind—and the kite kept on climbing higher and higher until it landed in a tree halfway down the hill. It seemed to be standing between two branches looking down at them and Charley, his mouth in a tight, straight line, said, "Well, that's that!"

"Can we climb the tree to get it back," Lily asked.

"Nope! Nobody's going to climb that tree," he said. "It's about eighty feet high. That kite is never going to come down."

Then with a stony face and tight lips, he walked back to the cottage in the way that he always did when he wanted to say *the end* without words. And Lily, who hadn't moved at all, stood in exactly the same spot, looking at the kite in the tree.

As Charley said, that was that, and Lily did her best not to look miserable, but it seemed to her that it was strange to be given a birthday present that she had never even touched—that she never would touch. For several days afterwards, when she got home from school, she stood looking up at the tree and wondered if magic could happen. If it could come down of its own accord, she thought, it really would be magic.

On the day after her birthday, a parcel arrived at the big house and it had her name on it. It was a birthday present from her grandmother in Oxford—the grandmother that they didn't stop to see on the day when they went to the red house.

Everyone was there that day to see her open her present—Aunt Agneta and Eva and Uncle Will and her parents and Matty, and this time Lily was allowed to open her present by herself. Her parents were standing on the other side of the room, as if it wasn't any business of theirs, but she never noticed any of that until she had taken her present out of the box and was holding it up in front of her, thinking that it was the most beautiful present ever.

It was a dress with short puffed sleeves and a band around the waist above a full skirt. It was brown—just a bit darker than her hair, and there were patterns above the waist, around the hem, and on the sleeves. They were all in light brown and creamy colours. At the back it was tied in a beautiful big bow, and when she held it up it seemed to her that it was made especially for her, as if she was a girl with creamy skin and brown eyes and light brown hair.

And while she was still looking at her wonderful present, she heard her mother say in a grumpy voice, to her father, "Trust your mother to be spoiling her! It will go to her head."

That might have been enough to put another dent in Lily's birthday, except that her grandmother had written her such a lovely note and had sent her such a beautiful present, and she knew that her grandmother really loved her. Nothing that her mother said could spoil that. She knew that her mother would never let her wear the dress to school—even though the other girls wore pretty dresses—but she also knew that she could wear it to church because it was the only nice dress she had and she would have to look good in front of her mother's friends.

But all of her mother's friends lived in Oxford and her family hadn't gone to church since they left Park Street—and she still had no idea where they might be living next.

After her birthday it seemed to Lily that everything around her was moving faster, as if in a hurry. The end of the school year was approaching fast, and everyone, especially the teachers, seemed to be rushing to get things done.

As far as she was concerned, nothing much had changed. She was still going to the library after school and Jerry was still coming to let her know that Mr. Carey was there, but it wasn't the same. Even though she had never managed to feel that she belonged at that school, no one was bothering her anymore and, perhaps because of that, other things competed with the books and took over a part of her brain—or her brain took over a part of her. One way or another she began to be aware of things that she had never noticed before.

There was an auditorium at the school that she never noticed, or perhaps she had seen it, but never thought that it was relevant to second graders, or at least she had never seen a second grader go into it. But now she took notice of it because there was to be a special program in the auditorium to celebrate the end of the school year and Irene

Prentiss was going to sing, because she had a beautiful voice. Everyone said so, and it was true. She knew it because she was there and Irene sang *Pack up your troubles in your old kit bag*, and it was clear and sweet and true, and she knew that she could never sing like that.

It was only a few days later when her whole class was told that they had to go to another room that Lily had never been to, because they were going to have a special treat. All the students were going to see the Walt Disney film *Cinderella*. It was the first time she had ever seen a film and it was beautiful and like magic it fixed itself in her mind and she went around for days with Cinderella in a beautiful gown dancing in her head, and she could still hear the music, and for a little while it really was magic.

And then the next day her mother told her that she "had better" take her book back to the library and not come home with another one, because they were going to move. It would be a little while yet, she said, but it was the end of the school year, so it was time to tell her that she wouldn't be going back to that school, because they were going to live in the red house.

For a moment Lily didn't know what to think. She had been wondering for weeks, until she had finally concluded that she would never see that house again, and now she didn't know what to say because it was such a surprise.

"Well," Betsy said, "do you not like that house?"

"Oh yes," Lily exclaimed. "I love it, but I thought you weren't going to buy it. You never said."

Betsy smiled. "Your father and I decided not to tell you too soon because you would be asking 'when' every few minutes. As it is we won't be moving for a few weeks more, because there is so much that has to be done, and the people who live in the house also have to pack up their things."

"Can I join the library in Oxford?" Lily asked.

174

Betsy laughed and it was so unusual to hear her mother laugh that Lily didn't know what it meant.

"Of course you can," Betsy said, "but you'll have to wait until we are settled again."

On the last day of school, Miss Maddock gave the class a little lecture about how pleased she was to have had them as pupils in her class, and how different it would be for them when they all went into the third grade.

"You will be learning more difficult things then," she said, "because you will be older, and you are all ready to learn more difficult things."

She looked around the class and smiled as if she was about to hand them all a wonderful gift, and when she could see that they were all waiting eagerly to hear more, she went on:

"One of the things you will learn," (she smiled again) "is the multiplication tables. They are very different from adding and subtraction, but I am sure that you will all find it very interesting to be learning something harder. Of course, you won't need to worry, because you will only learn half of them to begin with. You won't begin to learn the other half until you are in fourth grade, but I am sure that by the end of third grade, if a teacher asks you to give the answer to '10 times 5' you will all be able to give the right answer."

And Lily, who was sitting, looking out the window and wondering whether Miss Maddock would ever stop, suddenly heard her saying— out of the blue, it seemed—'10 times 5' and without a thought, she called out, "50."

Of course she didn't mean to be rude. It was just an automatic response, but she certainly managed to interrupt Miss Maddock's speech, for there she was, staring at Lily with a very peculiar look on her face.

It was a bit unnerving to have Miss Maddock staring at her so, and Lily wondered whether she would be sent out to stand behind the door again, but instead she turned her back on Lily, smiled at her class and wished them a happy summer. Then she told them they could all go home.

From Lily's point of view she saw it in her mind as "The End," and it was bliss, but she would have liked to tell Miss Maddock—and the whole class as well—that she knew all of the multiplication tables up to twelve, and it wasn't hard at all.

CHAPTER 12

1953

Another New World

When it came to changes, those relevant to Lily always seemed to sneak up on her without notice, leaving her with uncertainties at best and at worst a world of nervousness which she carried about like a backpack filled with fear and confusion. Even as she was still breathing a sigh of relief at the knowledge that she would never have to go to that school again—or sit in the mean teacher's classroom—or ride in the car with the pointy-nosed Ellen—the devil himself was busily conjuring up enough other worries to keep her in a state of jitters for several years to come.

She had thought they would be moving to the red house as soon as school was over, but no, it was a summer of *Not Yets*. Every day, it seemed, Betsy would say, "Not yet," until finally she shrieked "ENOUGH!" and it was loud enough for Eva to come out and see if there was a problem.

"Yes," Betsy shouted. "The problem is this child! She never stops wanting to know when and it's driving me mad!"

Eva offered to entertain Lily for a while, which was a good thing, because there was enough entertainment in her way of seeing the world to keep Lily happy for whole days. In fact, spending time with Eva was the best thing that happened all summer because Lily really liked her and besides what else could she do? She didn't have a book to read, and she had given up looking at the tree with the kite still in it and there really wasn't much else to do.

Sometimes she just sat quietly with her doll Fred, watching Aunt Agneta cutting and folding pieces of old clothes and braiding them into rugs, but it was Eva, bustling about the kitchen as usual, who told her that she couldn't move to the new house until the people who already lived there had taken all their things to another house—and when all that was done and the house was empty her mother and father would pack up their things and a man would come and put them all on a truck and drive them to the new house.

"You will know when it happens," she said, "because everybody will be awfully busy and you will have to stay out of the way if you don't want your parents yelling at you."

In the end it happened more or less in the way that Eva said, although other things happened first and Lily and Matty weren't there at all when the truck came. On one of those waiting days, Charley came home from work early—possibly because they would be moving soon, or perhaps he just thought it would be fun to go swimming in the lake where he used to swim when he was a child. Isn't that what he said when he came home early that day? But how could Lily know what he was thinking? She never knew what he thought, or what he might do, but she knew that she had to be cautious when he suddenly did something unusual and unexpected.

On that particular day, what began as a good idea turned into a tremendous rush because, while her mother was still gathering the things they might need for swimming, or sitting on the ground when not swimming, Charley heard the sound of the train some distance away and he was determined to get to the crossing first.

In those days, great long trains went by very slowly while the people in cars sat and waited and waited until every single carriage passed by them, and there was nothing to do in all that time but sit and count the carriages. More often than not there would be a hundred or so—and that is why they hurried—all of them, even Matty. They were all gathering up their things in a rush—changing into bathing suits fast—dashing to the car.

Charley had all the doors open by then and was waiting to go. Seatbelts didn't exist in those days. You just hung on tight when you went around corners fast, and with Charley's foot flat to the floor, his entire family was hanging on tight. They could all hear the train hooting in the distance and Charley was counting off each crossing by its hoot, and each hoot got louder as the train got closer. It was nearly a mile from the farm to the railroad crossing and he knew that there would be five good long hoots before they reached it.

From the look on Betsy's face as she watched Charley driving like a maniac, Lily knew that her mother wasn't a bit pleased, but not a word did she say. In fact, there wasn't a sound from anyone—no doubt because it was not possible to hold your breath and squawk at the same time, and perhaps also because by that time everyone had counted the five hoots and they all knew that their crossing would be next.

And there it was! They were crossing the tracks and the train was coming straight at them. It seemed to happen all at once—the train almost on top of them, much too close, and the train driver, who appeared to be shouting at them—even though they couldn't hear him—was also pushing whatever it was that made the train hoot, and from where they sat it was the loudest hoot they had ever heard.

To Lily, who was sitting on the side nearest the train, it looked like a monster—a great reddish-brown monster that loomed over them just feet away. It was enormous and frightful and ferocious and the hooting never stopped, and she had never been so close to a moving train, yet somewhere in the back of her mind, scarcely audible to her brain, it was very interesting to be seeing it all, even though she was certain that it would swallow them up—every bit of them, even the car.

Charley with his foot on the floor as hard as it could go somehow managed to fly across the tracks in midair as the train passed by behind them with room to spare by at least a yard. They landed on the other side of the tracks with a great bump—followed by several bounces, then silence. The car had stopped smack in the middle of the road and for a moment even that seemed miraculous, but then Betsy, who had plenty of voice to spare by then, sent it all to Charley in such a great flood of outrage that he had to pull off the road for fear of drowning in it.

It was at least three or four minutes before he dared to move on again and in that time Lily sat watching a headless chicken wandering around the barnyard of the farm across the road. She had never seen anything like it before. To her knowledge it was completely impossible, and it was the impossibility of it that fixed her attention on it. How could she be sure it was true? It was like a fairy tale, because all sorts of strange things happened in fairy tales. Perhaps, if her father's car could fly across railroad tracks, a headless chicken walking might be possible. She closed and opened her eyes several times to be sure it was true, and every time she opened them the chicken was still walking without a head. By the time her father had started the car again, the chicken's wanderings had lasted long enough for her to gather a whole batch of questions about headless chickens, but her mother was not yet finished with what she had to say about trains and railroad tracks and dangerous men, so she kept the chicken in her mind—specifically in the part where she stored interesting things to remember.

Lily knew that there were two lakes on the southern side of Hubbardston and both of them were very large and beautiful, but she had no idea that there was a third lake, because she had never seen it. It was off to the right, about half a mile perhaps beyond the road, and when they got there she saw that there was a place to park, and beyond that there were a great many pine trees with picnic tables scattered around them. There was also a well-worn path to the water, but when they got there it seemed odd, because although there was plenty of water in the distance, at the edge of the lake, where there was an embankment with perhaps eight men sitting on it, it seemed strangely closed in, as if all the water in that spot was sitting in a large bathtub—but much deeper.

The men were all about the same age as her father. A couple of them moved aside so that Betsy would have a spot where she could sit on her blanket, but beyond that they had nothing to say. They just nodded their heads.

On the side opposite the men, there was another embankment, but it had a sharp slope and no one was sitting there. The distance between the two was about six feet, so it wasn't at all like a swimming pool or even part of a lake. It seemed that real swimmers would need to go to a different spot if they wanted to swim in the lake.

For Lily it was all about seeming. She had no idea what it was really like. Nobody was swimming, not even out on the lake, and the men were looking displeased. Perhaps Betsy and Charley had interrupted a meeting. Perhaps the thought never entered her mind, or it vanished when Charley stepped into the water and said to her, "Come here! It's time for you to learn how to swim. Come on, hop in the water. Let's get moving—on the double!"

She hesitated because she wasn't at all sure what might happen next. It may have been irrational, but the hooting train was still in her head and the addition of "On the double" made her nervous. She hunched her shoulders and Charley reached over and grabbed her arm. In a wink she was standing in water up to her armpits.

"That's better," he said. "It's not even cold. Now, the first thing you need to know about swimming is to learn how to hold your breath under water—like this..." and without any warning he put his hand on her head and pushed her under the water and held her there.

For how long? It couldn't have been very long or she would have drowned, but it was long enough to scare the wits out of her, and when he let go she came up coughing and spluttering and gasping for breath—and hoping that someone might come to her rescue, but no one did. Her mother was absorbed in some knitting and the watching men were frowning.

She had scarcely stopped coughing when Charley said, "I told you to hold your breath. You won't ever be able to swim if you can't hold your breath under water" and again without warning he put his hand on her head and pushed her under.

And the same thing happened except that the moment she surfaced, coughing and gasping, she scrambled out of the water and fled as far and fast as she could go. Regardless of her bare feet and her struggle to breathe, she ran to the furthest deep corner of the pine trees and climbed as high as she could up one of them and even then she didn't feel safe. She was shaking all over and there were scrapes and cuts on her arms and legs and it didn't matter at all, because she was breathing. She had no idea what would happen next.

After a few minutes her mother came to the tree. She had packed up her blanket and knitting and Lily's shoes, and she stood looking at Lily.

"Come down," she said. "We're going home now. Your father and Matty are already in the car."

Perhaps it was the look on Lily's face when her mother mentioned her father—a frozen look perhaps—because Betsy assured her that she would be safe and that it was okay to come down.

Climbing down was much more difficult, especially without shoes, and not knowing what her father would do next she remained awfully nervous. At the bottom of the tree, her mother handed her the shoes and they walked back to the car without a word between them. It was the same in the car. Not a word was spoken the whole way home.

Even at home Lily stayed as far away as possible from her father. She was skittish, like a wild animal, and Charley in turn paid her so little attention that she could have been invisible. When he was home she would slip away and hide behind apple trees in the orchard, or talk to Eva if she wasn't too busy.

The siege ended one morning when Betsy filled two large bags with clothes belonging to Lily and Matty and told them to get in the car.

"The house is ready," she said. We will be moving there within a week or so. We are going there today to have a look at everything and after that the two of you will be staying with your grandparents until it's all done. I expect you will be pleased with that."

Charley in the front seat started singing the song about the Salvation Army, "Away with the rum by gum…" He was looking mighty pleased with himself.

Lily and Matty in the back seat, knowing that their mother didn't like their grandmother, tried not to look too pleased. They just laughed a lot. It was easy to laugh when their father was singing silly songs.

When they went through their bags later that day, Lily found Fred in her bag and she knew that her mother had put her there so that she wouldn't be lonely.

Fred means 'peace' in Swedish. It is pronounced like 'Frayed'. The doll named Fred is a girl. She appears for the first time in Chapter 6. She may have been a part of Lily's life much earlier, but she didn't become a character until Charley took her away from Lily on a cold, dark night in Hubbardston. With all that was going on at that time, she had really needed Fred for comfort.

CHAPTER 13

1953

And Then What

And so they went to the house which on the surface was much the same as the last time Lily had seen it, weeks ago. And yet in a contradictory way, nothing was quite as she had thought it would be. All the rooms were there in the same places, but she hadn't expected them to be so empty. Of course it would be different she had thought, because a truck had come and taken all the things that belonged to the other people. She knew that and she had expected to see an empty house, but still it seemed strangely different—perhaps because now it was a big empty house with a hollow sound, not quite as quiet as it had been.

Betsy and Charley—with Lily and Matty tagging along—walked through every part of it, including the cellar, and they seemed pleased at every turn—checking this and that as they went, talking about how it would be when their own truck came. They went through it all very slowly and thoughtfully, talking the whole time about how it would be here and there—this piece of furniture and that piece...

For the children who had to be quiet during the whole long process, it seemed an awfully long time to be more or less invisible.

185

And when finally it was done and her parents were pleased with it, Betsy went upstairs to do it all again.

It was such a long time since they had lived in a real house and it seemed such a big house in comparison with the fruit pickers' cottage. It was necessary, Lily thought, to examine and remark about everything and plot it all so carefully, and yes there was so much talk about where this and that should be done, and which part of a room would have this piece of furniture or that one, and it was especially important where there were angles to consider, but somewhere in the midst of it all she began to feel a bit confused.

She had been so eagerly looking forward to seeing her grandparents again. Her mother had said that they would look at it all, but she hadn't expected this to take so long. Perhaps it hadn't been so long, but at that moment it seemed to be taking forever. Usually her parents would hurry her away so that they could have 'some peace,' so it seemed awfully strange to be doing it all again except, as it turned out, the second trip upstairs was entirely different. There was no doubt about it.

This time Betsy stood halfway between the two end rooms, looking from one to the other, and then, with scarcely a hint of what next, she turned to Lily and asked, "Which room would you like to have?"

No one had ever asked Lily a question like that. She was accustomed to doing what she was told, not deciding for herself, so of course she was bemused. She didn't know what to say and she was afraid that she would get it wrong.

Betsy, who was watching Lily with a piercing look said, "You can have whichever one you like. Choose!"

"Can I look at them again," Lily asked, not at all certain what her mother had in mind.

"Of course," Betsy said.

So Lily, still bemused, went into the one that overlooked the driveway, and she walked around the room thoughtfully to see how much space there was for the furniture, and she looked inside the closet to see how big it was, and then she looked out at the driveway and the yard and the field and house up the road from them, and she put it all in her mind. She didn't take very much time. She took only enough to imagine what it would be like with furniture in it, and where the bed would be and how she would feel when she lived in it.

And then she did the same thing with the other room. She saw immediately that it was much smaller than the first one, but in that room there were windows that looked out on the fields, and the fields went all the way to the woods, and there was a small, brown house down the road a bit below them. She could see the cars coming up the road before they vanished behind the great overgrown blackberry patch. She looked at the brown house again. It looked nice. She had seen a house like that in a fairy tale and she could imagine the kind of people who might live there. And then she looked inside the closet and was surprised to find that it was big. She thought that if there was enough room to open the closet door and have the bed alongside the window, she could sit or lie on the bed and read, or just look at the world below.

She thought of the other room where the only place for a bed was in the large space alongside the closet and there would be no view of any kind from there. In this room she could look out the window whenever she wanted to see what was happening. If she looked towards the end of the field she might see a deer, she thought, maybe even a bear. It would be very interesting.

"Well," said Betsy. "Have you decided yet?"

"Yes," Lily said. "I would like to have the room that looks down the hill."

"The small one," Betsy exclaimed.

"Yes," Lily said.

Betsy frowned. "Why would you want that one?" she asked.

"Because I like it," Lily said.

And there began a conversation that lasted for some time. Lily was quite sure what she wanted and Betsy kept demanding that she explain why.

It never occurred to Lily to count how many times her mother asked "Why," but by the time Betsy had challenged every reason she had given Lily was thoroughly bemused and on the verge of tears. Not knowing what else to say, she finally said, "Okay, I will have the other room if you want."

"I told you to choose the room you want, not the room I want," Betsy said. "So why would you change your mind?"

"Because you want me to have the big room," Lily replied, "even though I like the other one better,"

"Okay," Betsy said, "you shall have the small room, and you had better not complain about it when you decide you don't like it after all."

The question of not liking it after all never entered Lily's head—not then, not ever. As she saw it, it wasn't a question of size. It was about what she saw, both inside and out—and that was all in her head. It was the books she read that created her ability to see the magic. Within a year almost every tree of interest in the woods had names—and the children down the hill, who had joined her in discovering the wonders of cow paddocks, knew all the names, and had added a few of their own.

Lily's mother, who loved classical music and opera, and spent hours listening to it, was also a fine knitter, a wizard with embroidery and sewing, and not a bad cook—but her greatest talent was organizing people and money. She could put both together in her head and get it right every time, all except Lily perhaps, who didn't always fit the equation of the moment. Who knows why? It wasn't until Lily was grown up with children of her own that Betsy took to saying—always in front of company—"You were an awful child!"

Just once in one of her rambling conversations, Betsy had said,

"If it weren't for you I would have gone back to Australia, but they wouldn't let me take you with me."

It was the only glimpse of some kind of truth that Lily ever had, and that was immediately banished by a chore—the dishes perhaps.

CHAPTER 14

1954

To Grandma's House at Last

It may have been hunger that brought the long examination of the house to an end. In the whole time that Betsy quizzed Lily about her choice of bedroom, Charley's stomach had been rumbling until finally hunger came to the rescue.

"Let's go to the diner in Auburn," he said, in a seriously hungry tone. "We haven't eaten for hours. Not even a cup of coffee."

"We'll have to take the children to your parents', first." Betsy said. "Then we can enjoy ourselves."

"Of course," he agreed. "They've probably been waiting for hours too."

"That would be just like them," she replied. "Hmmf! At least it will be convenient and that child won't be bothering me every five minutes."

'That child' was in the car in seconds, sitting quietly in the back seat, a perfect example of well-behaved—although inside that very same well-behaved face, her head was spinning with excitement. She too was hungry but she could easily manage the ten minutes or so it

191

would take to get there. She knew that it wouldn't be much longer—not if her father was hungry.

When ten or perhaps fifteen minutes later they drove up the driveway, her grandparents were out the door and welcoming them so fast that it was as if they had been leaning against the screen door, just waiting and waiting. For Lily it was almost overwhelming. It wasn't the excitement of seeing them again, or the fuss of adults talking and organizing and bringing in bags and so on... It was the place itself. It was the one place in the whole world where it was as perfect as anything could be. It was the place where Lily was happy all the time and nobody ever yelled at her.

For a few minutes it was all very busy. Grownups always talked in circles, or that's how it seemed to Lily. They had to make sure that everything would be done the right way. At least Betsy talked like that. 'These are their clothes,' she said, 'and their shoes' and so on... There was nothing in the bags that Lily couldn't have told her grandparents about, and they would have known it themselves just by looking.

But of course there was the grownups talk about the house and when they would move in—information—all very precise and so on... By the time they were driving out of the driveway, Charley must have been twice as hungry, and even then Betsy managed to call out the last important reminder to the children, "You had better behave yourselves properly and if you don't, I will be sure to hear about it!"

They all watched as the car reached the road and Charley turned left in the direction of the diner, and then there were four great sighs of happiness and everybody smiled enormous smiles, which were interrupted by her grandmother who said, "Would you like to have some lunch? It's ready and waiting."

And lickity-split, as they say, they were all sitting at the kitchen table.

The kitchen was an unusually big one, with the sink in the far corner, looking down the hill to her grandfather's garden. Between the table and the sink there was a door to the laundry room. It was a room that seemed to hang over the very steep slope below. Perhaps it seemed that way because Lily wasn't tall enough to see what was underneath that room, but she always thought that if there was nothing underneath, it could fall into the nothing.

"It can't fall," her grandmother had said—a long time ago as Lily remembered it. "Just look at me! If I can walk here without falling, a little girl like you could never fall through those great heavy planks."

Of course it never happened, but still she kept looking at it and wondering about the bottom of the hill where there was, as she saw it, another amazing thing. Sometime long ago someone had managed to put a great high pole, with two holes in the top of it, at the bottom of the slope, and that pole was somehow connected to the window above by great long ropes that could be moved around one way or another, depending on the wind. On that great high rope, the clothes could flap around in the breeze all day—or until it rained.

It was magic. She was sure of it. All those clothes went out wet and came in dry, and her grandmother never had to carry a bag of clothes—wet or dry. Electric clothes dryers hadn't been invented yet and the clothesline may not have been the most exciting thing at her grandparents' house, but it invariably drew her to the simple cleverness of it—and the height—and the nothingness under that height.

The table where they ate was quite long and always against the wall, so Lily and Matty both sat on the side away from the wall. It was where they had always sat. Their grandmother sat on the side nearest the sink and stoves and work benches, and Lily was the nearest to her. Matty sat at their grandfather's end of the table. It was a perfectly fine arrangement and everyone was happy with it.

The children had sat in those seats many times before, so there was no fuss at all. In fact, it was just like coming home again, although they would never say such a thing aloud. Even Matty knew better, but it was no trouble at all to keep their thoughts inside their heads. Inside thoughts had a wonderful feeling to them—a bit like Christmas.

On the wall opposite—three feet or so closer to the door which led to the cellar below, there were two stoves. One was a wood stove and the other electric, and although it seemed a bit odd to Lily, she could see that her grandparents knew exactly what to do with both of them, and she always watched them carefully so that she could learn why they were different. She was too small to do anything else, but it was such an interesting process to watch, especially when her grandfather, standing in front of the electric stove, was flipping flapjacks high in the air and laughing like crazy and saying "You can have the first one that falls on the floor."

It never happened. Every single one of them landed in exactly the place he meant it to, but every time a flapjack flew up in the air, it was fun to think that it might land somewhere else. But today wasn't a flapjack day. It was just a good food and lots of talking and laughing day.

"I saw a cowboy on a horse on *El Capitan*," Matty said. "He said hello to us. We went down the mountain and it was very steep and the trailer was pushing us. It was scary."

"That was in Texas," Lily said.

"We went to Mexico too," Matty said. "We weren't allowed to talk to the children. Dad said they were dangerous. But it was fun..."

And so the conversation went this way and that, with mouthfuls of food in between. There were several months worth of things to talk about and it just kept on going, mostly in all directions—whatever came to mind, and their grandparents, William Stearns and Linnea, née Malmquist (always known as Grandpa and Grandma—no matter what anyone else called them), listened to every word they said and sometimes they asked questions—and everyone was happy.

Somewhere near the end of the very long lunch, Lily said, "I read

The Story of Aladdin or the Wonderful Lamp. In the library next to the school, there was a nice lady and she let me read the book, but first I had to prove that I could read it."

"Hmm," her grandfather said, "I have that book upstairs, I think. Your father read it when he was a child, but he was older when he read it. Ah yes, you are a clever girl if you can read that. I'll have a look upstairs. Maybe I can find it."

"I'm going to join the library," Lily said, "as soon as we finish moving into the new house."

"And I'm going to do the dishes," her grandmother said. "You should all go outside and get some fresh air. There are some baby chicks you might like to see.

And that was just the beginning of the most loveliest time, as Lily called it, even though she knew it was grammatically incorrect. It made perfect sense to her, and Matty agreed.

So then....

CHAPTER 15

When Once There Were Barns

Lily had always been interested in the barns. There are some still. You see them here and there, spruced up, turned into homes or antique shops, and you never think how it was then. You never think how it was to be up every morning before five for the milking and the same again in the evening. How could you know how heavy those milk pans were—how exhausting it was to carry them to the dairy and back twice a day—how it could get to be so endlessly hard that it seemed sometimes that the barns themselves began to carry the weight of it? Each trek represented one or two cows only out of fifty, more or less, depending on the size of the farm.

So it was with the Woodart's barn. She remembered how every time she went past in the school bus, she could see how it sagged a little more each year. The house too. It was just a matter of time until one of them collapsed. In the end they both did—house and barn. They had waited it seemed for just the right moment. The boys had got through college and had jobs elsewhere. Their parents were getting old by then and needed a rest, so they took an apartment in town and managed somehow on the old-age pension. As if that had been the plan all along.

She remembered her grandfather's barn. It was marvelous—built on the side of a hill and four stories high at the back—cows at the bottom, chickens at the top and all manner of other things stored in the middle. And *the pièce de résistance* was a room above all the rest. There was a special flight of stairs for just that one room overlooking the valley as if it were a balcony. That room was filled with jigsaw puzzles—every one of them belonging to her grandfather and every one of them solved by him. For her, just the sight of those boxes was magical. She had sat at the same table finding pieces with her grandfather many times. He was infinitely patient and quite often wonderfully funny.

At house level, her grandmother parked her car in the barn. There was plenty of room. The floor was sturdy and the car was safe from every kind of weather. There were sliding doors on the inside that stood open every day in the summer to let in the light. In the winter, they were closed to keep the animals snug and warm. On the left hand side near her grandmother's car was a door, behind which was quite a large room where the poultry lived. It always seemed to her that the floor was carpeted with feathers and the chickens were fidgety and so skittish. Here they made her nervous, but there were always eggs and occasionally chicken soup. Her grandfather had his own extraordinary way of beheading and he would often bring the feet so that she could entertain herself pulling the tendons and watching the feet opening up and closing again. It was, she thought, both weird and fascinating—seeing how the feet worked.

Beyond her grandmother's car, and next to the hen house, was a three-story drop into the area where her grandfather heaped great piles of hay for the winter. She was bewitched once—standing at the top and looking down at her grandfather tossing the hay in with his pitchfork. She counted the seconds between one toss and another and without a thought, she jumped. It was quite an adventure. To this day she can still see it in her mind—the grandfather's fork piled with hay on an incoming track—and he, not seeing but sensing her movement, whisking his fork away in a last minute blur. He stood back for a moment as she landed and he waited, as if to see if she still had legs to walk on, and then he shook his head and said, "Don't ever do that again. Do you want your mother to kill me?" That was all he said, which in itself seemed like a miracle. And then, for a few minutes or so, he abandoned the fork and took her over to his garden to get her opinion on whether or not he should be cutting the cucumbers that day. He surely was the only grown-up she knew who didn't slice pieces off her for doing some silly thing. She never said a thing about her amazing jump to anyone else, but to this day she treasures the look on the grandfather's face as she came flying in.

One day, when Matty was thirteen and Lily was sixteen, the barn caught fire and was burnt to the ground. There had been a phone call at their house and Betsy had rushed down to their grandparents' place, leaving her behind to watch little Immy. Lily never knew what caused that fire. To her the barn had been so rock-solid that burning it seemed impossible. All she knew was that her brother and another boy—whose name was never mentioned—had been playing in the barn just before the fire started.

They had left their bicycles in a stall to the right of her grandmother's car, but no one ever said where they had been playing when the fire started. Near the haystack perhaps? Experimenting with cigarettes? Who knows? No one ever said. It was the failure to say—to give any kind of information—that made her ask herself questions, but she knew better than to ask.

Wasn't it lucky, they said, that the boys were okay? And they shuddered when they told us that they had been in the barn when the fire started.

Matty's bicycle was destroyed in the fire. Such a pity they said—but it could have been so much worse. He could have been burned, poor boy. And they sighed and hugged him close. You could buy another bicycle with the insurance money, they said, but you couldn't buy another boy. And sure enough, in that very same week, their father bought him another bicycle.

The inspector came by afterwards to figure out exactly what had happened. How? It might have been caused by an electrical fault, he said, although he wasn't certain. Who knows? It was just a lucky thing that the fire didn't take the house as well. The house and the barn were at right angles—not quite touching at their corners. Lucky, they said, that it had only scorched one corner of it.

Lily's grandfather was never the same after that barn burned. Her parents always said it was losing the puzzles that had meant so much to him. There were so many and they would have been worth something by then. Without the puzzles to occupy his mind, they said, his life had lost its meaning. Yes, that is how they saw things.

How, she wondered, could her parents have so easily forgotten how it had been every summer, when the morning glories had climbed across the entire front of the barn all the way to the top—they were a glorious blue—and the hollyhocks in their glorious red had stood so tall at the foot of the morning glories—and the raspberries and strawberries had filled the whole space down the side below the chicken coops—and every summer they ate bowls filled with glorious berries and milk and sugar? Did they think that her grandfather could do nothing but jigsaw puzzles? Did they not know that he spent no less time reading books? Did they not know...?

All of grandfather's garden tools were destroyed. And the milk pans. And the chickens were dead. And the cows were sold. What good were cows without a barn in the bitter winter? But her grandmother's car was saved, which was a good thing because you could write a whole book about her grandmother's car and where she went and what she did. Even so, it never had a roof over its head again, but like all truly stoic people they knew that all you had to do in the deep winter was to scrape the ice off before you drove it.

There was the Petersen's barn too—another wonderful barn—only a short walk down the hill from where they lived, past the pond and the pignut hickory tree at the foot of their driveway. The difference is that when that barn burned down, everyone knew it had been caused by Johnnie Potts smoking in the hay. To Johnnie, it was just another barn. After all, his father owned two of them.

When the Petersens—and Mrs. Petersen's brother, Martin Hurst—lived there, it was a model farm, so well kept that it seemed to sparkle inside and out. There were two barns—one for the cows and the scary bull and one for the poultry. Between the two there must have been well over a hundred animals, not including the dogs and cats. There was a spotless dairy as well. The kids scrambled all over the whole property inside and out as if it was their second home—and the Petersens never once complained. They seemed to like them.

There were pastures on both sides of the farmhouse and barns, and a huge field at the top, where the grain for the cows was grown. In the fall the children—at least six of them—followed the tractors and the truck up and down the seemingly endless field in the grain harvest. Of course, children were of no use whatsoever. All they could do was breathe in the excitement and the goodness of it. No one ever shooed them away. They seemed to think it was all part of the fun of working like the devil to bring in the grain.

In the winter they slid down the same great hill to the far corner where the snow had piled up over the barbed wire fence and frozen solid. In that particular year, everywhere on that hill the snow was deep and frozen so hard that they could walk on it without making a dent—and on a sled it was fast, very fast. And knowing how solid it was, they marked the one safe spot where they could fly over the fence in the far bottom corner without hitting a tree on one side or toppling over a cliff on the other. And when they were satisfied that they had done all they had to do, they began at the top—a very long way to the fence it seemed—and with a one-foot push, in no time at all the children on six sleds of various sizes, one after the other, gathered such speed that when they reached the faraway fence, they literally flew over the top of it like birds soaring on the breeze. And in their brief mid-air moment on their way back to earth, they prepared themselves for the long and twisty track through the trees and rocks of the cow pasture below, knowing which leg to push with when they needed to avoid a fast approaching tree, and the brook at the bottom, over which they leaped and headed upwards on the other side until they stopped just short of the road. Then they turned round and walked all the way to the top again.

This they did for days on end—for as long as the snow remained sturdy. No one was ever hurt. It was their idea of heaven and the Petersens seemed perfectly happy with that. After all, their granddaughter was one of the crowd. What did their parents know of daring adventures? Nothing. They went home when it began to get dark with scarcely a dent on them. All they had to do was arrive home on time. Where they went and what they did was neither here nor there as long as they 'behaved' themselves. In those days no one had ever heard of 'helicopter parents.'

After the Petersens died, William Potts bought the farm. He already owned a farm much further up the hill—a good mile away at least—but apparently one farm wasn't enough for him. He needed more. What his young son Johnnie needed was a cigarette! He never took the trouble to discover the hundred other places in the rocks and woods around where a boy could smoke and never disturb a soul—or burn down a barn. He was, Lily thought, about the same age Matty was when her grandfather's barn was burned.

There is one barn still standing at the very top of the great long and winding hill where all of these children once lived. If you turn left just before you reach what was the Potts farm and walk another half mile, you will come to the barn on what once was a farm. Quite a few children grew up there. But of course nothing is the same as it used to be. The barn is still there, but by some unexpected shift in thought, it has now become a hanger for an airport—just a small, local airport from which small planes can come and go and young men can go tearing through the local sky and perhaps dream.

Times have changed. Curiously, in this part of town the houses are all pretty much the same and the land around them is also the same. On the other side of town, the farms seem to have shrunk and the fields around them have disappeared altogether—submerged by great housing developments. But not surprisingly the one truly significant barn on that side of town is still there, although without any fields to graze cattle, it has become a piece of the past. A hanger-on you might think, in the midst of much debate about what to do with such a useless thing—or that is how some people see it—a thing that lacks charm or purpose.

Of course there is a reason for its prolonged existence. It is the third barn on that particular spot. The first two, possibly reaching back to the seventeenth or eighteenth century, were struck by lightning and burnt to the ground. The twentieth-century owners decided to bypass what they saw as bad luck and built a most impressive barn made entirely of concrete and steel. Even the stalls for the cattle were made of steel.

As it happened, Lily had some experience of that barn. Her friend Eva lived there and they often played together. There was a great deal to explore—from the brook at the bottom of the hill to the rocky remnants of the ice age tossed onto the top of the same hill. It happened one afternoon, when Eva and Lily were clambering about those boulders not long before the cows were due in for milking, when there was a sudden and unexpected crash of thunder.

"We'd better get the cows in," said Eva.

And they ran down to the barn, where the cows, having heard the same thunder, had already begun to get themselves ready for shelter. It was a lovely warm summer day. All of the barn windows were wide open to let the warm air in. At the end of the barn was an unusually large door—about eight feet above the ground. It was where the sweepings from the barn floor were regularly pushed overboard, and it too was open that day.

Eva had grabbed a long metal pole as she entered the barn. She used it to make sure that the cows—all of whom knew which stall was theirs—would take their place in an orderly manner. She sent Lily to the other end to stand in front of the open door, just in case the thunder spooked them, but they were most cooperative that day— indeed anxious to be in their stalls. The storm was moving fast and in a very noisy way. Eva was also moving fast, and, once certain that the cows were properly in their stalls, she dropped the bar that held the whole line of them in their place. They could move about, but they couldn't get loose. The bar was just a few feet from the open door.

As she stood catching her breath—about three feet from Lily— there was suddenly the most extraordinary flash and crash, and the entire barn was instantaneously filled with lightning from one end to the other—dashing all over the place it seemed, up and down the cattle stalls and around and about every bit of metal there was, windows, doors, ceiling, in and out and around the whole great thing—and all of it was wide open. And the most dramatic thing of all was to see Eva with the metal pole still in her hand and lightning simultaneously zipping up and down the pole and racing around and about her at a tremendous speed as she stood as if frozen with pole in hand, seemingly unable to move. It danced around Lily as well, which was nothing in comparison, but it seemed to her in those few split seconds that it was all really quite harmless—a mere game that the gods were playing, for surely, if it had been the real thing they wouldn't have known it.

It was only seconds, but when it stopped, Phyllis, white in the face, dropped the pole and raced down the whole row of more or less hysterical cows trying to flee, backing out of their stalls, feet in the air, kicking in all directions. For a moment Lily moved to follow Phyllis, but seeing all those feet and frantically swaying backsides, the thought of being kicked in the head or trampled by a cow was much worse than the grand display of fireworks that she had just seen. She stayed behind until they settled down. Through one of the many open windows, she could see Phyllis in the pouring rain and flashes of lightning, running faster than she had ever seen her run before. By the time Lily got back to the house, all the excitement had worked its way out. The lightning had hit a transformer about thirty feet from the barn, they said. It wasn't unusual.

It happened in a surprisingly short time that everything changed. Dairy farming entered a whole new world. Milking cows became a part of the technological age. Farmers no longer had to carry heavy milk pans to the dairy. They had been replaced with hoses which hooked up to modern technology and required nothing more from a farmer than to attach the hose connections to each cow and check to see that it was all working properly. Electricity did the rest. Electricity set the hose in motion and the hose carried the milk to the dairy.

It was a brave new world for the farmer just to think about it, but in a relatively small country town, even farmers who were living quite comfortably would have needed to recreate their whole system—and the costs could be overwhelming. Only one or two farmers in an area could have done it. Lily had no real knowledge at all of the shift from simple families with barns, and cows who produced milk in those barns, to corporate farming enterprises, but in the world today you can Google dairy farms in any state in the country and you will get dairy farms with a plural attached, for example:

From our Farms to Your Fridge—Massachusetts Dairy...

Phyllis's family left the farm years ago, but the barn is still there, sitting as if in the middle of nowhere and not knowing how it came to be so. How could a barn know that the cows were long gone because their pastures are now housing developments with rows and rows of 'New Homes!'

There have been debates about tearing down that barn. It is an eyesore, say those on one side. It is history, say those on the other... Perhaps one could argue that the spot on which the barn sits is in itself scientifically significant. It is possible. Surely two burned barns and one still standing could amount to proof positive that lightning can strike any number of times on the one spot.

CHAPTER 16

Ages and Thrashing

For most of her early existence, in matters social, political, historical—all that existed outside her mind and her immediate physical environment—she was decidedly naive. She had a sense of others as enemies or friends to the extent that they made her feel comfortable or uncomfortable, but she was never able to apply herself to dealing with either. She could not tackle the problem. She would have been afraid to hit back and the thought of striding up to a person and laying a ghost, or offering friendship, never occurred to her. In most things of this kind, she was afraid. More often than not, she shrank into herself at school, and on the bus, at church even. And when she shrank she was elsewhere—not invisible just elsewhere. Elsewhere was a place somewhere in her mind. While her peers were out dealing with the world, pushing and shoving, taking charge of a jump rope, chalking out hopscotch in the schoolyard, lining up all the skippers and jumpers in order, she held back and waited to be noticed. Mostly she hoped she would be noticed. Without doubt, they had trained her very well in Hubbardston—and her parents before that.

She was almost out of high school before it occurred to her one day in a Latin class, or, to be precise, in the middle of an ablative, that her mother was the youngest mother of all her classmates by several months. Even Carrie Wheelock's mother, who, according to Betsy, *had* to get married, was older than hers. Not that it was such a surprising thing. Her mother never let her forget for a moment how *young* she was. Really! After all, her daughter would be finishing high school soon and she herself was only thirty-six years old.

It was true. What's more, no thoughts of mortality had entered her head yet. Marilyn Monroe was still alive. And didn't Betsy's tail twitch with pleasure at her new-found body—and those legs that never let her down—so slim and shapely. Illness had some advantages after all. The weight had just poured off her during her last illness. But, as usual, it added another scar. Yes, it was a lovely thing to be so slim, but after appendicitis, three caesarean sections, a hysterectomy, and a gall bladder operation, with their resulting adhesions and sagging abdomen, Betsy knew to keep her middle section well covered at all times, but her legs—so slim and shapely—ran rings around the other, mostly sturdy, women in town. She wore peddle-pushers or short shorts, always with sandals in the summer season, and basked in the admiration of the television repair man, the farmer up the road and even the vicar and anyone else who might care to wink.

But after the gall bladder operation, when Charley had brought the children to the hospital for just one quick visit and Betsy showed them the small bag of gallstones, "twelve of them" she boasted, as if she was proud to have produced so many, Lily, her mouth pulled tight to obliterate expression, remained silent. She was afraid that her mother would see herself on Lily's face—as in a mirror—yellow and drawn and exhausted. She had never seen her mother looking so ill, and it frightened her. Perhaps this is what made her mother complain, on a number of occasions, that she was so unfeeling—that she was so like her grandmother.

It was true. She and her grandmother had this in common—the

ability to see the truth of a matter and respond awkwardly, because neither of them was a good liar. Matty, on the other hand, had no trouble at all. He entertained his mother wonderfully with a great long tale of what happened at school that day, and the day before that ... and she found it amusing.

Lily thought of her own children. She always thought of them, and she knew exactly where she got her ideas about how they should be treated. How old was she—fourteen or fifteen perhaps—when, in the midst of one of Betsy's hitting, hair-pulling, shrieking tirades—which had seemed as usual to come out of nowhere for no reason—Lily had shouted, "I will NEVER do this to my children!"? That was the one thing she made a point of remembering. How could she forget? She got an awful beating that evening when her father came home. And later in her room with the door shut, she repeated the promise she had made to herself and her future children—so that she wouldn't forget. It would remain in her head for a long time—forever perhaps. She had meant what she said.

Why did her father beat her? Because Betsy told him to. Usually it was both Lily and Matty getting a beating, or as Charley preferred to call it, a 'thrashing'. Was there a difference between one kind of beating and another? Either way, there was no doubt in Lily's mind that when Charley said *thrashing* it had a much more ominous sound to it than a humble beating, but it always added up to the same thing. There was always a kind of ritual in the order of things. It began with Betsy, who shouted at them until she was red in the face and then banished them to their rooms, where they were to sit for hours and consider their "atrocious behaviour."

More often than not it was about nothing more than a minor sibling dispute. They never knew what Betsy told Charley when he came home. They were upstairs with their doors shut and never heard a word of what their mother had to say, but they could hear Charley's car coming into the driveway and they could hear Betsy's voice—speaking in a lower register—a register of discontent, Lily thought. It seemed to be saying, "Nya, nya, nya, nya... According to her ritual, they would be called to dinner on the last 'nya' and Charley would always give them his grim death stare. They sat through the heavy silence over dinner, eating reluctantly, knowing what was to come. And they knew from the look on their father's face that Betsy had painted them black—or was it red—the colour of the devil?

In the meantime, before Charley came home, they waited in their rooms in anxious silence—or that is what Lily did. How could she know what Matty did when their doors were shut? On a number of such banishments she had seriously contemplated the slope of the roof over the porch below and the thickness of the blue spruces that grew next to it. It would be easy, she had thought, to climb out her window and slide down into the trees and run away to... where? There was nowhere to go. There were only ramifications. Regardless of which room they were in, both she and Matty knew that in Charley's eyes their mother could do no wrong. He was a good, loyal husband—blind as a bat when it came to his children.

It was always the same. It had become a ritual. Charley, who finished his dinner long before the others, would put down his knife and fork and ask his children to explain themselves and before they could say more than a word, he would order Lily to get the belt from the broom closet and take it *down cellar*. His Marine Corps belt—three inches wide—was his weapon of choice. Matty—also ordered by Charley—followed Lily—and they waited together in the cold, damp cellar. Charley always kept them waiting. There was power in that. It was part of the ritual. When finally he came down, he asked them to explain themselves. They were only children, but even then they knew it was a trap. How could they argue their case when neither of them had heard what their mother had said? They remained silent because they knew that if they protested, the beating would be much worse. They knew it from experience. And there was also something hateful—or was it self-righteous—a good Christian sort of self-righteous—in the way that Charley looked at them when he asked the question? When all was said and done, the ritual ended when Lily and Matty, each with their new set of welts, were ordered to go upstairs and finish their dinner. And then do the dishes.

Betsy, who was always sitting in her chair waiting for them to come upstairs with ragged, tear-soaked faces, invariably looked pleased at the sight. She had perfected the art of looking pleased without smiling. It was just a look—her best superior look—and then she turned her back on them and went to the living room to watch television. She did this every time.

The welts lingered for days—a work of art of sorts—red, swollen stripes neatly arranged on a diagonal across her back curved around her bottom and finished with a snap around her thigh. It was the snap that gave it distinction—neat, round, swollen marks in the shape of the belt—the end that went through the buckle. Neat.

Quite often, on a thrashing night, Lily remembered the first time she had heard the word 'thrashing'. She was about eight years old, going on nine. They had already moved to Federal Hill by that time and were at Hubbardston again—visiting this time. Why was it that she and Matty—who had been in and out of the old farmhouse countless times—were no longer permitted to sit inside with the grown-ups? They had been told by their parents that they were to stay outside near the house and they were to behave themselves, which, of course, left them with nothing to do and nowhere to go. For hours, it seemed, they lingered near Aunt Agneta's window while their parents were in the house talking the usual talk, talk, talk. It went on until they began to feel tired and restless and unhappy. It wasn't until they had lingered to the edge of being obstreperous that they were truly noticed. Then there was a sudden silence on the other side of Aunt Agneta's window, followed by thumps as Charley stamped his way through the house and out the door. That was when he threatened them with a *thrashing*. It was another new word for Lily.

Now, years later, she wondered whether Betsy, marrying at such a young age—scarcely an adult herself at the time—may have needed to make such a distinction between herself and her children. Distinction was the word for it, she thought, the difference between the one who does what she's told and the one who does the telling. A generous word distinction—sliding as it did from one parent to the other. Her mother never let her forget who did the telling in her family. The danger time always occurred when things seemed normal. One wrong word or action could unleash the devil. Lily knew this and yet she would be carried along by a word or thought of a moment. In the midst of a seemingly normal, interesting or useful, funny or serious situation or conversation the world could turn upside down in a wink. Is that what happened on that day so long ago—the hitting, hair-pulling, shrieking day? She must have said something and triggered a tornado of fury.

CHAPTER 17

1992/1961

~~

The Facts of Life, with a
Twist of Lime and Bitters

Memory is a peculiar thing. It can come out of nowhere and haunt you with some piece of your life long forgotten. It can arrive all smudged, vague and wrinkled, or cracked like an old photograph, a thing once known and now a stranger. Sometimes a memory is welcome, sometimes not. Sometimes when it emerges it takes on an unexpected shape. In this case, it appeared like a bubble, opaque and wafting in the air between them—her and him—a distraction in the midst of distractions.

This particular memory appeared most unexpectedly at a class reunion—the first Lily had been to. Thirty years had gone by since the last time she had seen her fellow classmates all in the one place. She should have been enjoying herself, celebrating the chance to meet again, but it was all so strange for her, and it seemed at first that there was no connection at all between them, past or present. Except for a handful of women with whom she had remained friends over the years—despite the distance of ten thousand miles between them—

her former classmates were, as she saw them that night, just people—strangers in a sea of vaguely familiar faces.

She was grateful to the unknown person who had organized name tags for everyone. She had fidgeted through her handbag, hunting for her glasses, which she wore only for reading, although she soon realized that they would have to stay on for the whole evening if she didn't want to offend people by failing to recognize them—especially, given that the moment she arrived, everyone seemed to recognize her. She had been overwhelmed with hellos and welcome backs and you haven't changed a bit, and how do you manage it? And there she was again, wanting to crawl under a table, because it was so embarrassing that she couldn't remember them in turn. What could she do? Smile and hope for the best.

It was some time before she was able to ask Lucy—her most regular contact amongst her old friends, "How can they recognize me so easily when I am struggling even to remember names, let alone faces?"

Lucy laughed. She always laughed. Perhaps that is why she was still a friend. "Oh," she laughed again, "of course they remember you! You are the only one they don't see all the time and they knew you were coming."

And then, being a thoroughly practical person, Lucy took her over to a large board on which there was a photograph of each person in the class with their name underneath.

Lily stood there for some time, remembering the young faces and putting names to them, and while Lucy laughed and chattered, several other old classmates joined them—all very jolly and commenting on faces then and now, until Lily began to feel a bit less... less...? *Uptight* was the word she was looking for. It came to her in the middle of some conversation ten or fifteen minutes later.

But before that, while she was still peering at old photographs, she had come to Frederick—otherwise known as Ricky. I hadn't realized, she thought, what calculating eyes he has. I suppose it's perfectly logical. After all, he was a wizard at maths, wasn't he?

"Ah! Ricky," Lucy chimed in, as if she had been listening in on Lily's thoughts. "Yes," she said, "and he's coming this way right now. You will get to meet his new young wife and I would advise you not to mention Ginger."

Then, seeing how puzzled Lily looked, Lucy added in a whisper, "He's had three wives. Ginger was his first. It appears that they each have a place on a rising scale relevant to his career. As his career took off, Ginger, so I've heard, was found to be not sufficiently educated for his dinner party conversations, and there was no place for her amongst his brilliant colleagues. As if it was *her* fault. It happened with the second one too..."

And there they were all at once—Frederick and his new, young wife—come to say hello to Lily. His wife's name was Gabrielle and she was French, he told her. She was both young and beautiful and, as anyone could see in a wink, much more interesting than he was. Perhaps, Lily thought, that's why he married her. A person whose very appearance would make him seem more interesting would be of considerable value to him, wouldn't it?

Lily smiled, chatted pleasantly and watched Gabrielle carefully, wondering if she was happy. After thirty years of living as an adult, she had learned something about reading faces. What she saw in Gabrielle was a very nice person—the real thing, in fact—a person who had no need to put on an act. The thought flashed through her mind that Gabrielle would outlast Frederick, and she was sure the same thought would occur to him one day—and he would have to get used it. But there she was, thinking catty thoughts, all aimed at him, not Gabrielle. Why? It was Lucy, she told herself, who had put them in her head.

And that was when the opaque bubble of memory wafted in—fully there and then gone in a wink. How curious it was that it could have come and gone without leaving a flicker on her face or a glitch in the conversation. She never ceased to be amazed by the power of the brain to work on its own—without a prompt—but always leaving her wondering.

She thought about it later at home and wondered why it had come to her after all those years. There was nothing to it really, even if it had left a sour taste at the time. In fact, the more she thought about it, it wasn't even a bad memory. It was just that it was so blatant ... so arrogant ... and nothing like it had ever happened to her before. Even at the time, when she thought about it afterwards, she could see that it was of no importance, that it didn't matter in the least but still, it had made her feel used and foolish. And later, weeks later, she had wondered whether she was meant to feel foolish, whether it had been a grand joke on her—something he could laugh about with his friends. Or perhaps it never entered his head.

In retrospect, the one certain thing was that she knew exactly what he was, even if he didn't. That was the end of it as far as she was concerned, and she had buried it so well that she had forgotten all about it until she met his new wife and heard about the others, and the memory woke up. So once again, on the day after the reunion, she gathered up that memory, because she was curious to see it from an entirely different position in time.

She had been about seventeen years old then. It was a Saturday morning and thirty or so students were about to board the bus which was to take them to Boston. It was to be a "cultural" day, planned to enlighten students in their last two years of high school by introducing them to art, history, and a fine restaurant. It would begin with a visit to the Museum of Fine Arts, and Lily, who was very interested in art, had been looking forward to it. But when she saw the students who were milling around that morning while they waited for the bus to arrive, she wasn't so sure she wanted to go, because although she knew them all by name at least, there wasn't a friend amongst them and it had made her feel uncomfortable—a bit bleak and lonely—and the trip hadn't even started yet. She was still thinking she had made a mistake in agreeing to go, when it occurred to her that once she was inside the museum it wouldn't matter whether she was alone or not. There would be much more interesting things to see and think about.

Nevertheless, she remembered how taken aback she had been when her friends had all come up with excuses. She had been so certain that they would enjoy the excursion even if they weren't interested in art. Despite their excuses and the fact that she knew they weren't coming, it hadn't occurred to her until the moment when she looked around to see who was boarding the bus, that she might not have anyone to sit with, and it worried her.

That day is what she remembered when the bubble of memory wafted past in a wink—and it all came to mind again. It wasn't just about Frederick, she thought. It also had something to do with other people, fellow students in particular, and her tendency to shut the door on them, metaphorically speaking. There were times, she was sorry to remember, when if a nice young man was coming towards her, she would cross the street rather than have to say hello. Why? Was it because 'hello' wasn't enough? More words might have been required, and she would be found wanting?

She knew that some people thought she was shy, and some thought she was snooty, but she was neither. It was something more like having stage fright amongst people she didn't really know, even people from her own town—especially people from her town. Strangers were somehow easier. But she was too young to understand why at the time.

Her friends would have told you—if you had asked—that she was really very lively and quite good fun—although somewhat silly at times. They told her so themselves. They were good, down-to-earth New Englanders who would have put both the question and the answer in a box labelled: 'After all, what are friends for?'

It was true, she thought. She was a bit silly some of the time, but not in the way they saw it. Their lives had a practical base, quite different from hers. They lived on farms—dairy and chickens both—where there was scarcely a minute to spare for mischief—or dreaming. Lily lived well out of town, in a perfectly beautiful spot, surrounded by woods and farms and plenty of food for the imagination, but no people of her own age. She had a grand time with the younger ones, exploring the woods dense around them, scrambling over great boulders tossed up by the ice age, playing games invented and inspired by the moment itself, naming everything.

It was Lily who did the naming and it was, she thought, the thing that made her friends think she was silly. But how could she not name it all? She had read *Anne of Green Gables* in the bleak dark days of one winter and well before the spring was over she had white ways of delight and every other thing that Anne had conjured up, plus a few of her own, all verbally attached to spots of great interest to her from one end of the woods to the other. The magic of life was right there in those woods. The town was a different thing altogether.

She didn't really like the town, except occasionally when there was a holiday and there were parades, and sometimes circuses or carnivals. Once upon a time it had been a small country town situated on a highway, which in those days was really just a road. And then it grew— sprawled out in all directions and filled up with new houses and the people to go with them, who all seemed to have invisible stamps on them saying 'City'. It had seemed a bit much even then, but by the time of the class reunion most of the farms had gone—replaced with housing developments—and bigger schools had been built, and nothing was the same. Why bother remembering, she wondered, if nothing was the same? "Because," she said to her empty room, "the memory came to me of its own accord."

She had decided that day, even before the bus arrived, that she would shuffle vaguely through the crowd until she was in line to be the fifth or six person to board the bus. That way, she could be sure of getting a window seat and it wouldn't matter at all who sat next to her.

She was mighty pleased with herself as she sat down and looked out the window. It was quite a new thing for her to be in charge of an outcome and she couldn't help smiling—just a little bit and only at the window. And then there was a thump as someone sat down in the seat next to her, and a male voice was asking if she would mind if he sat there, or had she perhaps already promised it to someone else?

She had recognized the voice immediately. It was Frederick. How could she be in the same class with him every day without knowing his voice—aggressive, even strident at times? But what was he doing there? In all the time she had been at school with him—nearly eleven years—he had never once had a real conversation with her, or chosen to sit with her. Talk between them had always been limited to the least possible number of words—whatever was necessary at the time. So what was he up to?

"The seat isn't taken," Lily replied. "You can sit there if you want."

"Oh good," he said, "because this is exactly where I'd like to be."

Lily frowned and looked out the window.

"Seeing that the seat was empty," he said, "I thought perhaps we might get a chance to talk for a bit. You don't mind, do you? After all, it's a good long drive into Boston and there will be plenty of time to talk. You are really a very interesting person, you know."

Lily frowned. "You have known me since I was six years old," she said. "Why now? You have plenty of friends on this bus—at the back I suppose, although I haven't looked."

For a moment she felt a tremor of despair. What was the point of saying such a thing, when it was too late? All the seats on the bus had already been taken and, like it or not, Frederick would be sitting next to her the whole way to Boston. She couldn't complain, of course, but she wasn't pleased. Of all the people who might have sat next to her if she'd had a choice, he would have been the last on her list. It wasn't that she particularly disliked him, it was that he was so smart, so pleased with himself, so sure of getting what he wanted. Why was he sitting there? Was it a dare, or a joke?

What she remembered, when she thought about it on the day after the reunion, was that he had behaved like a perfect gentleman that day. He had been courteous, interested, curious, pleasant, and there wasn't a single word of their conversation that she could fault. Not that she could remember a single word of what had been said so long ago—just that it had been pleasant.

And it wasn't over when they arrived in Boston. Oh no, it just kept on going! He followed her everywhere that day, took her by the arm, asked politely if she would mind if he walked with her through the museum, and sat with her at lunch, and so on... And Lily didn't know what to make of it. This was a side of him she had never seen before and, and although it unnerved her, it was really rather lovely.

Imagine a girl like me getting so much attention all at once, she exclaimed quietly, in her head. What is a girl like me to think? I've never had a real boyfriend? But why did he choose me?

That was the real question and it bounced around her all day until, in the end, she decided to stop worrying and let him have his way. What could he do except go on chattering and flattering and imitating Prince Charming? She was safe, she thought. She hadn't fallen head over heels for him, as the girls she knew always said. She was much too wary for that. In fact, she told herself, once she had got used to it and screwed her head on tight just in case, it was quite unreal—but it was a very nice sort of unreal and she was willing to let it happen for that day at least.

In the end her question was answered. Why choose me? Because he thought she would be so flattered—an easy target. And he carried it out right up to the door of the bus at the end of the day. And then, quite suddenly, he told her to hop on the bus and save him a seat, and he dashed off to retrieve a lost item, or so he said. It wasn't until he boarded the bus again and walked right past her to the back, without so much as glance in her direction that she realized she had been used. Ginger Krauss, who followed not far behind, glanced at Lily with a sweet little smile.

What else did her bubble memory have to offer of that day? A sturdy, somewhat matronly girl from the senior class, who was the last on the bus, had sat down beside her with a smile, and asked, "Are you okay? It was a bit nasty using you like that just to get Ginger. He's been after her for weeks, you know. I don't know how she came to be on this excursion. She's just a sophomore. Perhaps she's old for her class."

Is that really what she said? It was something like it. And Lily's reply was also something like, "It's insulting to be used in that way, but I am awfully lucky that it's Ginger he's after and not me."

"Good girl!" her new companion said. "I'm Nancy. Let's enjoy the rest of this day."

And they did, chattering merrily the whole way home.

A bit over a year later, the gossip buzzing through the school was that Ginger Krauss was pregnant and the sympathy seemed to linger over Frederick. What will Ricky do, was the question. It will ruin his life if he has to give up his studies, they said.

The answers always come in time. They married. He studied. The rest was buried in a cloud. All sorts of things must have happened. She was just his first wife. Things were still happening.

On the day after the class reunion, Lily went to visit her mother, who was very anxious to hear all about it. She couldn't remember her mother being a gossip-monger in the past, but she certainly was eager to hear it all now—at just the right time for a highball. She had looked at her watch to be sure it wasn't too soon.

"So, tell me all about it," she said as she mixed the drinks, nice and strong as usual. Very strong, Lily thought as she took her first sip.

"Well," said Lily, "I was more or less caught in a corner by that awful Adam Parker, forever it seemed. I had no idea who he was at first. Fortunately, he had a name tag. I thought it would be a brief and passing conversation, but he wasn't about to let me go easily. So there I was, a prisoner of his endless talk—mostly boasting. I kept hoping that William would come and rescue me, but he was giving me 'leeway'— he told me later—to renew old friendships. Goodness knows there was never a friendship with Adam!"

"Ah!" Betsy exclaimed, looking pleased. "I remember him. We drove him home one night. Years ago now."

Lily stared in amazement, wondering how on earth her parents could possibly have had anything to do with him.

"Why?" she asked.

"Oh, he was so drunk he could hardly stand up, let alone drive. Your father put him in our car and drove him home. It was quite an experience—not at all what we expected. He seemed a rather sweet young man, just drunk. We wouldn't have offered to take him home otherwise. Once he was in the car, he alternated between moaning and groaning or being downright aggressive, mostly complaining about you. It went on the whole way home, and that was no easy thing, because he couldn't remember where he lived at first, and your father was getting impatient driving around in circles and him in the back seat moaning and grumbling. As I said, it was all about you. 'I always wanted to ask her out,' he said—kept on saying—'but she was such a snob that I never dared to ask her.' Hmmph! I'll bet he's an alcoholic by now.

"I was never a snob," Lily said, "but if he had asked me I would have said no. I would still say no."

There followed a few moments of silence, which to Betsy, who was all prepared to leave no stone unturned, seemed like a great black hole.

"Is that all you have to say?" she demanded. "After thirty years?"

"Just about," Lily replied. "They were mostly all nice, although it was a bit confusing at times. I had trouble remembering names and faces. And it didn't help that there was so much noise. It wasn't too bad at first. People were gathering and all that—laughing, talking. But once everyone was there, they started the music and that went on the whole time, awfully loud, even while we were eating dinner. I suppose it was meant to be a nostalgia thing, but the music seemed to be from some other time. I thought I knew the music from our year, but whatever it was they were playing didn't seem to fit. Not that it matters, but it made it almost impossible to talk. I could scarcely hear a word anyone said, and then there was dancing—some new pop thing maybe. Strange. I don't recall ever seeing it before. Heaven knows where it came from! It was all a bit distracting."

"Strange dancing," Betsy exclaimed, after another sip of her highball. "Sounds like line dancing to me."

"Of course," Lily said, "how silly of me! Why was I thinking of pop? It must be jetlag—the mother of confusion—fries your brains! Perhaps if I had expected it... Perhaps not. Just as well I didn't join them. What a mess I would have made of that!"

Again there were a few moments of silence which left Betsy frowning—gulping her drink rather than sipping it. It was understandable. She had been thoroughly prepared for a grand gossip session and her horse, it seemed, had stumbled at the races. A fizzer! And seeing this, Lily offered her mother a small scrap—the only thing she could think of. "I met Frederick McKiver's new wife. She's very nice. I like her."

"Hmm!" said Betsy, her eyes lighting up again. "I remember him too—you do mean Ricky, don't you? He's done very well for himself! Although—in recent times—perhaps not so well. Didn't he lose his job? Something to do with a government department abandoning that area of research? What was it about? Space travel? Star wars? And wasn't there a bit of a scramble to find another job—not quite so illustrious?"

Lily had no idea what Frederick did or didn't do, but she thought it must have had something to do with maths. Should she have asked him at the reunion? Why? The thought had never entered her head. Was it something she needed to know...?

"Did you know," Betsy was asking across her thoughts, "that his parents are getting a divorce. After all these years! There's all sorts of talk about them. His father, it seems, is an incredible bully. Always has been. Used to beat the boys mercilessly. They must have had a miserable time growing up. Probably beat his wife once they were gone. Their house is for sale, you know. Perhaps *you* could buy it. It's on the main road, just beyond the bridge..."

"Bridge!" Lily exclaimed.

How did her mother know these things? She was the one who had gone to school with Frederick, and yet she had no idea where he lived as a child. She didn't even know he had brothers. Or had she known once long ago? Perhaps it all vanished when she moved to the southern hemisphere and her mind became so full of information that after a time it got busy one day and put all the useless bits into the cardboard box corner of her brain, and spiders had come along and hidden it all under dust-covered webs.

Was that possible? Didn't people talk about clearing the cobwebs out of their mind? Did the brain really have its own agenda? Why not? It gave her something to think about when her conversation with her mother, having twisted and turned its way through the mazes of small town life, became a monologue in which Betsy delivered the gossip on virtually everyone in the town, while Lily wondered how it was that this small woman, who lived high up on the hill beyond the town, could possibly have come to know so much about so many in such detail. It was truly extraordinary, hypnotic in fact, until quite suddenly a great gust of wind cracked a branch off a nearby tree with a sound like a shot and Lily, no longer spellbound, found that her mind was wandering about in a worrisome confusion which—her mind being what it was—resolved itself quite of its own accord by switching gears and taking her instead to the large old birch tree in the hollow below the great ice age boulders—a place where her mother had never been. She wondered if there would be time enough to find those boulders and nestle into the hollow once more. If she slipped out the door quietly and disappeared for a bit, would her absence be noticed? Would it matter?

Why not? It was always the place where she could be safe from her parents when Betsy was flirting with the devil again. Did Frederick's father really beat his boys mercilessly, or was Betsy conjuring as usual? If at that moment, Lily—a grown woman with grown children—had reminded her mother that she and her brother had also been beaten by their father and it was always because she—her mother—had set him up for it, would Betsy have thrown a hysterical fit or set the non-existent dog on her? How could her father have known what his children had done or not done when he was miles away—wending his way home after a long days' work. How could he have known what was true and what wasn't true when Betsy filled him in on the evils of their children? It was always late in the day—just before dinner, and the children had been banished to their rooms—long ago it seemed.

How could she and Matty have known what their mother was saying, when all they could hear from their rooms upstairs was a dull complaining noise that sounded like 'nyeh nyeh nyeh...? And every time he beat them, the look on their father's face when he swung his great leather belt had always been self-righteous and hateful. The one thing that she and Matty never knew was just what Betsy had told their father.

If her parents could look in the mirror while they told stories and gossip about other people, would they perchance see the monster in themselves? Of course not! Why would she ask herself such a question? Hadn't she read the Icelandic sagas, fairy tales and ancient history, Shakespeare and Charles Dickens—every one of them filled with the worst and best of people—and always, the worst was the most memorable? She could never think of poor Little Dorrit without worrying about her.

She looked at her mother, whose glass was about to slip out of her hand and smash on the floor, and she caught it and put it aside. Betsy had fallen asleep, and seeing that there was plenty of sun left outside, Lily quietly left the house and headed for the old birch tree in the hollow where, if nothing else, she might come face to face with herself again. She might even say hello.

CHAPTER 18

2007

Being Ethereal—As It Were

With yet another reunion pending, Lily was once again thinking of her old friends and fellow classmates, which of course reminded her of the last reunion—the one that she and William had attended before they returned to the antipodes. And now another was looming—the second since they had all slid into the twenty-first century.

She was not at all sure she wanted to go. In fact, she was certain that she didn't want to go. It was such a long way, and years of travelling back and forth hadn't made the trip any less daunting. No matter what she did, she always arrived at the other end shredded and rickety on her feet and not entirely convinced that she wasn't someone else, that *she* had been left behind somewhere—at the dismal Sheremetjevo perhaps, or Singapore with its enormous carpet with the brilliant pattern of seamless repeats stretching to the horizon—or faraway wall—a work of genius and nowhere to sit. Not a chair in sight except for those in the dark and dismal areas where there were empty gates—or the handful at Starbucks—walking—walking—Starbucks in Singapore—standing with Styrofoam cup in hand—a lost soul—the modern world...

She thought about the last reunion. She'd had a horrible headache that night and everyone else was merrily line dancing while she watched in puzzlement. Why had that stuck in her mind? She could not for the life of her remember a single occasion when anyone in her class had ever done anything like line dancing—except perhaps the Virginia Reel when they were twelve or thirteen years old and coerced into a dance class designed to prepare miniature adults for the world to come. Yet, despite the fact that everyone seemed intent on remembering how it had been then—when they were young—they also seemed to know exactly how line dancing was done. But wasn't that a modern thing? She didn't have a clue. She wondered if they had been doing this kind of thing the whole time and she had never noticed. Perhaps she had blinked—or just "been away."

She thought of her class yearbook and the page with herself on it. There she was in the ghastly photo her parents had imposed on her against her wishes. She cringed to think of it. She was the only person in the whole yearbook looking back over her shoulder, for which she blamed the photographer, who just when she thought they were finished, was suddenly inspired to experiment with a different pose— something more artistic, he'd said. It seemed harmless enough at the time, sitting there in a demure little shirt with a Peter Pan collar— looking backwards. How could she know that she would be stuck with it forever?

She remembered the day when the photos arrived in the mail. There it was on the top of the pile—the first to catch the eye of the beholder. Her face seemed oddly stretched and reshaped as if only part of her was there—or the part of her that was intrinsically *herself* as she understood it—seemed to be missing. Her heart sank. If that was the best, she thought, how awful would the others be?

She was relieved to find that there were several other perfectly good, *normal* photos to choose from, but of course, once Betsy saw them there was no choice to be had. In scarcely the wink of an eye, she had zoomed in on the one aberration and that was that. She insisted that it was the best and Charley agreed with her as he always did. And just in case Lily thought about protesting, Betsy closed the deal on the spot. "You can argue till you're blue in the face," she had told her, "but it won't make a jot of difference because," as she said with a smirk, "he who pays the piper calls the tune."

Lily was quite upset at the time and could never forget how her friends had reacted when she complained about it. "But surely," they'd said, almost as a refrain, "it is your choice isn't it? It's your yearbook!" and, "*My* parents would never..."

Ah well! What could she do?

She still has the yearbook. It emerges occasionally from the back of a cupboard. She scarcely ever looks at it except to refresh her memory when there is news about one of her former classmates, but she can never look at the entry for herself without seeing it as a belated lesson in being careful what you say, how you look, and what you agree to. It always seemed to her that in the world of that book there was no escape from the prying eyes or clever remarks of those who take pleasure in inventing you as something other. Yes *other*, because it wasn't just that photograph. There was also a list of her attributes, of the things she did, clubs she belonged to and *precisely* what kind of person she was. Of course it was the same for every other student in her graduating class. They had all given information about themselves, their clubs, etc., but she was the only one who was described, on the very top line, as "ethereal." It was the first thing she saw when the yearbooks were handed out all those years ago.

Where on earth did they get that from, she had wondered. Do they know what it means? Or, for that matter, what do they mean by it? Me! Ethereal?

She had thought about it from time to time over the years, not offended, just puzzled, and she had asked herself, 'How could I have been at school with my fellow classmates for twelve years without them having the least idea of who or what I am?' But then she thought, they didn't know. They weren't there. Only I was there. After all, it was my life.

She remembered it as if it were yesterday. It was, she thought, just about the best time in the world— those bits of it that belonged entirely to her, *sans* parental interference. It was a wonderful way to grow up— tramping through woods, sitting in the tops of trees, vaulting over broken tree limbs, leaping from one great rock to another—arriving home scraped, scratched and bruised just as the sun went down. How often did I walk into the house—she asked herself—all caked with mud, or coated with burrs, and my mother had been calling me for the past half hour or more? I always told her I was sorry, I hadn't heard her.

But sitting there with yearbook in hand, there was still that word. Perhaps, she thought, it was true in the mind of the person who wrote it. She wondered whether it was just one person or the product of a committee. If they had consulted Betsy no doubt she too would have been puzzled. She would probably have told him or her or them that I was nothing but a heathen. Although perhaps not. After all, hadn't she spent so much time trying to civilize me—trying to make me potentially marriageable? Why would she admit failure? Besides, she would surely have fallen over laughing at the thought of me being ethereal.

Then she wondered, how could my mother have known one way or the other what I really was? Didn't she tell me once that I was the most impossible teenager on earth—that I had gone around 'for four whole years with a stone-cold face and nothing at all to say'?

A remark like that tends to stitch you up and render you mute— and without doubt Betsy was a dab hand with a needle. What's more, she had needles of all kinds. Her comfort zone was inside the house— knitting—sewing—doing embroidery—talking on the phone or listening to music for hours on end and she believed that the face of a teenage girl, who had to wait until it was over, however long it took for her conversation or opera or requiem or symphony or whatever else to end—was stone cold?

When she thought about it later, Lily admitted to herself that it was probably true—but only *when the wind was in the east*—when Betsy was being utterly unreasonable or just plain unfair. One way or another, it was a matter of perception. There was and always would be a hurdle between herself and her mother—lifted occasionally by a 'good mood.' Betsy lived in a circumscribed world of her own design. Lily, on the other hand, was *out there*—somewhere ethereal perhaps— and from her point of view, *out there* was a perfectly fine place to be. How could her mother know such a thing?

Not only did Lily know it, she had no trouble getting there. What's more, she could do it in her mind as well as in reality. It was a thing she had learned from reading books. A mere child she was when she found herself *out there* for the first time. She remembered it clearly. It was that awful afternoon when nasty boys had pelted her with rock-hard snowballs and she had escaped into a library where she discovered the story of Aladdin and his wonderful lamp. At the top of the first page was the word 'Aladdin' and at the bottom was the word 'incorrigible.' She remembered trying to sound it out. 'In-corri-gible' is what she thought it said and she wasn't sure what it meant.

She had begun to read very slowly and carefully and it was hard, but something about the story had made her want to read more, because even though she didn't know all the words, she could understand what was happening—and that was when the world around her vanished and all that was left was the strange and wonderful world of Aladdin. Outside the library, the air was thick with snow, piling up in heavy drifts. Inside, Lily was busy following Aladdin through the streets of Arabia, somewhere near China.

Ah yes, she remembered! Even then—only seven years old—she

knew that it wasn't just about reading, that when the world vanished like that it was a special kind of magic, and the more she read the more wonderful the magic became. It was like belonging to a secret society with a membership of two—herself and a book. After a while, when she was a little older, if there was no book to be had, she could go one step further. She could create whole new worlds in her head— and take up residence in them—especially on those days when her mother ordered her to stay in the car while she did the supermarket shopping, or when she went into the drugstore and chatted, for ages it seemed—or like now, standing there, waiting for her mother to stop being difficult. She created whole villages on such days—built houses, furnished them, made them hers—quite certain that she would move into one—someday.

She knew that her mother—sitting with phone in hand—could see her but she was quite certain that she herself wasn't there—or at the very least that her mind was elsewhere, and that was almost as good as being in the woods entirely alone except for the creatures who lived there. She had been working for some time on the idea of being accepted by them, those small, intrinsically honest creatures who had never seen a telephone. In that world, when she wasn't climbing trees, she practiced walking quiet, like an Indian. On a good day, scarcely a twig snapped.

And there it was again, with yet another reunion invitation in hand, that word was staring her in the face and she was still wondering what had prompted it. Perhaps it was the school play. She hadn't thought of it for a long time. Why not? She had played the lead role. But that had happened only because she had checked the cast list and chose to audition for the last thing on it, simply because it was the only listing that had just one sentence by way of description: *A girl named Clementine who is a tomboy*. She was sure she could do that and a one-sentence description suited her just fine. It would please her mother, who had been urging her to audition for something—*anything* to get her out of the house—or her hair.

It turned out to be fun. But ethereal, surely not! In fact, when she discovered that she had the lead role in a three-act play, she felt that she had been tricked, and the thought of learning all those lines nearly overwhelmed her. If Matty hadn't listened to her every night after the dishes were done, she could never have done it. She hadn't forgotten that. But she also remembered those anxious flutterings in her mind during rehearsals, every time she looked out at the vast auditorium and saw all those empty seats. She imagined them full of people and herself on stage struck dumb—all those lines she had worked so hard to learn—gone—a blank—not one of them to be found anywhere— not even a flicker of them. At the back of her mind at every rehearsal, no matter how well it went, there was always that troublesome 'What if...' It stayed there right up to the final dress rehearsal, which had been so well organized that there was even a small audience sitting in the first few rows—a setting as close to the real thing as it could get.

Of that evening only one thing stuck in her mind. As she had walked on stage, thinking of her first line, there had been a sudden and utterly unexpected flash of light in front of her and she had stopped dead in confusion, wondering if thunder might follow. And as she stood blinking, the director—Mrs. Blomgren, a most lovely woman— came rushing on stage apologizing.

"Oh, I am so sorry!" she exclaimed. "I completely forgot to tell you about the footlights. You mustn't let them worry you. You don't have to look at them. You look above and beyond them. They are only there for the audience—so that they will be able to see the actors clearly— because, without the lighting of a real room, there are often dark patches on a stage and from where the audience sits you can fade out at times—which makes it much harder for those sitting at the back. You can't see it of course, but they can."

At that point, Mrs. Blomgren frowned, then stopped for a few moments and looked beyond the footlights, thinking, it seemed. Then, as if raring to go again, she said, "Okay! Let's practise becoming accustomed to the footlights."

Thence followed a few minutes of becoming accustomed. The entire cast was called on stage so that they too might get used to the lights. For Lily, it took less than a minute to see the point. What she had discovered, when she had stood there and looked beyond the footlights, was the dazzling gift of the gods, for no matter where she stood on the stage, on any angle, all she could see of the rehearsal audience was vague, shadowy shapes, recognizable only in the first five rows, and only if she looked hard, which with all that she had to do and remember was most unlikely. Beyond the first five rows she could see nothing but a dark blank. Not even the chairs were visible and, having seen it—or not seen it—for herself, all her fears vanished in a wink. What a grand thing that was!

"I think," said Lily, as they were getting ready to start again, "the footlights are really for us. If we can't see the audience, we won't get nervous and forget our lines. Even if all the seats are full, we can pretend there's no one there."

"Of course," said Mrs. Blomgren. "Why didn't I think of that myself?"

Lily remembered—Mrs. Blomgren—the patience of an angel.

Apart from the photograph episode and the school play, what else was there that could possibly be regarded as ethereal, she asked herself. The answer was 'nothing.' The only thing that stood out in her mind was ice, because that particular winter was among the longest and coldest in the region for more than a hundred years. There was ice everywhere. All the lakes and ponds were thoroughly, gloriously frozen and she was in love with ice skating. She was also a girl on a mission.

Not long before, her parents (not knowing what else to do with her, particularly since she showed no sign of attracting a serious boyfriend), took note of her interest in ice skating and joined her up in a skating club at a rink in Worcester. Then they kindly drove her there on a regular basis.

It wasn't really a good idea. Lily was the youngest person in the club and thoroughly outclassed. She also tended to be rather shy, especially with older strangers—and the ice at the rink was filled with older strangers, all of whom knew each other and were, moreover, absorbed in honing their own skills.

But she tried. She really did. She had to. Didn't she have the expense of it all hanging over her—the price of the membership—all that driving. Even the cost of her brand new 'ice-rink ice skates' was hanging over her—especially the cost of those skates, which were, in her parents' opinion, an uncalled-for extravagance—one which they would long remember.

Hadn't her father in his wisdom, prior to enrolling her in the club, bought her a perfectly suitable pair of skates, two sizes too large, so that she (a fifteen-year-old who had already stopped growing) might grow into them? Lily had not been able to persuade him otherwise. He always knew better and in the face of the intractable, she had convinced herself that skates too large were probably better than skates too small. But when it came to the point of trying them out on the ice, they were impossible. She could not get used to them. She couldn't find the point of balance. Her feet moved around inside them. She tended to lurch from one side to the other and was in danger of spraining an ankle or cracking her skull. She fell frequently, as though she was just a beginner, and she was miserable. It seemed to her that in the eyes of all at the rink, her skates were making a fool of her.

In an attempt to solve the problem, she consulted the man who sold skates from the stall in the corner near the ice-rink café—thinking that with the right advice she might be able to skate in her too-large skates if she just did this or that.

"Good heavens!" he exclaimed when he saw them. "These are

terrible! Your feet will never grow so large. You will never be able to skate in these. And the blades! Oh! They are awful—cheap and awful! Just look at the edges! Can't you see...? They won't even sharpen properly."

He went on to explain in detail, and from every point of view, exactly how dreadful her skates were. Then, reaching into his stock, he pulled out a pair of Hyde skates, made for the Canadian market, and just the right size for her. They were brilliant in every way and five times the price of her too-large skates. He got her to try them on. The difference was immediately apparent, which made her feel even worse.

"My father will never agree," she told him sadly. "He has only just bought my skates."

The man shrugged and put the skates back in the box.

Somehow—Lily couldn't remember exactly how—she managed to introduce her father to the man and to her astonishment he did agree to buy the skates, although it took a week or so to get him to that point. And then, because she thought she had just used up all her miracles at once, she stood there with her wonderful new skates in her arms and thanked him a dozen times over, while he, with the grimmest of faces, told her that she had better get used to the idea that they were her Christmas and birthday presents for the next three years.

She cheerfully agreed, although she couldn't help wondering what he would think if she were to wrap the skates in bright paper and ribbons each time. One can get carried away with the imagery of a thing like "for the next three years!" But that was a minor thing— Charley's idea of a joke perhaps. It really didn't matter. Nothing could dull the joy of actually owning such skates.

The feeling of indebtedness hung over her, nevertheless, and she soon found herself on the horns of a dilemma, as they say, because even in her dazzling white, professional quality, comfortable, sturdy and brand new Canadian skates, she could not banish the discomfort she felt at the obvious gap between her abilities and those of the other club members marking up impressive patterns on the ice all around her. And as usual, no one paid her any attention. It seemed that one way or the other, whether she stayed or went, she was bound to embarrass herself. But after all that expense she believed she had no choice but to stay. So stay she did, and since choice was an issue even then, she chose to ignore the snooty skaters, skate where she wanted and even get in their way at times. It was a challenge of sorts and there was nothing ethereal about it.

As it happened, the early arrival of the long winter solved the problem. Charley, as has already been suggested, was a true-blue, penny-pinching New Englander, although to be fair to him, there were penny-pinching New Englanders all over the place at the time. They had lived through the Great Depression and the War and crop failures, gone without jobs and long ago learned to be cautious about money. They would remain so for the rest of their lives, no matter how rich they became. So of course Charley couldn't see the point in paying for Lily to skate on ice twelve miles away, when there was perfectly good ice just down the road for free. Besides, he had probably got tired of driving an extra twelve miles each way just so that she could skate at night—and she hadn't even met some nice young man. Is that what he thought? How could she know? But there had been hints. After all, she was only two years younger than her mother was when *she* was married!

But before that, when the lakes were 'not quite safe enough' for skaters, and Lily was still struggling to justify her membership in the skating club, a man whom she had never seen before at the rink suddenly appeared one evening on the ice in front of her and began spinning—brilliantly spinning. She stopped to watch him and he came to a halt right in front of her.

"How do you do that?" she asked, so astounded that she entirely forgot her shyness. "Will you teach me to do it?"

"Sure," he said, "you just do this." And he spread his arms out wide and skated backwards in a circle, and when he had picked up some speed, he flung out his right leg, turned in the opposite direction, and began to spin, and as he spun he gradually pulled in his out-flung leg and arms. She could see him speeding up as he did this and, with his arms crossed over his waist, he went on spinning faster and faster until he began to blur. He put his foot out then, loosened his arms, and came to a sudden stop without any apparent effort. "There!" he said, flinging out his arms, as you would to an audience. "That's how you do it."

Lily tried it herself—concentrated on getting it right, exactly the way he had done it. She landed on her backside.

"Good!" he said. "You've got it right. Now you just need to keep on doing it until you've got the hang of it. And don't forget to give yourself a focus point. Regardless of where your body is, you need to keep your eyes on that point. Otherwise, you will get dizzy and fall over."

She did it again. She crashed. He laughed. "Just keep up the good work," he said, as he skated off.

As it turned out, that was her last day at the rink, although she didn't know it at the time.

For the whole of that winter, as long as there was ice to skate on and light enough to see by, Lily was out there in the cold on McKinstry's pond and her parents never seemed to mind at all. "Why should she be at home helping around the house," Betsy argued, "when she needs to justify the great expense of those skates?"

So there she was, every day, on the pond skating backwards in a circle, flinging out her leg, turning, crashing, trying again, teetering, wobbling, lurching—over and over again.

All winter long, the pond continued to freeze, and as it froze, great cracks appeared in the ice as it contracted, and with each contraction there were thunderous booms which sent people skittering off the ice for fear of falling through.

"Don't you know," Lily said to them, "that the ice must be all of five feet thick by now?"

They ignored her, which didn't worry her at all. "The thicker the ice, the louder the boom," she shouted at them, but they made it clear, from the safety of the embankment, that they thought she was mad—besides which it was evident from where Lily stood, that standing on firm land—all the boys and girls in a huddle and squeezed together for warmth, was much more interesting to them than a freezing pond, or a frozen-toed fanatic.

She smiled blissfully at the thought, because now she had the ice all to herself. The real danger, she knew, lay in the cracks, because if she happened to skate into one, regardless of the direction she was going, she would be violently arrested and make a mess of herself, one way or the other. It had happened to her more than once. Even so, she persisted. At the beginning of each day's skating, she took the time to find herself an island of ice, bound by widening cracks and large enough in the middle to spin on, if she should be so lucky.

It happened one day much to her amazement, not long before the ice turned to water again. On one of those little islands, she skated backwards in a circle, flung out her leg, turned in the opposite direction and began to spin, and as she pulled in her arms and leg, she knew for the first time that she was going to keep on spinning until she put out her foot to stop herself, and all the while, focussing furiously on her chosen spot and feeling giddy with excitement at the speed of it, she told herself over and over, "Don't lose your nerve! Keep on going!"

She stood still for a few moments after she stopped, not at all dizzy, just thinking with great satisfaction about what she had done, and about how easy it would be to do it again, now that she had finally "got the hang of it."

She did it again just to be sure, and then again, after which she

looked all around her, eager to take in the whole scene of her triumph—
the great panorama of McKinstry's pond, cracks and all. Only then
did she see that she had an audience. A small crowd of fellow skaters
had stopped to look, no less surprised than she was, when they saw her
spinning faster and faster, just like a real skater.

"How did you do that?" someone asked.

Lily thought of the man at the skating club—her great teacher—
and she laughed.

"Well, you just do this," she said, and she put out her arms and
began to skate backwards in a circle...

Now, so many years later, she asked herself again, how ethereal can a
person be who bruised and dented just about every part of her body,
and her skates as well, at least three hundred times in the space of one
winter, all for the sake of a spin?

With the reunion looming, on a whim, on one of the hottest days
of an Australian summer, Lily reached into the back of her closet and
pulled out her old Canadian skates just to have a look at them. It was
shocking. Not only did they look positively ancient, but every inch
of them was bumped, battered and scraped, the result of long, hard
skating and endless falls. Worse still, they had turned a sad shade of
gray and dried out so badly that she thought they would crack if she
tried to put a foot into one.

She tried anyway and to her surprise, as she slipped her foot in,
the boot bent beautifully, as if to say, "Hello again, where have you
been?" And when she had put on both of them and stood up, she
knew immediately why she had slid all over the place when she first
stepped on the ice in Canada the year before, wearing a pair of "Made
in China" rented skates. The difference between those and her own
'Hydes', made in America for the Canadian market long ago, in the
time when China had wrapped itself in a "bamboo curtain" and its
dominant economy was way over the horizon, was like night and

day. It was all in the fit, the comfort, the balance and the shape of the blades. There was no doubt about it: Hyde made wonderful skates! And standing there on that hot Australian afternoon in her old skates (with the guards on, so that she wouldn't scrape the floor), she was suddenly filled with questions, like, "Do they still make them? Does Google know about Hyde?"

She Googled. She asked. And Google answered politely as usual: "Ice skates Hyde." And bingo, there they were on her screen. No, said Google, they do not make them any longer. But they live on nevertheless as 'antiques'.

"Imagine that!" Lily exclaimed to herself. "My old skates are now regarded as genuine, bona-fide antiques—just like me! How splendidly ethereal!"

And then, on a whim, she Googled 'ethereal' and came up with: 'Extremely delicate and light in a way that seems not to be of this world.' She looked at her battered old skates again, and was speechless! She would write to her former classmates: "I apologize for not being able to attend the class reunion. I have taken up mountain climbing. I have set my sights on Mt. Everest, which is as close to ethereal as I can get."

CHAPTER 19

Jack Frost

Lily was sitting at her desk writing. She was trying to deal with the problem of putting her thoughts down on paper at the same time as she was trying to close her mind to the music which came at her endlessly from the direction of her side fence. It was a fact of suburbia. Houses were built too close together. Driveways on one side of a fence mirrored driveways on the other side. There was nothing but concrete and a six-foot fence between them—and the awful ivy that grew all over it and pulled it out of shape, no matter how much she hacked at it. She sat thinking about the neighbour's music and wondering why she found it so offensive. It's not the music which offends me so, she told herself. It's that it is so intrusive—so incessant. It was also that she felt betrayed. Because it was classical music, it seemed to her that she was being assaulted by a friend. She would have understood if it had been Led Zeppelin or some such, but for her, classical music was the food of life. She had grown up on it. Beethoven, Mozart, Puccini, Verdi, Berlioz and countless other composers had been fellow inhabitants of her mother's house from the time she was born. She knew them before she could speak. She also knew that they belonged to her mother. Her father would sing riotously of Ivan Skavinsky Skvar and a woman, who would be coming down the mountain wearing red pajamas, and her mother would frown and say that he should stop singing; it was unsuitable for the ears of children. Her father would sneer at Mozart— and say "it's tweedle tweedle dum music," but he would tolerate it— with a studiously tolerant look on his face—because he had no choice.

Despite Betsy's declared ownership of the household music, it managed to find a place in Lily's heart as well. She was perfectly happy with that and there wasn't a thing her mother could do about it, except perhaps turn it off, which she never did. As long as no one disturbed her when she was listening, Betsy was happy. Sometimes she would listen to the radio. Sometimes she played a record. Sometimes the children would come home from school to a dark house and there would be music filling every corner of it. There would be a note on the kitchen table saying something like, "I am listening to *The Damnation of Faust*. Do not disturb me," and Lily and her brother would tiptoe upstairs, carefully avoiding the creaky steps. This didn't happen all the time. But there were many such days, filled with grand operas or requiems, and the children were never notified in advance that they would be coming home to an unfriendly house that day. On the day when they broadcast the monumental *Boris Godunov*, Betsy not only left a note on the table, she had also called all her friends in advance to tell them exactly how long the opera would last and ask them not to call her during that time. By the time she was ten years old, Lily could have told anyone—if they had asked—who all the great singers of the time were. She could also have told them that her mother preferred a Contralto to a Soprano, and a Bass Baritone to a Tenor.

She had always thought there was a gap between herself and her mother on the question of music—of who owned it, who had the right to listen to it, or to listen with some degree of authority. But then, when she was twelve, her mother bought her a small record for Christmas with Mozart's *Eine Kleine Nachtmusik* on one side and Haydn's *Toy*

Symphony on the other. It amazed her—the thought that for the first time, she had her very own music to play, provided, of course that her mother would permit her to play it on the sacred HiFi. When she was fourteen, her mother began taking her to symphony concerts at night. What she liked best when the Detroit Symphony Orchestra came to town, was watching the conductor, Paul Paray, bouncing up and down in time to the music, both feet at a time. She was absolutely fascinated by the thought that he might come bouncing into the audience one night. She remembered also the night when Van Cliburn came out on stage, bowed graciously and sat down at the piano. It was a gala occasion. Everyone wore evening dress. He had won the Tchaikovsky prize and was in headlines everywhere. An American from Texas had won a major Russian prize. It had caused a big stir in Russia too. It was their first International Tchaikovsky Competition and the judges needed to ask permission of Nikita Khrushchev himself before they could give their precious prize to an American. It was the middle of the Cold War. Everyone was so excited. He is here in our town, people exclaimed, on our stage, and he is only twenty-three years old! When he sat down, there was a moment of quiet anticipation in the audience, and then, a look of consternation passed between him and the conductor, and they both rushed off the stage together, leaving the audience in a buzz of confusion. They returned a minute or so later, smiling, the conductor waving his music at the audience. Lily scarcely heard the concert. She was utterly struck by the discovery that a person so heralded and admired could do something so human.

What upset her so much about the music coming over the fence wasn't just that it was repetitious; it was that she had no choice in it. On still hot summer days like this one on which she was struggling to write, all the windows in the neighbourhood were open in case there might be a breeze. On such days, people all over Melbourne welcomed the tiniest bit of wind. She wondered whether they would welcome her neighbour's music as well. Today it was Bach—over and over again. She was trying to come to terms with a scene from her past—long buried and recently brought to life again. It wasn't the past that troubled her as much as the problem of seeing it again in her mind and representing it clearly on paper—as something real. It was also the disjunction between her memory and her mother's. This, she thought, was about something else, but what? On the surface, it seemed to be a battle between two memories, but as far as her mother was concerned there was no memory because nothing had happened—and her memory, as she often reminded Lily, was considered by all who knew her to be exceptional. Or, as her father frequently said, "You'd better believe it!" But this wasn't just about memory, or the past, or even her mother's ubiquitous possession of a trump card. There was more to it, Lily thought. She was certain that it had as much to do with the present as the past, but the more she thought about it, the more elusive it became, and the more she tried to sort it out the more her thoughts raced off in all directions, too fast for her to catch. They bounced off perimeters, got caught up with repetitions of Bach, and spun themselves into a tangled mess every time she reached for them. They ended up on her page as something so dull that it seemed they were smirking at her. They left blotches of ink behind them.

She looked down at her page with a feeling of disgruntlement. "There are episodes in a life," she read, "which in retrospect, have more meaning than others, even though they are not necessarily marked in photograph albums momentously, as one does with graduations, weddings and births. Neither are they necessarily the unforgettable and inescapable catastrophes that accompany life—the deaths and funerals, accidents and storms. Rather they are the moments of a period which, together, mark the soul. Scar it if you like, or stamp it in some way—like a product. You might call these the stretch marks of a life expanding in spite of itself. However you may choose to distinguish it, these moments linger in the mind. Or perhaps they lurk — like prowlers or thieves on a dark night, hidden behind trees, waiting to pounce on some vulnerable soul."

Oh Lord! Lily exclaimed to herself. This is awful! So bloody pompous! It's not what I want at all ... although ... I do rather like the idea of prowlers and thieves lurking somewhere in the mind ...

Bach continued to make his way into the room. She began writing on a different tack. She made up her mind to tackle the Harp Lady head-on, as an antidote. Is it true, she wondered, that a little poison is a cure for poisoning? She tried to think about what it is that makes a person what they are. She cast her mind over recent magazine articles and advertisements which asserted the me-ness of a person—the who I am and what I need and, most particularly, what I want. Me! Me! Me! What makes a person, she thought, has nothing—or very little—to do with the perfume that lingers, or those myriad sensations which can trigger a memory long after the event. The lyrics of a popular song might stick in the mind, although these days it's the sound that matters not the words. It's the car radio rhythm—the ba-boom, ba-boom, ba-boom pulsating at traffic lights everywhere. She remembered a magazine article which had caught her eye. It gave timely advice to sixteen-year-olds: "Be unforgettable. Drive him crazy. Wear 'Poison' on that first date. He will never smell it again without thinking of you." That might be true, Lily wrote, for a time at least. It happens with colours too. Autumn leaves, blue dresses, black stockings. Music. Oh yes! Music. That woman! The Harp Lady—the woman who lives on the other side of the fence. She is a thin, sour-faced, blonde woman. She is also a professional harpist who practises for up to twelve hours at a time. You may think this a good thing. Some people might even say, "If music be the food of love, play on," but whenever I think of the Harp Lady, which is what we have called her for want of knowing her real name, I cannot make the equation work. Is it music = love, or love = music? Or neither? What about food? Love = food and/or music.

But the Harp Lady is thin, like a stick. She is no voluptuary. Spaghetti is out of the question. A diet of fish fingers perhaps?

What then is the ratio of love to music, or music to love, when these are measured in relation to time, that is, the number of hours in which one person can practise in a day without collapsing in a heap from exhaustion? Twelve hours should be equal to a flood of love, you might think. So why, whenever I meet her in the street, is she so sour—so cold? Is there another equation in this? No smiles = no wrinkles? This seems to add up, especially if you take into account the fact that she dyes her hair, but the dye is obvious and the hair is short and severely trimmed, which may equate in its own peculiar way with the stick-thin image. Or is it possible that the music I hear over my fence is a CD? The same CD played over and over all day?

Lily was horrified at the thought, because to determine whether or not it was a CD, she would need to concentrate on it. Listen more carefully. She listened. It could be, she told herself. She is not playing scales. But how can I be sure? I would need to listen for breaks in the music, or practice repetitions—and that would drive me mad. Either way, she sighed as she wrote, I have no doubt that for the rest of my life—or for a while at least, whenever I hear Bach, I shall think of fish fingers. It is perfectly logical. The sum of the equation is equal to the impression that remains when the Harp Lady has gone past me and turned the corner.

This, Lily thought, was getting out of hand, but her mind was working in its own way and she had very little control of it just then. She was still annoyed with what she took to be a discrepancy between the personality of the musician and the beauty of the music. She was also frustrated by the fact that she had no choice in the matter. This would go on until one of them moved, or died. There wasn't enough room to plant a tree between them. Well, at least I am not the only one, she thought. Everyone in our family feels the same way about her, which is a good thing because it means that I am not alone in my negativity.

And on the positive side, we are all in agreement about *Casablanca* too. You only need to say, "Play it again, Sam," and it doesn't matter in the least if that's not what Humphrey Bogart actually said. It's the voice. He could have said 'pickled onions' and it would still be interesting.

Right! Lily thought. Have I done it? Have I finally put the Harp Lady and her music out of my mind? Can I get back to my own thoughts now? It's a time that I am thinking of, she told herself. Pay attention! It's about a time and events in my own history. It is also about the fact that my parents and my brother lived in the same time and the same place and yet, as I have only recently discovered, my memories of that time apparently have no place at all in their minds. Why was I so shocked to discover this? Do I need to remind myself that my memory is about what happened to me, not them? And who else can live my life but me? But still, there should be some common recollection—shouldn't there? Of course I wouldn't expect Matty to remember much; he was only four years old. Nor would I expect Mother or Dad to remember things that happened when I was at school, but at home—surely they would remember those things. I don't understand it.

Lily thought of the day that had disturbed her so. She had gone to visit her parents. Her mother had wanted help with an embroidery project. "Be prepared to work," she had said when she asked her to come. Lily wondered what help her mother could possibly want. After all, when it came to embroidery, her mother was a widely-acknowledged expert. No one disputed that. The proof of it was everywhere.

As it turned out, the embroidery had already been finished some days earlier. Her mother was making a chasuble for the local vicar in a deep purplish-red Thai silk. On the back of it, she had embroidered the flames of the Holy Spirit in a fiery mix of gold, red and orange, and she had highlighted it with threads of pure gold and tiny crystal beads. From any angle, it was dazzling. And when the cloth was moved, even in the smallest way, the flames sparked and glittered and seemed dangerously alive. It was enough to put the fear of God into the Bishop himself. Lily was amazed. She walked around the table, admired it from one side and the other, asked whether something so fine should be worn at all, and wondered what it was her mother wanted her to do. Her mother—always a mind-reader—handed her a large, neatly-folded piece of pinkish-red Bem silk. "I want you to do the lining for me," she said.

Lily took the silk and smelled it, felt the weight of it, tested the colour against the Thai silk. Her mother reached into a cupboard and pulled out the original paper pattern. In no time at all they were busy measuring, marking, cutting ... the two of them. "You need to add a bit extra to the lining, all around" Lily said. "There has to be space for the body to move inside it without it pulling the chasuble out of shape on the outside. And you need to pin it horizontally. It should bubble a bit when you pin it."

Her mother nodded and looked pleased. It occurred to Lily that her mother had done the linings herself many times, and she felt rather silly. What a dumbcluck I am, she told herself in a silent admonition. Fancy me telling my mother how it should be done! Ah well... Perhaps she is just tired of doing this kind of thing. Or maybe she wants us to work together for a change. What a nice idea!

She was delighted at the thought and, without a moment's hesitation she jumped wholeheartedly into the spirit of things. She consulted with her mother on every detail. She was afraid to make a single cut or tuck without a second opinion. It had to be perfect. They worked together, discussed options, made decisions, admired, chatted. As Lily ran basting threads across the centre to keep the silk from slipping, they talked about the people they knew. As she pinned, they spoke of bishops—the current one and the one before that. No piece of gossip was left unturned. When she began to sew the lining to the Thai silk, she worked carefully and concentrated on every stitch. It all had to be done by hand, using an invisible stitch. It was not difficult, just slow—so there was plenty of time for Betsy's stories. Betsy was almost as well-known in the district for the stories she told as she was for her embroideries. They were in her mind—whole generations of them, all of them invariably elaborate, sometimes outrageous. They took off in all directions, twisted and turned their way through mazes, backed up on themselves unexpectedly, or were hatched, like little birds, one story out of another, and then, when it all seemed impossibly complicated, with something like the sudden, seemingly careless flick of a magician, she would gather up all the loose ends at once and tie them off in a perfectly sublime and indestructible knot.

On this day, she spoke about the man who had bought the old Eames farm, and about his relations and forebears and all the trouble they caused everywhere they went. This led her to the topic of their own family genealogy—which had always been a splendid source of entertainment for her. She could create whole new lives and grand confabulations out of great-great grandfathers and their aunts and uncles. She didn't need to know exactly when or where they lived. The fact that they did live once was enough. And not only could she tell a story, she could also invite Lily to join it as part of a parallel dialogue, with the result that, during the whole time Lily worked on the lining, there was a constant stream of chatter between them—and never once did Betsy take her eyes off the work. She could have signed an affidavit as a witness to every single stitch of it. When, finally, they stopped for a cup of tea, Betsy handed Lily one end of a large, white bed sheet and between them they spread it out wide and placed it carefully over the entire work table. Only then, when they were certain that it was safe from all flying insects and the sticky fingers of ghosts, did they go into the other room.

It was a bitterly cold day. The snow lay in drifts seven or eight feet high and Lily's father kept piling more wood into the stove. Not that they needed the stove, Lily thought, as she sat there soaking up the warmth, both hands wrapped around her tea mug. The house had perfectly adequate central heating, her mother always said, but her father preferred the wood stove and he would argue that it saved them a whole lot of money in a year. From where she sat, Lily believed him. But even if it didn't save them a penny, she told herself, it's worth it. There is something so satisfying about a wood stove—something deliciously homely.

On that particular day, it was so cold that the stove was barely holding its own. Even with the central heating it was consuming wood at a great rate. Lily sat watching the flames as they burst out in one spot, flickered in another, leaped, mingled and travelled the length of a log, and she thought of another fire, long ago, in another place.

"Do you remember?" she asked her mother, "when I burnt my arm on the stove at Hubbardston?"

Her mother look up at her, momentarily startled—and then her face went blank. "No," she answered.

"Oh, but surely you do!" Lily exclaimed. "It was when we lived in Hubbardston. Don't you remember how cold it was?"

"No," Betsy replied. Her voice sounded flat, and cold.

"How could you possibly forget?" Lily asked.

She was more surprised than she cared to be. There was something in her mother's face—something like a sudden wind change. After such a lovely morning, it seemed that a spell had just been broken. She knew at once that she should change the subject. There was something about the past, even the very recent past, something to do with Betsy's mind, or the effect that other people had on her... She couldn't put a finger on it. It wasn't a specific thing. If it had been, she would have known what pitfalls to avoid. Whatever it was, it had been happening more frequently and the closest she could ever get to an explanation was her father's stock response, "Your mother is a very sick woman." He would set his face tight at that and she couldn't get another word out of him. She looked at the flames again, flickering and popping in the wood stove. She breathed in quietly—a long, slow and deep breath. It would not be wise to pursue this, she told herself, but still she could not resist asking, "Surely you couldn't forget that we lived in Hubbardston?"

"Oh yes. I remember that," Betsy answered. "But it was so long ago. And I don't remember anyone getting burnt. Not at all."

Lily sipped her tea and thought about the past. Her mother always claimed to have a perfect elephant memory, and no one ever disputed that. But why doesn't she remember this? Surely my arm was something to remember. Not that it matters now. It wasn't even tragic at the time. So why doesn't she remember? She looked at her father—Charley. He was wearing his tight, closed face.

Lily looked at the fire again. "The weather was just like this," she said. "Incredibly cold. You couldn't see out of the windows at all. Not because of the snowdrifts, but because of the patterns on them. Jack Frost had come in the night and left them entirely covered with patterns. They were like etchings in ice, the most exquisite and intricate etchings imaginable. I remember you telling me about Jack Frost the first time I ever saw windows like that. I believed in him even more than Santa Claus—because he left magic behind him wherever he went. Nobody could ever have convinced me that it was really my parents making those patterns. I kept thinking that I might catch him at it one night. I was perfectly certain that he was somewhere inside the house, hiding in some dark corner, blowing on his fingers and sitting back like a guest at his own exhibit. I knew he must be in the house, because if you touched the windows, the ice of his patterns was all on the inside."

Lily knew that her mother was listening, even if she couldn't see her face properly. She was bending over her knitting, very close, examining it with a look of great concentration. Like a Jack Frost with wool, she was making one of those wonderful, complicated Aran patterns. But Lily knew her mother had already made the same pattern so many times that she could probably do it in her sleep. Jack Frost, on the other hand, was different every time. She watched her mother for a moment, hesitated, then stepped in a little deeper.

"The day I burned my arm," she said, "was a school day. I wanted to stay home. It was so cold that I thought I might freeze before I got to the end of the road. I was only seven. Do you remember?"

Her mother looked up at her for a moment—expressionless, then she went back to her knitting. Her father got up, put on his fireproof gloves, opened the door of the stove and moved a piece of wood to a better spot. Neither of them said a word.

"You remember the cottage, surely?" Lily asked, and this time, she didn't wait for a response. "You wouldn't let me stay at home that day. It wasn't snowing and they hadn't called off school. All the same, you know how long it takes to thaw out a chunk of frozen meat! That's how I felt when I came out of the bedroom. All stiff and frozen. Even my head felt frozen. If I remember it right, I was walking in slow motion and you were getting cross with me. "Hurry up!" you said. "Get moving! Mr. Carey will go without you. Move! Quick! There's no excuse for being lazy." Or words to that effect. As you said, it was a long time ago. My memory may be a bit corroded by now.

"To this day I don't know why, but I had a delusion about that stove—for want of a better word. Yes, I believe I was deluded. I think I was so cold when I was getting dressed that my mind played a trick on me. Without thinking what I was doing—I remember it as though I had done it in slow motion—perhaps I did—I leaned forward—slowly—and laid my arm across the stove to see if it was warm."

Betsy stopped knitting and looked up. She stared at Lily for a minute, saying nothing. She seemed to be waiting. Then, as if she hadn't meant to get interested, she returned to her knitting with a "Hmmph!"

"I am certain," Lily went on, "that it couldn't have happened if it had given me a warning. If it had been really hot when I got to within three or four inches of it, I would have known that it was hot. The moment it happened I knew how silly I had been, because then I remembered that I had seen you lighting it earlier. I must have forgotten because I was so cold.

"It sure did make a great mess of my arm. Funny! I don't remember if it hurt. It must have. I remember though that it was the whole inside of my forearm. I remember also that I couldn't believe it at first. I felt as though I had just been bitten by my own dog, which was a silly thought because we didn't have a dog."

Betsy went on knitting. Charley appeared to be asleep.

Lily took another step—deeper still into dangerous waters. "Well," she said. "You might not remember it, but it sure did make you hop around at the time. You made such a fuss. I didn't even have time to finish dressing myself. You did it for me. You pushed me this way and that, as though you were kneading dough in a hurry to have a loaf of bread in time for dinner. I was so thoroughly kneaded and shaped into my mittens and boots and all the rest that when you pushed me out the door to go to school, it was as if you were shoving a loaf tin into the oven. And then you could breathe a sigh of relief and say, "Done!" Not, of course, that you ever made a loaf of bread. It was me that made the bread, wasn't it?

Lily looked at her mother again. She was knitting still—eternally knitting—and silent.

"Ah well," Lily said, "it's just an image. An idea of what it felt like at the time. What a rush it was to get me off to school once I'd made a mess of myself! Of course, you didn't just shove me into my clothes and push me out the door. You hurried about for a minute trying to think what to do about my arm, and then you opened the door and scooped up some snow, and you brought it into the house and piled it onto my arm "to cool it down fast," you said. And then, when it seemed cool enough, you put something gooey on it—some

255

kind of cream. Burn cream perhaps. And you wrapped a whole roll of gauze bandage around it from elbow to wrist. I remember watching you do it. It was fascinating to see my burn disappearing under the bandage, and somehow, I think, it felt better—warm and comfortable. I remember that when you had nearly used up the whole roll, you cut the end in half—several inches deep, and then wound the two halves in opposite directions till they met again on the other side. Then you tied them together in a bow and pulled my sweater down over it. You did it so well that nobody would ever guess there was a bandage underneath that sweater. It's amazing to think that after all that I did manage to get to school on time.

"School was something else though. Somehow I have no memory of getting to school that day. I must have been a bit shell shocked. It wasn't until I was actually sitting at my desk that I noticed how much it hurt. Perhaps it was just more noticeable at school because there was nothing else to think about. I remember thinking that I was sitting there with a very large burn on my arm and nobody could see it under my sweater. Well of course, I knew that if no one could see the burn—or the bandage, there would be no one to sympathize with me, and a little sympathy would have been a good thing just then. So I kept trying to sneak a look at it—just a wee look. I didn't mean to disturb it. I certainly knew that you couldn't make a fuss in that class. At least I couldn't. Miss Maddock was a horrible woman and she hated me. I'm sure of that. If ever she noticed me at all, it was to be cross with me about something. I wonder if I really was so bad. Do you know that in the whole of that year, no matter how many times I raised my hand, she never once called on me to answer a question? Irene Prentiss, on the other hand, could just blink her eyes and smile sweetly, and Miss Maddock would ask her every time. It didn't seem fair to me."

She paused, as another thought struck her, and then she said, "Irene was killed a year later. Do you remember that?"

Betsy looked up from her knitting—a bit wide-eyed. "Oh yes! I remember that," she said. "A man who was backing out of his driveway hit her when she rode past on her bicycle."

"Yes," Lily said. "It was you who told me about it at the time. You had read it in the paper. She was such a pretty girl. That wasn't fair either. I mean to say that her death wasn't fair. It wasn't her fault if Miss Maddock was a stupid, horrible, and thoroughly biased woman. Irene of course came from an old town family. To this day, the name Prentiss is on mailboxes all over the town. She and Miss Maddock probably went to the same church."

She saw that her mother was looking at her still, waiting for more. For a moment, Lily couldn't remember what she had been saying. She shivered, quite unexpectedly and wondered if the fire had died down. But no, she could see that it was burning to its limit and it was warm in the room—almost too warm. She gazed at the flames.

"Yes" she said—slowly, and rather uncertain. "Yes... Well... I think that... as I remember it, the day I leaned on the stove was the day when things took a turn for the worse at school. Yes... I know it did. Before I burned my arm, I had been more or less invisible. After I burned it, I became something like a leper. The bandage kept coming unravelled. For days, every time I played at recess or lunch, there would be a long white tail hanging out of my sweater."

She looked at her mother again, as if searching for something. Then as her memory filled in, she said, "I remember now. You would check my burn every night to make sure that it was healing properly. You would put more cream on it, and every day you put a clean bandage on it. But I could never figure out a way to keep it from unravelling and, although I would wind it back around my arm, I couldn't make it stay. It always came undone again. Each time, it became more ragged. Once or twice a teacher helped me with it, but in the end they didn't want to know about it. After a while, nobody wanted to play with me. Really. Nobody. Not even the couple of kids who usually did. Perhaps it was all too much for them. They weren't really friends anyway. I was the new kid at school and it was such a very small country town—and we lived a good way out of it. I often thought that the kids who did play with me were either dimwitted, or just being kind. Whatever the reason, I certainly wasn't popular in those days. You would have thought I had lice."

Betsy looked up with a frown and stared at Lily for a moment. She tilted her chin upwards with a little jerk, and then looked down at her knitting with a puzzled look. Lily had the impression that she wondered what it was doing there. Quite suddenly, her mother looked up again and spoke in a loud voice to the wood stove, "Charley!" she said, "There's tuna in the fridge. We could have tuna sandwiches for lunch."

Charley got up and went into the kitchen without a sideways glance or a word to either of them.

There was nothing unpleasant about the lunch. Betsy and Lily chatted amiably about nothing in particular. It was a time for eating, not talking.

After lunch, Betsy said that she was very tired and would need to lie down for a bit. Charley went off to his workshop. He had something he wanted to do, he told Betsy.

Lily went back to work on the chasuble. She worked as carefully as before. It was a quiet afternoon and it seemed to pass quickly. The sun was nearly down before she noticed it. She would need a light, she thought. She stood up and stretched her back. As she reached for the switch, she saw in the far bottom corner of one of the windows a tiny patch of ice where Jack Frost had left his mark. It was all on the outside. There was no ice inside this house. And even on that one outer window, there was so little ice that it seemed as though Jack Frost had been apprehended by the laws of the modern world—caught, constrained, and truncated by double-glazed windows and the warmth of oil heating.

The thought passed through Lily's mind as she stood staring at the window that her father had not said a single word to her since she and her mother had sat down for their cup of tea. She had no idea whether he remembered her burnt arm or not. She would not ask him. He would never say.

CHAPTER 20

1994

A Very Sick Woman

I don't think I can stand much more of this," he said.

Sometimes it is the end and not the beginning. Sometimes it dawns on you that beginnings are a thing of the past. It puts an entirely different perspective on things, but it rarely changes anything. All the more so to a person who has been blessed with the life of nine cats, who has stepped forth virtually unscathed from all manner of catastrophes—jungle battles, car wrecks, and even the blizzard of '78. These things give an even greater sense of shock when the end really is in sight. So what can be done about it? A man who has always led an exemplary existence can hardly take off on a whole new adventure upon his retirement if his wife is a very sick woman. Not even if he can trick the physicians' lie detectors, the machines and the tests—heart, lungs, and all that. "You have the body of a forty-year-old sir," they said. "You will have to come back for more tests. We do not believe it."

Charley Stearns did not believe it was the end, and he did not want to believe it. Here he was, such a healthy man, and he had a wife who was said to be, and who possibly was, such a very sick woman.

He stood in the doorway looking at her—Betsy. He looked tired. He had just put down the phone, having refused to allow his son Matt to speak with her again. "Your Mother is a very sick woman," he had recited, loading each word with an excess of gravity.

It is what he always said when he was under orders not to call her to the phone—always with the same heavy emphasis. It was the way he excused himself for excluding his own children from the family— or blamed his children for having upset their mother—or both. Sometimes this went on for weeks at a time—always in exactly the same way. And always, if his children tried to talk to him instead, he sounded evasive, impatient, menacing, or critical.

Lily called him the guard dog when he was like that. "Oh, no, I didn't get to speak with Mother when I rang. I got the guard dog, and you can never get anything out of him," she would say. Everyone knew what she meant, but no one knew whether it was his idea of loyalty, or righteousness, or whether *she* was listening.

Lily knew that when Charley started acting like the guard dog, Mother was off again. Something had got into her. Some idea, or conviction, or persuasion. Some sibling rivalry perhaps. A little poison in her ear without doubt, and Betsy's imagination working overtime on it—re-writing her will in her mind, even as the poison took effect. Occasionally, Betsy was suffering guilt pangs—if she was cutting one of them out of some celebration or other—if she didn't want to cramp her style. She always picked a fight then.

Betsy had just about perfected the art of replacing guilt with justification. All she needed was some story she could spread from one end of town to the other, or to the end of the state, or even to relatives on the other side of the world. All she needed was a story that would make people realize immediately how unsuitable it would be to invite your own child, under the circumstances.

This was not a happy family. But there was something in its persistent unhappiness, or the management of it, that set it apart from others, marked it with a "B", you might say. As unhappy families go, this one distinguished itself in this respect at least: it was hell-bent on being unhappy in its own way.

Charley stood in the doorway waiting for an answer. Betsy ignored him. She set her face tight against him and refused to be drawn into this. It wasn't her problem how he felt about not calling her to the phone.

"I just don't think I can stand much more of this," he said. "You are alienating all the children. If you keep this up, we won't have anything left. We'll be all alone."

"We've been all alone for years," she answered, and, looking at him with her cold face, she added, "I like it better this way."

"No! You do not. I do not."

He stood with defeat and exasperation visibly etched into him. He did not know what more to say. He did not have the words, or the strategies, to handle her. He could never overcome her hard arrogance. And she always won. He waited a moment, then shrugged his shoulders and turned to go into the kitchen.

Since his retirement the year before, he had taken on nearly all the housework. Mostly he did as he was told, like a high-class, brilliantly-programmed automaton. He cooked exactly according to the instructions she called out from the TV room, and then he served the product of her instruction precisely in keeping with her timing. He stoked the fire in the wood stove when she complained that her feet were cold. He changed her CD for her whenever she wanted a new one. And he made her drinks according to her instructions—her endless instructions.

At times he worked like a martyr to his own private cause,

long-suffering and silent. Furiously silent. Stubbornly silent. Self-righteously silent. He washed the dishes, the benches, the table, the floor, and he simmered inwardly. He straightened the chairs as if everything depended on him getting them right. In their proper place. And then someone would come and sit on one, moving it out of place and it spoiled his work. He would sigh and look grim at the trouble of it all.

There had been a time when he had laughed—a huge, roaring laugh, full of the sheer exhilaration of a healthy young life that was still heading into the future. No one had heard him laugh like that in years.

Those were the days when he had sometimes played silly practical jokes. Like the time when Ozzie—his old Marine Corps buddy—and his wife, Charlotte, came to dinner, and everyone ate corn-on-the-cob until they started joking that it would soon be coming out of their ears. And he went into the bathroom near the dining room and lit a bunch of firecrackers on such a long fuse that when they exploded he was already back at the table again eating more corn. At the explosion he wore a face like a surprised angel. Ozzie, who was a policeman, jumped up from the table and headed out the front door, reaching automatically for his absent gun—all in the one crazy, unthinking, reflex action. And Charley laughed—roaring like a bull. And Ozzie got mad and then he laughed too. They laughed until they cried. It was such a joke.

He used to be like that once. In those days his friends called him Lucky, even though they were poor and he was sometimes out of work. In time his nickname—and his friends—faded away.

In the kitchen, he picked up a wooden bowl. Thought he might get himself some peanuts. He wasn't drinking these days. He had always enjoyed a beer or two, but in the last year he had been acting like an ascetic. Stuck to water and got thin.

"I need another drink," she called out. "You didn't make this strong enough."

Obediently, he reached for the bottle of gin, unconsciously pulling his face into a tight grimace—the face he always made when they had visitors and she made a fool of him. He pulled his mouth back into a fixed grin that showed nearly all his teeth clamped together hard and his eyes squinted up in wrinkles at the corners. He had been doing it for years—as if he thought it somehow passed for the real thing. But he had never seen himself doing it in the mirror. Had never noticed how wild it made him look. Like a tiger in anguish. But in answer to the proverbial question, how are you, he always said with the same grin, "Neva betta!" Another of his jokes.

She sat and waited in her chair—the only chair in the room that nobody else would dare to sit on. It was hers alone. No guest would have made the mistake of trying to sit there. She saw to that. Guests—including her children—were directed to their places according to her whim, or plan. It depended on how she intended to hold her audience, or manipulate it.

But today she was alone except for him. And so she waited with her feet up on her hassock—bare-footed as usual. She turned her little foot this way and that—admired the shape—the daintiness—the perfection, and she let her knitting slide off her lap onto the floor as she lost the shape of her foot in a momentary blur. It was halfway through a row. Several stitches unraveled and she would have to pick them up later. But now she forgot it. She was on the edge. Not far off the snap.

The snap! Battered women have often described this: the instant, that is, when husbands or boyfriends or fathers having drunk too much have snapped from the slightly alarming into the absolutely terrifying as if someone has pushed a button—the *Pithecanthropus*, fully automatic and mechanized and agitated in an instant into a violent, uncontrollable basher.

She did this too when she'd had too much. Snapped! But she was

265

less than five feet tall. So all the power of her, and all the violence of her, lay in her tongue. She could flay you with that. Zip you open! Rip out your heart and leave you hollow. Apart from the knitting, it was her thing, but you had to have seen this to believe it. Who would ever believe it otherwise? That dear little old lady with the knitting! That dear, sweet lady who covered the Christmas tree at church every year with mittens and hats for the poor, cold, neglected children of the town?

Charley made the gin and tonic with a slice of lemon for nicety—just as she liked it, double strength as usual. If it weren't for the grin, still fixed, you might have thought him an exemplar of butlerhood—an excellent servant indeed. But you could never know what he thought beneath that unreadable grin. He might have been quietly praying that this would be the gin that would take her off into oblivion once and for all.

Charley had other faces. There was his deaf face, for example. The one he had when he had turned off his hearing aid—the genuinely uncomprehending blank face. There must be some advantage to being deaf, after all. But a peculiar blindness seemed to go with that face. It was as if you became invisible to him once he was really deaf. You had to try harder to get his attention, and when you did get it, he would look at you quizzically, like a cocker spaniel to which you had just spoken French. Once he'd switched off his hearing aids, he did everything methodically. So much more carefully. As if he was deliberately making a show of his righteousness. As if nobody but he could ever wash a dish with such perfect saintliness. Sometimes it seemed that he felt like a victim. Or a drudge. A kitchen slave. Doing all the work that nobody else would do. Grandfather Cinderella looking out the back window at his pumpkins! But you couldn't very well turn a giant Blue Hubbard into a coach, could you? That enormous, misshapen squash that you had to cut open with an axe. It wouldn't do.

Occasionally, you could have mistaken him for a Florence

Nightingale working wonders with his patient. Poor Betsy in the other room with her bare feet, waiting for her gin and tonic. Betsy with the heart condition, "or at least that was what the doctor hinted that I might have." Betsy with diabetes sometime soon if she kept on drinking. Betsy whose doctors had lost count of all her illnesses. Betsy, who had begun to lose count of all her doctors. She could do whatever she wanted, if she had the strength. If she had gone easy on the gin the night before, she didn't even need her cane when she bustled about the house doing her morning chores. The ones she didn't trust Charley to get right: the machine washing and the disinfected bathroom. The ironing she left for Charley.

But at night what she wanted was to sit in that chair with her drink. And sometimes watch television quiz shows to prove to herself that she was brilliant. It went together, the sitting and the drinking. It never was any fun to walk around with a drink. Once you had a drink in your hands you sat. And every day for thirty-five years, at an hour that crept forward by imperceptible degrees each year, Betsy sat with her drink. Sometimes with friends. Sometimes alone. Sometimes it was whisky. Sometimes gin. At one time "a highball" had meant mixing whisky with ginger ale and ice. Now it meant just ice. But gin went with tonic. And be sure to double the gin!

Today Betsy sat brooding over her drink while Charley complained about alienation. He must have felt very strongly about it if he complained. It wasn't his style to stray so far from silence. He had felt a little surprised even as he said it. But he had also felt cold. A shiver had run through him that he couldn't account for. Even now, adding that slice of lemon, he felt cold. Outside the roses were in bloom— the roses his daughter Lily had given him at his last birthday. The bees were still at work in the evening light. The borage and bergamot performed in a profusion of blue and red along the path opposite the roses. In his garden he was no martyr. In his garden he hummed quietly as he worked, lighting up with childish joy at each new shoot and bud. When she allowed him. In the wood at the end of the field, he could hear the woodpecker at work. Juncos and chickadees still ate at his bird feeders. He fed the birds the whole year round these days. And he almost smiled at the memory of the hummingbird in the summertime, feeding at his bergamot—a miracle it seemed—always. Every year without fail, the tiniest bird imaginable travelled thousands of miles to feed in his garden.

But Lily was out of favour again. Betsy was "put-out" with her. Hated the sight of her. That brown hair that she wouldn't dye. And her clothes—her plain, dull all-one-colour clothes. Betsy listened eagerly when Matt complained against her. Eager to confirm her own opinion. Sometimes when those two got together, they just about lied Lily to death. They had been doing it for years. If only she had known! Lily's little brother Matty. Betsy's son Matt.

But now something had happened which had never happened before. They were all out of favour. Lily and Matt and Immy. All of them.

That was it, Charley realized. It had never happened before. Usually, it was only one at a time. The one piece you could remove without causing any disturbance to the main structure. Betsy's game of blocks. She moved people—her children, her neighbours, her friends—in and out of her world, like a child playing with blocks. No! It was much more sophisticated than that. Much more devastating. But only for the one block at a time. The block that was put aside indefinitely. To be attacked. Or ignored. To have other blocks thrown at it. To be hated by all the other blocks. To be put away in a cupboard for a while, and then suddenly brought out again without any kind of explanation.

There was never an explanation. No apology. Ever. What a game! It was all so uneasy for a while afterwards for the others, but it was never a trouble for Betsy. It was, after all, her game. That was the whole point of it. Inventing the game and controlling it; being in charge of it and the centre of it at the same time. When she finally called it off, she came out like the sunshine, heaping bounty on you, beaming at you for a time. She always called it off with a *thing*. A gift that you had to thank her for. Or a newspaper cutting that you had to acknowledge. And Lily, especially, was slow to learn that during the periods of Betsy's beneficence, you had to watch her face diligently for the gathering of the next cloud.

This time it was different though. This time Betsy had put them all away in the cupboard and turned her back entirely. Not, of course, until she had made sure that they had all turned their backs on each other first. This time, she amused herself with frequent visits to the vicar. Teaching his wife to do ecclesiastical embroidery. Her other thing. And Charley felt cold in the depths of his soul.

"Clare told me today that all my children are mad," Betsy said, as Charley handed her the drink.

He closed his face up tight and went back into the kitchen.

"Oh, you don't think so!" she shouted in a sharp voice. "Well she did! So it's true. I told her about them. All of them. I told her what they've been doing and she said they must be mad. All of them."

Charley came back and stood silently in the doorway, looking at her with no expression. She lifted her chin, made a sudden sideways movement, like a bird, and fixed him with a beady, piercing stare. "And anyway," she said, "I don't like any of them. They haven't pleased me."

The last time Lily was out of favour, Charley had gone out to the garden and dug up all the roses she had given him on another birthday, and thrown them into the heap of cuttings at the back. He remembered this now. He remembered too, a few months ago when he had been driving her over to stay the night with them. Betsy had been in a clouding-over phase, and Lily had felt uncertain. He had felt it too. Out of the blue, and staring straight ahead as he drove, and enunciating each word carefully and slowly as if it were *she* who was deaf, he had announced, "Your—mother—is—a—wonderful—woman."

Lily had said nothing. As if she hadn't heard him.

"I don't know anyone who does the things for other people that she does," he had gone on, talking faster—like a salesman trying to clinch a deal before closing time. "Anyone so generous."

Lily had remained silent.

"Just think of the Christmas tree at the church!" he had insisted. "That in itself. Every year it is covered with things. And every year it is nearly all your mother's things. You can see them all. No one else does so much. Cares so much."

Of course, that Christmas tree, Lily had thought later—after the game had started all over again and she was it. That tree was an indisputable fact. She wondered later on what she should have said, and asked herself why he had come out with it so aggressively just then? Who had he been trying to convince?

Looking at Betsy, Charley remembered too. He opened his mouth as if to speak and then shut it again. He never could find the words to say what he really meant. He shrugged again and went upstairs to his bathroom. Betsy sat drinking alone until she fell asleep in her chair.

Appendices

❧ ～ ☙

Appendix 1

The problem with my so-called Lily stories, is that they never were meant to be stories. I began writing a book. My first chapter was written from the adult Lily point of view. I then stepped back in time and wrote a number of chapters from the point of view of the child Lily. All of the stories (or chapters) about Lily as a child tend to be episodic, mainly because she is a child, but more importantly, I think, it's because the incident, or episode, that sticks in her mind sufficiently for her to remember it as an adult, has had an impact on both the child and the adult character, and has shaped her in some way. When I wrote the first of these, and Robyn Gardner wanted to publish it in Mattoid, I tinkered with it to make it stand independently as a story (and then published it under the pseudonym, Jenny Hillersten—after my great-great grandmother). Since then, I've kept the early chapters within the bounds of "story" so that they might be heard (partly because feedback can be useful). Thus "Charley Flies South" was published in the last anthology as a story. I have another chapter (in the midst of the early stories) written from Betsy's point of view, in which Lily isn't present. "Jack Frost" is the first of the chapters that I have allowed to take off a bit—move into another mode, because by the time I finally get past the early episodes, I want to shift the pace of the whole thing considerably—to make a very clear distinction between the mind of a child and the mind of an adult. But since I never have time to read more than a page or two at a meeting, none of this is ever clear to the listener. To add to that the question of autobiography or fiction: the answer is that it's fiction. But it is fiction based in part on things that have happened. It is also, I think, fiction which takes liberties, both with style and with what is true or not true. The things that are true in "Jack Frost" are like props: the wood stove, the cottage, the burned arm, the embroidery, the harp lady, but these 'props' were taken from various scenes which occurred over a number of years. The rest is what I did with it - or invented. I can't remember which famous author wrote that "fiction is beautiful lies," but that raises another question: If you succeed in writing something that appears to be "real", will people always assume that it's true? Or, if you write a complete fiction, in which nothing is true, but you write in the first person, using your own name, and make it seem real, will people assume that it's autobiography, even insist on it? What then are we to make of Somerset Maugham's, The Razor's Edge? He writes in the first person. He is the narrator. His characters refer to him as Maugham. The character/narrator in the novel is a writer of novels. What about the rest—all the other characters, their lives, etc.? Is it truth, or is it fiction? One thing is clear; it's not autobiography, because he is not speaking of himself except as an observer. Of course, I can ask these questions, but when I read it, the thought never entered my mind that it could be anything but fiction. Perhaps fiction isn't just beautiful lies. Perhaps it's also beautiful inventions, or beautiful accidents - things the pen wrote when you weren't looking.

Appendix 2

I wouldn't call myself a "major" international scholar. For me, it's always a struggle—especially a struggle to say exactly what I want. To create a scene in which everything becomes authentic. Not realistic. Just authentic.

It's true, I believe, that children only gather their wholeness into themselves by degrees. If it's true that a child doesn't become responsible until about the age of seven, then it really is as though we come in parts which only gradually make a whole. This surely would explain those adults who never quite make it to a full and rational adulthood, because trauma of one kind or another was never adequately dealt with. Perhaps those adults of our past who felt that children shouldn't be told things that "they wouldn't understand" have inadvertently been the cause of much grief along the way. Aunt Marjorie, for example, in deciding that we shouldn't ever speak of Alison's grandmother again, because, at the age of four, in Marjorie's opinion, Alison wasn't capable of understanding the concept of death. What about the adult idea of children being seen and not heard? Does this also mask an adult belief that when it comes to adult issues, children should neither see nor hear?

This brings to my mind, once again, the question of "point of view." Those three words worry me considerably, because in my mind they represent something like the "rule of law" of fiction writing, and I visualize teachers everywhere telling students what the rules or guidelines are and how they must be obeyed. But to me, when I write, the criteria are that the writing must be interesting, must achieve something that rings true in the mind of the reader (and more particularly, in my own mind), and must move in such a way as to put the necessary whole of the picture before the reader, even if it shifts and transitions along the way. Sometimes you can only get to a place by a winding path. By "necessary whole", I don't mean that it is about telling all. "All" is impossible, or if it were possible, it would be deadly. I mean all the necessary threads that combine in one way or another and lead to that particular moment or situation in the mind or experience of the character, even if the character is not capable of seeing this combination him/herself. It was necessary, I thought, to step back at that particular point—at the moment of waking from a nightmare—and place the child in the setting and sequence of events that preceded the nightmare. It was necessary, because, amongst other things, nightmare

273

of one kind or another was a constant and recurring thing in that child's life at the time.

I don't know what exactly Raymond Carver means by his title, "Where I'm Coming From," but it seems singularly appropriate for me, because when I write, it's where I'm coming from. I believe that we are remarkably fortunate to be writing today, with a whole world of astonishing writers preceding us. In my mind, every writer before me who has truly achieved a breakthrough in style or thought gives me a license to write in such a way as to create my own style and way of thinking, in my own time. It even gives me a license, I believe, to send echoes of my predecessors running through my own work. In my other book, Heaven Feathers, for a moment, when Diana is in disarray, both in mind and body, I have allowed Gertrude Stein to sneak into my writing—just a faint echo. Something of her style. It's my writing, not hers. I've done the same with Faulkner in "Charlie Flies South." And a few others along the way. It's my belief that anything of this sort should be rare, but when it occurs, a light touch is in order. It should be a natural part of the writing. Preening is not what it's all about. My writing is about me and my way of telling a story—or finding a solution. I just happen to love the fact that people like Calvino, Garcia Marquez, Strindberg, Maeterlinck, Pirandello, Mark Twain, Cheever, Dickens, Dickinson, Jewett, Kate Chopin, George Eliot, Arundhati Roy, Joyce, Kipling, Hugo, Poe, Hardy, James, hundreds... have given me permission to write in my own way—because they did. And, as long as I can make the whole thing work, I think they have also given me permission to break rules—because they did. And it's not just about style, it's also about language, especially about the way that you create an impact with words—how you use them.

About writing of personal experiences which occurred a long time ago, and particularly of early childhood experiences, it is impossible to get a full and clear picture. You remember most clearly certain things—people, places, incidents, and objects (books, closets, teddy bears, wheelbarrows, whatever!), again, one might say, in flashes. Why you remember these things and not others is not known. But if you begin to work on that one memory and try to portray it, as if it were happening right now, you may find that your mind will release more of the memory. If not, your imagination will fill in what you can't discover in yourself—if you allow it to, and don't try to direct it with a heavy hand. But if it is true, as they say, that the brain stores every single piece of information or experience that has ever come our way, then you as a child exist somewhere inside your own brain. If all you have to go on is a feeling (fear, joy) and a flash of memory, if you begin to put the two together on the page, the words will come. If, from your earliest childhood memories, you've had a great love of buttercups—a whole field of buttercups, then probably there was something more to it. It's not just about buttercups. It's about a particular time or place, and possibly other people as well. If, as a writer, you want to portray this and find you just can't summon up a clear memory, then you invent it on the basis of how you feel when you think about it. In the end, it's about what you put on the page, not about your past history. When I wrote about a particular house at the end of Park Street—which I remembered very badly, but described in detail, Jeanne, who actually lived at that end of Park Street, said to me, "But that's not what the house was like at all!" I asked her describe it to me and she did. And then, after I'd thought for a bit, I said, "But my house—my creation of that house—is the right one for my story." Perhaps the problem of recalling events distant in time is the reason for all those long opaque sepia introductions to films that work in the then and the now.

That's really all I can say about this at the moment. Except that, according to the blurb on the back of Gorky's My Childhood, his "gift for recapturing the world of the child is uncanny." I agree with that. It's worth reading, and harsh beyond anything Lily ever experienced.

Appendix 3

How do you write about things that happened a long time ago when you were a child?

And more particularly, how do you deal with things which affected you immensely and which the adults around you dismissed as just plain silly, or at least unworthy of their attention?

How do you deal with the fact that adults failed to take action—or show any care or concern, when you were in need of love and support—when, in fact, you were a victim?

If you want to write about yourself, you can find any number of ways in which to do it. You can write an autobiography or a memoir, or a fictionalized truth. You can write anything you like about yourself. You can tell how funny it was when this happened, or how frightening or dangerous when that happened. You can write about your brave struggle towards the great success you ultimately achieved, or you can relate quite humbly how you came to be where you are now. There are endless possibilities.

But what if the things that happened to you left you damaged or vulnerable in some way? What if every time you put your pen to paper, wishing to write of those things, you find that your page is filled with anger and resentment? How do you write if such feelings dominate your writing? Well you either give up, or, if the story really matters to you, you take a different tack. You capture a different wind, one which will occupy you so completely that you will forget to be angry.

In my case, I chose to distance myself by creating third-person characters. I know exactly who I am writing about, but I choose to bury them in the immediate sense. I have given them different names so that, although I am telling their story, they aren't really the same people. They have become characters, complete only to the extent that I make them so. The question is no longer about what happened to me but about how Lily felt, or thought, or responded to various situations.

It is also about how Charley and Betsy thought and acted. In creating third-person characters, it became necessary for me to see and hear them in my own mind, because what they said and how they acted was no less important to the story than the child who is the protagonist. I have found that including the viewpoints of the adults who controlled the world of that child created a more rounded and seemingly authentic picture and this is important because there is never just one side to a story. It is also important to be aware that those adults might quite reasonably have been completely unaware of the things that frightened the child. They were not necessarily culpable. They had their own problems. Nevertheless, although I realize that adults, who are so taken up with their own affairs that they fail to see what is really happening, are not necessarily bad, but they are blind in this respect and like it or not they are the shapers of their children.

In the story "All Creatures Great and Small", I have written of the nightmare which was not only very real to the child but was a recurring one. It returned fairly often, albeit haphazardly, for two or three years and the child never knew when she went to bed whether she would sleep peacefully or wake up in the middle of a nightmare. There was no comfort in her knowing that the nightmare would always be the same. When I wrote this, I was concerned with the story of both the nightmare and its sources: Mr. Dooby with his knife, Aunt Agneta reading in the paper about the man who was impaled by a deer, Lily, who had to stand at the corner of the road in dark all alone, surrounded by thick woods and waiting for a man to come and take her to school, and Lily sleeping in the cold, dark room, isolated—as she saw it—from the rest of the house and the security of her parents. Putting the story together in a reasonable fashion was my main concern. Making it real was what mattered to me. I thought it would be a recognizable thing for a reader, because I am sure that nearly everyone has had a childhood experience which frightened them enough to be memorable years later. What never occurred to me until just now is that Lily's nightmare was actually a post-traumatic stress symptom in exactly the same way and no less real than the post-traumatic stress suffered by returning soldiers, but who would ever think that a seven-year-old girl might suffer in such a way? If you were to put such an idea to her parents they would call it ridiculous. To them she was just a silly, bothersome kid, but regardless of what they might have thought the stress was real enough and so was the recurring nightmare. How it came to be so is something I can't explain. It may have never occurred if there had been just Mr. Dooby and his knife, if there hadn't also been several other frightening things in her life at that time. Whether or not it was a combination of elements—the things that scared her brought on the nightmares and it would be many years before she could challenge her own fears and take command of them. She herself never once mentioned the nightmare to her parents. There was no point. She knew that, even as a child.

Appendix 4

My mother (a war bride) was a remarkable embroiderer. She had been doing it almost all her life. She grew up as an Anglican in Australia and when she married my father and went to live in Massachusetts (taking me with her), she began going to the Episcopal church in Oxford. After a time, she joined the Altar Guild and when she became exasperated with the quality of work that was being done, she began taking lessons in gold thread embroidery from a woman who was considered to be the very best in Massachusetts. Gold thread embroidery was primarily done for ecclesiastical garments—chasubles, copes, stoles, mitres, etc. She soon became an expert and, when not working for the church, she was also producing decorative work such as on the Christmas card. She was also a fine knitter and she could sew. And she was a voracious reader as well as a fanatic about music, especially opera.

Unfortunately, my family as a whole left a good deal to be desired. My father, who doted on my mother, was, in general, not a sympathetic *person to us children, and my brother and sister, who were younger than I, worked very hard against each other and against me, each of them wanting to be the most important and to get the most for themselves. My mother helped that along by talking about wills and inheritance more often than any person should.*

My mother made four small pieces of embroidery for me over the years, which I really cherish. It wasn't until I went to visit my brother in New Jersey that I discovered just what he had—a WHOLE WALL covered in my mother's embroideries. They would be worth a lot of money one day, he said. When I saw my mother next, I told her how impressed I was to see so much of her beautiful work all at once. She seemed a bit nonplussed for a moment, and then she said that she wasn't making any pieces for me because she knew that I didn't like her work. I was most taken aback—speechless in fact. But then I said that I would be most interested to know who had told her that, because I would never have said such a thing, What's more, I added, given that I am the only one of her children who ever did any kind of sewing or knitting or embroidery, I would surely know a good thing when I saw it.

She never did tell me who had made that remark, but a few weeks later she produced that most wonderful piece of embroidery—fully framed and done especially for me. "I have never used those colours before," she said when she gave it to me, "but I knew that they were the right colours for you." Of course, there is a religious message in the fish, but for me she called it "a Mexican rainbow trout." To this day I think it would be reasonable to say that it is almost certainly the most beautiful and creative of all her works. She died in the year 2000. The family fell apart and who knows what became of the rest of her work. It was my husband's idea to turn it into a Christmas card. It was a brilliant idea.

Appendix 5

I should also say that my Lily character is essentially autobiographical. I have named her Lily because my own name was just a horrible distraction to me. It interfered with my writing. In fact, it tended to muddle me thoroughly—so much so that I actually tore my first attempt into a hundred pieces and threw them away. My name clearly made everything seem to be askew. Much to my surprise, the moment I created Lily, I could do all sorts of things—tell the truth, exaggerate, lie, twist, invent. She's a mighty good character, and she's only partly me. I create the things she did and places where she went, but she is the one who lives it all. I have come to like her. Her full name is Lily Stearns. The Stearns came from one of my early American Boston ancestors. Sometimes you get very good information from a genealogy, but mostly you just get dates. The one thing that I find a genealogy useful for is stealing names and attaching them to characters.

Apart from our writing group and my daughter Ingrid, no one else has read some of the chapters. You may be the first, and I probably won't send it to anyone else. I have twenty-four smaller pieces which are complete in themselves. Sometimes I send one out to someone. Not very often. I also have five chapters of another book about a character named Diana. She is a complete fiction. She came fully named in a dream that stuck in my head, so I wrote the dream and it grew from there. That really is all I've got.

Acknowledgments

Without such friends, contributors and supporters this book would never have been written:

Our extended family in Victoria Australia, especially Christine Mackay, Grahame and Lynda Code, who supported and advised me so strongly.

The energetic arts and writing community of Worcester Massachusetts, including our really dear friend Marilyn Butler, the board of WCPA, and Dan Lewis, Eve Rifkah, Michael Milligan, with others.

Friends and colleagues at the American Antiquarian Society, especially Doris O'Keefe who taught me so much, and my workmate, Carol Fisher Crosby with whom I have much in common, and Lorri Magnussan, my great assistant and supporter.

Carol Klekotka, Jeanne Rodier Hayes, Anne Tatum, Cilla Olson, Maureen Marcotta Gatto, Ruth Kneier, Doug Vizard, Judy Todd, Albert Pelletier, and all my other classmates of Oxford 1962 (the Pirates). Many have remained loyal friends through good times and bad for so many years.

Grace Church Oxford was a special place. Rev. Paul Goranson who gave a necessary warning on one crisis occasion: "Den som supsar med djävul borde ha en lång sked." (He who sups with the devil should have a long spoon.) He was right, of course.

Professor Brian Edwards and Robyn Gardner. Brian is director of Deakin Literary Society, a scholar, poet and editor. His work and his weekend conferences were a great stimulus and inspiration. Robyn and Brian published the first of these chapters in embryo.

A chapter of DLS was Deakin Literary Society-Melbourne, chaired by Trevor and Jennifer Code. Members of this group have contributed much, including responses to drafts of the Lily Stories. Special tribute to Tricia Veale, Marguerite Kisvardi, and thanks especially to Heather Tobias, Geoff Campbell, Jackey Coyle, Phil Constan, and Hon Bruce Atkinson. For many years we were hosted free by Writers Victoria at the Nicholas Building and The Wheeler Centre.

Sylvie Blair of BookPOD, who has made sure everything would come together and become the book that it is.

About the Author

Australian-born **Jennifer Code** is a linguist, researcher, and writer who grew up in Oxford, Massachusetts. The daughter of an Australian war-bride and a U.S. Marine, Jennifer's life and career have spanned two continents.

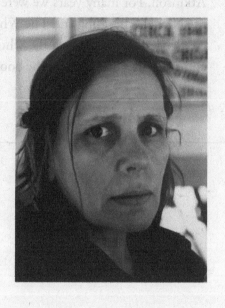

Jennifer holds both a Diploma in Arts and Design from the Royal Melbourne Institute of Technology (RMIT) and a Bachelor of Arts from the University of Melbourne, where she studied English and Scandinavian Literature and Languages. During her graduate studies she was the first woman and the first Australian to receive The Strindberg Scholarship and was invited to live and study at the Strindberg Museum in Stockholm. In 1993, she was awarded a PhD from the University of Melbourne for her dissertation on the post-inferno dramas of the Swedish writer, August Strindberg. Her translations and interpretations of Strindberg's work were highly recognized internationally.

In the 1990s, Jennifer returned to the United States where she worked as Manager of Acquisitions at the American Antiquarian

Society in Worcester, Massachusetts. During this period, she began writing short prose pieces and longer fiction works. Jennifer was a member of the Worcester County Poetry Association and contributed to publications and programming including a collaboration with the Worcester Arts Museum on their Hudson River paintings.

After more than a decade spent in the United States, she returned to Australia in 2004 where she served as co-chair of the Deakin Literary Society of Melbourne. Jennifer wrote and shared 'The Lily stories' with this group; many of these stories are found in the chapters of her book, *The Mad Angel*.

CPSIA information can be obtained
at www.ICGtesting.com
Printed in the USA
LVHW040507021121
702193LV00002B/29